HUDSON

R. M. Ballantyne

BAY

*Life on the
Canadian Frontier*

HUDSON

R. M. Ballantyne

BAY

*Life on the
Canadian Frontier*

cántaro
publications

www.cantaroinstitute.org

Hudson Bay: Life on the Canadian Frontier, R.M. Ballantyne
Published by Cántaro Publications, a publishing imprint of
Cántaro Institute, Jordan Station, ON. L0R 1S0, Canada

Book Design: Steven R. Martins

Library & Archives Canada
ISBN 978-1-990771-20-0

Printed in the United States of America

TABLE OF CONTENTS

INDIAN VILLAGE OF ROSSVILLE.

PREFACE

In publishing the present work, the Author rests his hopes of its favourable reception chiefly upon the fact that its subject is comparatively new. Although touched upon by other writers in narratives of Arctic discovery, and in works of general information, the very nature of those publications prohibited a lengthened or minute description of that *everyday life* whose delineation is the chief aim of the following pages.

Preface to Fourth Edition

Since this book was written, very considerable changes have taken place in the affairs and management of the Hudson Bay Company. The original charter of the Company is now extinct. Red River Settlement has become a much more important colony than it was, and bids fair to become still more important—for railway communication will doubtless, ere long, connect it with Canada on the one hand and the Pacific seaboard on the other, while the presence of gold in the Saskatchewan and elsewhere has already made the country much more generally known than it was when the Author sojourned there. Nevertheless, all these changes—actual and prospective—have only scratched the skirt of the vast wilderness occupied by the fur-traders; and as these still continue their work at the numerous and distant outposts in much the same style as in days of yore, it has been deemed advisable to reprint the book almost without alteration, but with a few corrections.

R.M. Ballantyne

1

APPOINTMENT TO THE SERVICE OF THE HUDSON BAY COMPANY

—The "Prince Rupert"—The Annual Dinner of the "H.B.C."
—Fellow-Voyagers—Threatening Weather
—A Squall—Island of Lewis

READER,—I TAKE FOR GRANTED that you are tolerably well acquainted with the different modes of life and travelling peculiar to European nations. I also presume that you know something of the inhabitants of the East; and, it may be, a good deal of the Americans in general. But I suspect—at least I would fain hope—that you have only a vague and indefinite knowledge of life in those wild, uncivilized regions of the northern continent of America that surround the shores of Hudson Bay. I would fain hope this, I say, that I may have the satisfaction of giving you information on the subject, and of showing you that there is a body of civilized men who move, and breathe (pretty cool air, by the way!), and spend their lives in a quarter of the globe as totally different, in most respects, from the part you inhabit, as a beaver, roaming among the ponds and marshes of his native home, is from that sagacious animal when converted into a fashionable hat.

About the middle of May eighteen hundred and forty-one, I was thrown into a state of ecstatic joy by the arrival of a letter appointing me to the enviable situation of apprentice clerk in the service of the Honourable Hudson Bay Company. To describe the immense extent to which I expanded, both mentally and bodily, upon the receipt of this letter, is impossible; it is sufficient to know that from that moment I fancied myself a complete man of business, and treated my old companions with the condescending suavity of one who knows that he is talking to his inferiors.

A few days after, however, my pride was brought very low indeed, as I lay tossing about in my berth on the tumbling waves of the German Ocean, eschewing breakfast as a dangerous meal, and looking upon dinner with a species of horror utterly incomprehensible by those who have not experienced an attack of sea-sickness. Miseries of this description, fortunately, do not last long. In a couple of days we got into the comparatively still water of the Thames; and I, with a host of pale-faced young ladies and cadaverous-looking young gentlemen, emerged for the first time from the interior of the ship, to behold the beauties and wonders of the great metropolis, as we glided slowly up the crowded river.

Leave-taking is a disagreeable subject either to reflect upon or to write about, so we will skip that part of the business and proceed at once to Gravesend, where I stood (having parted from all my friends) on the deck of the good ship *Prince Rupert*, contemplating the boats and crowds of shipping that passed continually before me, and thinking how soon I was to leave the scenes to which I had been so long accustomed for a far-distant land. I was a boy, however; and this, I think, is equivalent to saying that I did not sorrow long. My future companion and fellow-clerk, Mr Wiseacre, was pacing the deck near me. This turned my thoughts into another channel, and set me speculating upon his probable temper, qualities, and age; whether or not he was strong enough to thrash me, and if we were likely to be good friends. The captain, too, was chatting and laughing with the doctor as carelessly as if he had not the great responsibility of taking a huge ship across a boundless waste of waters, and through fields and islands of ice, to a distant country some three thousand miles to the north-west of England. Thus encouraged, my spirits began to rise, and when the cry arose on deck that the steamer containing the committee of the Honourable Hudson Bay Company was in sight, I sprang up the companion-ladder in a state of mind, if not happy, at least as nearly so as under the circumstances could be expected.

Upon gaining the deck, I beheld a small steamboat passing close under our stern, filled with a number of elderly-looking gentlemen, who eyed us with a very critical expression of countenance. I had a pretty good guess who these gentlemen were; but had I been entirely ignorant, I should soon have been enlightened by the remark of a sailor, who whispered to his comrade, "I say, Bill, them's the great guns!"

I suppose the fact of their being so had a sympathetic effect upon the guns of the Company's three ships—the *Prince Rupert, Prince Albert*, and *Prince of Wales*—for they all three fired a salute of blank cartridge at the steamer as she passed them in succession. The steamer then ranged alongside of us, and the elderly gentlemen came on board and shook hands with the captain and officers, smiling blandly as they observed the neat, trim appearance of the three fine vessels, which, with everything in readiness for setting sail on the following morning, strained at their cables, as if anxious to commence their struggle with the waves.

It is a custom of the directors of the Hudson Bay Company to give a public dinner annually to the officers of their ships upon the eve of their departure from Gravesend. Accordingly, one of the gentlemen of the committee, before leaving the vessel, invited the captain and officers to attend; and, to my astonishment and delight, also *begged me* to honour them with my company. I accepted the invitation with extreme politeness; and, from inability to express my joy in any other way, winked to my friend Wiseacre, with whom I had become, by this time, pretty familiar. He, being also invited, winked in return to me; and having disposed of this piece of juvenile freemasonry to our satisfaction, we assisted the crew in giving three hearty cheers, as the little steamer darted from the side and proceeded to the shore.

The dinner, like all other public dinners, was as good and substantial as a lavish expenditure of cash could make it; but really my recollections of it are very indistinct. The ceaseless din of plates, glasses, knives, forks, and tongues was tremendous; and this, together with the novelty of the scene, the heat of the room, and excellence of the viands, tended to render me oblivious of much that took place. Almost all the faces present were strange to me. Who were, and who were not, the gentlemen of the committee, was to me matter of the most perfect indifference; and as no one took the trouble to address me in particular, I confined myself to the interesting occupation of trying to make sense of a conversation held by upwards of fifty pairs of lungs at one and the same time. Nothing intelligible, however, was to be heard, except when a sudden lull in the noise gave a bald-headed old gentleman near the head of the table an opportunity of drinking the health of a red-faced old gentleman near the foot, upon whom he bestowed an amount of flattery perfectly bewildering; and after making the unfortunate red-faced gentleman writhe for half an hour in a fever of modesty, sat down amid thunders of applause. Whether the applause, by the way, was intended for the speaker or the *speakee*, I do not know; but being quite indifferent, I clapped my hands with the rest. The red-faced gentleman, now purple with excitement, then rose, and during a solemn silence delivered himself of a speech, to the effect that the day then passing was certainly the happiest in his mortal career, that he could not find words adequately to express the varied feelings which swelled his throbbing bosom, and that he felt quite faint with the mighty load of honour just thrown upon his delighted shoulders by his bald-headed friend. The red-faced gentleman then sat down to the national air of rat-tat-tat, played in full chorus with knives, forks, spoons, nut-crackers, and knuckles on the polished surface of the mahogany table.

We left the dinner-table at a late hour, and after I, in company with some other youngsters, had done as much mischief as we conveniently could without risking our detention by the strong arm of the law, we went down to the beach and embarked in a boat with the captain for the ship. How the sailors ever found her in the impenetrable darkness which prevailed all around is a mystery to me to this day. Find her, however, they did; and in half an hour I was in the land of Nod.

The sun was blazing high in the heavens next morning when I awoke, and gazed around for a few moments to discover where I was; but the rattling of ropes and blocks, the stamping of feet overhead, the shouts of gruff voices, and, above all, a certain strange and disagreeable motion in my dormitory, soon enlightened me on that point. We were going rapidly down the Thames with a fair breeze, and had actually set sail for the distant shores of Hudson Bay.

What took place during the next five or six days I know not. The demon of sea-sickness had completely prostrated my faculties, bodily and mental. Some faint recollections I have of stormy weather, horrible noises, and hurried dinners; but the greater part of that period is a miserable blank in my memory. Towards the sixth day, however, the savoury flavour of a splendid salmon-trout floated past my dried-up nostrils like "Afric's spicy gale," and caused my collapsed stomach to yearn with strong emotion. The ship, too, was going more quietly through the water; and a broad stream of sunshine shot through the small window of my berth, penetrated my breast, and went down into the centre of my heart, filling it with a calm, complacent pleasure quite indescribable. Sounds, however, of an attack upon the trout roused me, and with a mighty effort I tumbled out of bed, donned my clothes, and seated myself for the first time at the cabin table.

Our party consisted of the captain; Mr Carles, a chief factor in the Company's service; the doctor; young Mr Wiseacre, afore-mentioned; the first and second mates; and myself. The captain was a thin, middle-sized, offhand man; thoroughly acquainted with his profession; good-humoured and gruff by turns; and he always spoke with the air of an oracle. Mr Carles was a mild, good-natured man, of about fifty-five, with a smooth, bald head, encircled by a growth of long, thin hair. He was stoutly built, and possessed of that truly amiable and

THE "PRINCE RUPERT."

captivating disposition which enters earnestly and kindly into the affairs of others, and totally repudiates self. From early manhood he had roughed life in the very roughest and wildest scenes of the wilderness, and was now returning to those scenes after a short visit to his native land. The doctor was a nondescript; a compound of gravity, fun, seriousness, and humbug—the latter predominating. He had been everywhere (at least, so he said), had seen everything, knew everybody, and played the fiddle. It cannot be said, I fear, that he played it well; but, amid the various vicissitudes of his chequered life, the doctor had frequently found himself in company where his violin was almost idolised and himself deified; especially when the place chanced to be the American backwoods, where violins are scarce, the auditors semi-barbarous Highlanders, and the music Scotch reels. Mr Wiseacre was nothing! He never spoke except when compelled to do so; never read, and never cared for anything or anybody; wore very long hair, which almost hid his face, owing to a habit which he had of holding his head always down: and apparently lived but to eat, drink, and sleep. Sometimes, though very rarely, he became so far facetious as to indulge in a wink and a low giggle; but beyond this he seldom soared. The two mates were simply *mates*. Those who know the population of the sea will understand the description sufficiently; those who don't, will never, I fear, be made to understand by description. They worked the ship, hove the log, changed the watch, turned out and tumbled in, with the callous indifference and stern regularity of clock work; inhabited tarpaulin dreadnoughts and sou'-westers; came down to meals with modest diffidence, and walked the deck with bantam-cock-like assurance. Nevertheless, they were warm-hearted fellows, both of them, although the heat didn't often come to the surface. The first mate was a *broad* Scotchman, in every sense of the term; the second was a burly little Englishman.

"How's the wind, Collins?" said the captain, as the second mate sat down at the dinner-table, and brushed the spray from his face with the back of his brown hand.

"Changed a point to the s'uthard o' sou'-west, sir," he answered, "and looks as if it would blow hard."

"Humph!" ejaculated the captain, while he proceeded to help the fish. "I hope it'll only keep quiet till we get into blue water, and then it may blow like blazes for all I care,—Take some trout, doctor? It's the last you'll put your teeth through for six weeks to come, *I* know; so make the most of it.—I wish I were only through the Pentland Firth, and scudding under full sail for the ice—I do." And the captain looked fiercely at the compass which hung over his head, as if he had said something worthy of being recorded in history, and began to eat.

After a pause of five minutes or so—during which time the knives and forks had been clattering pretty vigorously, and the trout had become a miserable skeleton—the captain resumed his discourse.

"I tell you what it is now, gentlemen; if there's not going to be a change of some sort or other, I'm no sailor."

"It does look very threatening," said Mr Carles, peering through the stern window. "I don't much like the look of these clouds behind us. Look there, doctor!" he continued, pointing towards the window. "What do you think of that?"

"Nothing!" replied the doctor, through a mouthful of duff and potatoes. "A squall, I fancy; wish it'd only wait till after dinner."

"It never does," said the captain. "I've been to sea these fifteen years, and I always find that squalls come on at breakfast or dinner, like an unwelcome visitor. They've got a thorough contempt for tea—seem to know it's but swipes, and not worth pitching into one's lap; but dinner's sure to bring 'em on, if they're in the neighbourhood, and make 'em bu'st their cheeks at you. Remember once, when I was cruising in the Mediterranean, in Lord P—'s yacht, we'd been stewing on deck under an awning the whole forenoon, scarce able to breathe, when the bell rang for dinner. Well, down we all tumbled—about ten ladies and fifteen gentlemen, or thereabouts—and seated ourselves round the table. There was no end of grub of every kind. Lord P— was eccentric in that way, and was always at some new dodge or other in the way of cookery. At this time he had invented a new dumpling. Its jacket was much the same as usual—inch-thick duff; but its contents were beyond anything I ever saw, except the maw of an old shark. Well, just as the steward took off the cover, *hiss–iss* went the wind overhead, and one of those horrible squalls that come rattling down without a moment's warning in those parts, struck the ship, and gave her a heel over that sent the salt-cellars chasing the tumblers like all-possessed; and the great dumpling gave a heavy lurch to leeward, rolled fairly over on its beam-ends, and began to course straight down the table quite sedate and quiet-like. Several dives were made at it by the gentlemen as it passed, but they all missed; and finally, just as a youngster made a grab at it with both hands that bid fair to be successful, another howl of the squall changed its course, and sent it like a cannon-shot straight into the face of the steward, where it split its sides, and scattered its contents right and left. I don't know how it ended, for I bolted up the companion, and saw the squall splitting away to leeward, shrieking as it went, just as if it were rejoicing at the mischief it had done."

The laugh which greeted the captain's anecdote had scarce subsided when the tough sides of the good *Prince Rupert* gave a gentle creak, and the angle at which the active steward perambulated the cabin became absurdly acute.

Just then the doctor cast his eye up at the compass suspended above the captain's head. "Hallo!" said he—But before he could give utterance to the sentiments to which "hallo" was the preface, the hoarse voice of the first mate came

CAUGHT BY A SQUALL.

rolling down the companion-hatch,—"A squall, sir! scoorin' doon like mad! Wund's veered richt roond to the nor'-east."

The captain and second mate sprang hastily to their feet and rushed upon deck, where the rest of us joined them as speedily as possible.

On gaining the quarter-deck, the scene that presented itself was truly grand. Thick black clouds rolled heavily overhead, and cast a gloom upon the sea which caused it to look like ink. Not a breath of wind swelled the sails, which the men were actively engaged in taking in. Far away on our weather-quarter the clouds were thicker and darker; and just where they met the sea there was seen a bright streak of white, which rapidly grew broader and brighter, until we could perceive that it was the sea lashed into a seething foam by the gale which was sweeping over it.

"Mind your helm!" shouted the captain.

"Ay, ay, sir!" sang out the man at the wheel. And in another moment the squall burst upon us with all its fury, laying the huge vessel over on its side as if it had been a feather on the wave, and causing her to fly through the black water like a dolphin.

In a few minutes the first violence of the squall passed away, and was succeeded by a steady breeze, which bore us merrily along over the swelling billows.

"A stiff one, that," said the captain, turning to the doctor, who, with imperturbable nonchalance, was standing near him, holding on to a stanchion with one hand, while the other reposed in his breeches pocket.

"I hope it will last," replied the doctor. "If it does, we'll not be long of reaching the blue water you long so much for."

Young Wiseacre, who during the squall had been clutching the weather-shrouds with the tenacity of a drowning man, opened his eyes very wide on hearing this, to him, insane wish, and said to me in an undertone, "I say, do you think the doctor is quite right in his mind?"

"I have no doubt of it," replied I. "Why do you ask?"

"Because I heard him say to the captain he wished that this would last."

"Is that all?" said I, while a very vile spirit of vanity took possession of me, inducing me to speak in a tone which indicated a tranquillity of mind that I certainly did not enjoy. "Oh, this is nothing at all! I see you've never been on salt water before. Just wait a bit, old fellow!" And having given utterance to this somewhat dark and mysterious expression, I staggered across the deck, and amused myself in watching the thick volumes of spray that flew at every plunge from the sides of the bounding vessel.

The doctor's wish was granted. The breeze continued steady and strong, sending us through the Pentland Firth in grand style, and carrying us in a short time to the island of Lewis, where we hove-to for a pilot. After a little signalising we obtained one, who steered our good ship in safety through the narrow entrance to the bay of Stornoway into whose quiet waters we finally dropped our anchor.

2

STORNOWAY

*—The Ball—At Sea—Go Out to Tea on
the Atlantic—Among the Ice—Sighting Land
—A Sleepy Sight—York Factory and Bachelors' Hall*

THE HARBOUR OF STORNOWAY is surrounded by high hills, except at the entrance, where a passage—not more, I should think, than three hundred yards wide—admits vessels of any tonnage into its sheltering bosom. Stornoway, a pretty, modest-looking town, apparently pleased with its lot, and contented to be far away from the busy and bustling world, lies snugly at the bottom of the bay. Here we remained upwards of a week, engaging men for the wild Nor'-West, and cultivating the acquaintance of the people, who were extremely kind and very hospitable. Occasionally Wiseacre and I amused ourselves with fishing excursions to the middle of the bay in small boats; in which excursions we were usually accompanied by two or three very ragged little boys from the town. Our sport was generally good, and rendered extremely interesting by our uncertainty as to which of the monsters of the deep would first attack our hooks. Rock-codlings and flounders appeared the most voracious, and occasionally a skate or long-legged crab came struggling to the surface.

Just before leaving this peaceful little spot, our captain gave a grand ball on board, to which were invited the *élite* of Stornoway. Great preparations were made for the occasion. The quarter-deck was well washed and scrubbed; an awning was spread over it, which formed a capital ceiling; and representatives of almost every flag that waves formed the walls of the large and airy apartment. Oil lamps, placed upon the skylights, companion, and capstan, shed a mellow light upon the scene, the romantic effect of which was greatly heightened by a few flickering rays of the moon, which shot through various openings in the drapery, and disported playfully upon the deck. At an early and very unfashionable hour on the evening of the appointed night the guests arrived in detachments; and while the gentlemen scrambled up the side of the vessel, the ladies, amid a good deal of blushing and hesitation, were hoisted on board in a chair. Tea was served on deck; and after half an hour's laughing and chatting, during which time our violin-player was endeavouring to coax his first string to the proper pitch without breaking, the ball opened with a Scotch reel. Every one knows what Scotch reels are, but every one does not know how the belles of the Western Isles can dance them.

"Just look at that slip of thread-paper," said the doctor to the captain, pointing to a thin, flat young lady, still in her teens. "I've watched her from the first. She's been up at six successive rounds, flinging her shanks about worse than a teething baby; and she's up again for another, just as cool and serene as a night in the latter end of October. I wonder what she's made of?"

"Leather, p'r'aps, or gutta-percha," suggested the captain, who had himself been "flinging his legs" about pretty violently during the previous half-hour. "I wish that she had been my partner instead of the heavy fair one that you see over there leaning against the mizzen belaying-pins."

"Which?" inquired the doctor. "The old lady with the stu'n-sails set on her shoulders?"

"No, no," replied the captain—"the *young* lady; fat—*very* fat—fair, and twenty, with the big blue eyes like signal-lamps on a locomotive. She twisted me round just as if I'd been a fathom of pump-water, shouting and laughing all the time in my face, like a sou'-west gale, and never looking a bit where she was going till she pitched head-foremost into the union-jack, carrying it and me along with her off the quarter-deck and half-way down the companion. It's a blessing she fell undermost, else I should have been spread all over the deck like a capsized pail of slops."

"Hallo!" exclaimed the doctor; "what's wrong with the old lady over there? She's making very uncommon faces."

"She's sea-sick, I do believe," cried the captain, rushing across the deck towards her.

And, without doubt, the old lady in question was show-ing symptoms of that terrible malady, although the bay was as smooth as a mill-pond, and the *Prince Rupert* reposed on its quiet bosom without the slightest perceptible motion. With impressive nautical politeness the captain handed her below, and in the sudden sympathy of his heart proposed as a remedy a stiff glass of brandy and water.

"Or a pipe of cavendish," suggested the second mate, who met them on the ladder as they descended, and could not refrain from a facetious remark, even although he knew it would, as it did, call forth a thundering command from his superior to go on deck and mind his own business.

"Isn't it jolly," said a young Stornowite, coming up to Wiseacre, with a face blazing with glee—"isn't it jolly, Mr Wiseacre?"

"Oh, very!" replied Wiseacre, in a voice of such dismal melancholy that the young Stornowite's countenance instantly went out, and he wheeled suddenly round to light it again at the visage of some more sympathising companion.

Just at this point of the revelry the fiddler's first string, which had endured with a dogged tenacity that was wonderful even for catgut, gave way with a loud bang, causing an abrupt termination to the uproar, and producing a dead silence. A few minutes, however, soon rectified this mischance. The discordant tones of the violin, as the new string was tortured into tune, once more opened the safety-valve, and the ball began *de novo*.

Great was the fun, and numerous were the ludicrous incidents that happened during that eventful night; and loud were the noise and merriment of the dancers as they went with vigorous energy through the bewildering evolutions of country-dance and reel. Immense was the delight of the company when the funniest old gentleman there volunteered a song; and ecstatic the joy when he followed it up by a speech upon every subject that an ordinary mind could possibly embrace in a quarter of an hour. But who can describe the scene that ensued when supper was reported ready in the cabin!—a cabin that was very small indeed, with a stair leading down to it so steep that those who were pretty high up could have easily stepped upon the shoulders of those who were near the foot; and the unpleasant idea was painfully suggested that if any one of the heavy ladies (there were several of them) was to slip her foot on commencing the descent, she would infallibly sweep them all down in a mass, and cram them into the cook's pantry, the door of which stood wickedly open at the foot of the stair, as if it anticipated some such catastrophe. Such pushing, squeezing, laughing, shrieking, and joking, in the vain attempt made to get upwards of thirty people crammed into a room of twelve feet by ten! Such droll and cutting re-marks as were made when they were at last requested to sup in detachments! All this, however, was nothing to what ensued after supper, when the fiddler became more energetic, and the dancers more vigorous than ever. But enough. The first grey streaks of morning glimmered in the east ere the joyous party "tumbled down the sides" and departed to their homes.

There is a sweet yet melancholy pleasure, when far away from friends and home, in thinking over happy days gone by, and dwelling on the scenes and pleasures that have passed away, perhaps for ever. So I thought and felt as I recalled to mind the fun and frolic of the Stornoway ball, and the grav-er mirth of the Gravesend dinner, until memory traced my course backward, step by step, to the peaceful time when I dwelt in Scotland, surrounded by the gentle inmates of my happy home. We had left the shores and the green water be-hind us, and were now ploughing through the blue waves of the wide Atlantic; and when I turned my straining eyes to-wards the faint blue line of the lessening hills, "a tear unbidden trembled" as the thought arose that I looked perhaps for the last time upon my dear native land.

The sea has ever been an inexhaustible subject for the pens of most classes of writers. The poet, the traveller, and the novelist has each devoted a portion of his time and talents to the mighty ocean; but that part of it which it has fallen to my lot to describe is very different from those portions about which poets have sung with rapture. Here, none of the many wonders of the tropical latitudes beguile the tedium of the voyage; no glittering dolphins force the winged inhabitants of the deep to seek shelter on the vessel's deck; no ravenous sharks follow in our wake to eat us if we chance to fall overboard, or amuse us by swallowing our baited hook; no passing vessel cheers us with the knowledge that there are others besides ourselves roaming over the interminable waste of waters. All was dreary and monotonous; the same unvarying expanse of sky and water met our gaze each morning as we ascended to the deck, to walk for half an hour before breakfast, except when the topsails of the other two vessels fluttered for a moment on the distant horizon. Occasionally we approached closer to each other, and once or twice hailed with the trumpet; but these breaks in the solitude of our existence were few and far between.

Towards the end of July we approached Hudson Straits, having seen nothing on the way worth mentioning, except one whale, which passed close under the stern of the ship. This was a great novelty to me, being the first that I had ever seen, and it gave me something to talk of and think about for the next four days.

The ships now began to close in, as we neared the entrance of the straits, and we had the pleasure of sailing in company for a few days. The shores of the straits became visible occasionally, and soon we passed with perfect confidence and security among those narrow channels and mountains of ice that damped the ardour and retarded the progress of Hudson,

Button, Gibbons, and other navigators in days of yore.

One day, during a dead calm, our ship and the *Prince of Wales* lay close to each other, rolling in the swell of the glassy ocean. There seemed to be no prospect of a breeze, so the captain ordered his gig to be launched, and invited the doctor, Mr Carles, and myself to go on board the *Prince of Wales* with him. We accepted his offer, and were soon alongside. Old Captain Ryle, a veteran in the Company's service, received us kindly, and insisted on our staying to tea. The passengers on board were—a chief factor, (*The chief factorship is the highest rank attainable in the service, the chief trader being next*) who had been home on leave of absence, and was returning to end his days, perhaps, in the North-West; and Mr John Leagues, a young apprentice clerk, going, like myself, to try his fortune in Hudson Bay. He was a fine, candid young fellow, full of spirit, with a kind, engaging disposition. From the first moment I saw him I formed a friendship for him, which was destined to ripen into a lasting one many years after. I sighed on parting from him that evening, thinking that we should never meet again; but about six years from the time I bade him farewell in Hudson Straits, I again grasped his hand on the shores of the mighty St. Lawrence, and renewed a friendship which afforded me the greatest pleasure I enjoyed in the country, and which, I trust, neither time nor distance will ever lessen or destroy.

We spent the evening delightfully, the more so that we were not likely to have such an opportunity again, as the *Prince of Wales* would shortly part company from us, and direct her course to Moose Factory, in James Bay, while we should proceed across Hudson Bay to York Factory. We left the ship just as a few cats-paws on the surface of the water gave indications of a coming breeze.

Ice now began to surround us in all directions; and soon after this I saw, for the first time, that monster of the Polar Seas, an iceberg. It was a noble sight. We passed quite close, and had a fine opportunity of observing it. Though not so large as they are frequently seen, it was beautifully and fantastically formed. High peaks rose from it on various places, and down its sides streams of water and miniature cataracts flowed in torrents. The whole mass was of a delicate greenish-white colour, and its lofty pinnacles sparkled in the moonbeams as it floated past, bending majestically in the swell of the ocean. About this time, too, we met numerous fields and floes of ice, to get through which we often experienced considerable difficulty.

My favourite amusement, as we thus threaded our way through the ice, was to ascend to the royal-yard, and there to sit and cogitate whilst gazing on the most beautiful and romantic scenes.

It is impossible to convey a correct idea of the beauty, the magnificence, of some of the scenes through which we passed. Sometimes thousands of the most grotesque, fanciful, and beautiful icebergs and icefields surrounded us on all sides, intersected by numerous serpentine canals, which glittered in the sun (for the weather was fine nearly all the time we were in the straits), like threads of silver twining round ruined palaces of crystal. The masses assumed every variety of form and size; and many of them bore such a striking resemblance to cathedrals, churches, columns, arches, and spires, that I could almost fancy we had been transported to one of the floating cities of Fairyland. The rapid motion, too, of our ship, in what appeared a dead calm, added much to the magical effect of the scene. A light but steady breeze urged her along with considerable velocity through a maze of ponds and canals, which, from the immense quantity of ice that surrounded them, were calm and unruffled as the surface of a mill-pond.

Not a sound disturbed the delightful stillness of nature, save the gentle rippling of the vessel's bow as she sped on her way, or the occasional puffing of a lazy whale, awakened from a nap by our unceremonious intrusion on his domains. Now and then, however, my reveries were interrupted by the ship coming into sudden contact with huge lumps of ice. This happened occasionally when we arrived at the termination of one of those natural canals through which we passed, and found it necessary to force our way into the next. These concussions were occasionally very severe—so much so, at times, as to make the ship's bell ring; but we heeded this little, as the vessel was provided with huge blocks of timber on her bows, called ice-pieces, and was, besides, built expressly for sailing in the northern seas. It only became annoying at meal-times, when a spoonful of soup would sometimes make a little private excursion of its own over the shoulder of the owner instead of into his mouth.

As we proceeded, the ice became more closely packed, and at last compelled us to bore through it. The ship, however, was never altogether arrested, though often much retarded. I recollect, while thus surrounded, filling a bucket with water from a pool on the ice, to see whether it was fresh or not, as I had been rather sceptical upon this point. It was excellent, and might almost compete with the water from the famous spring of Crawley. In a few days we got out of the ice altogether; and in this, as the ships are frequently detained for weeks in the straits, we considered ourselves very fortunate.

We all experienced at this time a severe disappointment in the non-appearance of the Esquimaux from the coast. The captain said they would be sure to come off to us, as they had always been in the habit of doing so, for the purpose of exchanging ivory and oil for saws, files, needles, etcetera, a large chestful of which is put on board annually for this purpose. The ivory usually procured from them is walrus tusks. These are not very large, and are of inferior quality.

As we approached the shores of the straits, we shortened sail and fired three or four guns, but no noisy "*chimo*" floated across the water in answer to our salute; still we lingered for a while, but, as there was no sign of the natives on shore, the captain concluded they had gone off to the interior, and he steered out to sea again. I was very much disappointed at this, as it was wholly unexpected, and Wiseacre and I had promised ourselves much pleasure in trading with them; for which purpose all the buttons of our old waistcoats had been amputated. It was useless, however, to repine, so I contented myself with the hope that they would yet visit us in some other part of the straits. We afterwards learned that our guns had attracted them to the coast in time to board the *Prince Albert* (which was out of sight astern), though too late for us.

The passage across Hudson Bay was stormy, but no one on board cared for this, all having become accustomed to rough weather. For my part, I had become quite a sailor, and could ascend and descend easily to the truck without creeping through the *lubber's hole*. I shall not forget the first time I attempted this: our youngest apprentice had challenged me to try it, so up we went together—he on the fore and I on the main mast. The tops were gained easily, and we even made two or three steps up the top-mast shrouds with affected indiffer-

AMONG THE ICE.

ence; but, alas! our courage was failing—at least *mine* was—very fast. However, we gained the cross-trees pretty well, and then sat down for a little to recover breath. The topgallant-mast still reared its taper form high above me, and the worst was yet to come. The top-gallant shrouds had no ratlines on them, so I was obliged to *shin* up; and, as I worked myself up the two small ropes, the tenacity with which I grasped them was fearful. At last I reached the top, and with my feet on the small collar that fastens the ropes to the mast, and my arms circling the mast itself—for nothing but a bare pole, crossed by the royal-yard, now rose above me—I glanced upwards. After taking a long breath, and screwing up my courage, I slowly shinned up the slender pole, and, standing on the royal-yard, laid my hand upon the *truck*. After a time I became accustomed to it, and thought nothing of taking an airing on the royal-yard after breakfast.

About the 5th or 6th of August, the captain said we must be near the land. The deep-sea lead was rigged, and a sharp lookout kept, but no land appeared. At last, one fine day, while at the mast-head, I saw something like land on the horizon, and told them so on deck. They saw it too, but gave me no answer. Soon a hurried order to "Dowse top-gallant-sails and reef top-sails" made me slide down rather hastily from my elevated position. I had scarcely gained the deck, when a squall, the severest we had yet encountered, struck the ship, laying her almost on her beam-ends; and the sea, which had been nearly calm a few minutes before, foamed and hissed like a seething caldron, and became white as snow. This, I believe, was what sailors call a *white squall*. It was as short as it was severe, and great was our relief when the ship regained her natural position in the water. Next day we saw land in earnest, and in the afternoon anchored in "Five Fathom Hole," after passing in safety a sandbar, which renders the entrance into this roadstead rather difficult.

Here, then, for the first time I beheld the shores of Hudson Bay; and truly their appearance was anything but prepossessing. Though only at the distance of two miles, so low and flat was the land, that it appeared ten miles off, and scarcely a tree was to be seen. We could just see the tops of one or two houses in York Factory, the principal depôt of the country, which was seven miles up the river at the mouth of which we lay. In a short time the sails of a small schooner came in sight, and in half an hour more the *Frances* (named after the amiable lady of the governor, Sir George Simpson) was riding alongside.

The skipper came on board, and immediately there commenced between him and the captain a sharp fire of questions and answers, which roused me from a slumber in which I had been indulging, and hurried me on deck. Here the face of things had changed. The hatches were off, and bales of goods were scattered about in all directions. Another small schooner had arrived, and the process of discharging the vessel was going rapidly forward. A boat was then dispatched to the factory with the packet-box and letter-bag, and soon after the *Frances* stood in for the shore.

The *Prince Albert* had arrived almost at the same moment with the *Prince Rupert*, and was now visited by the second schooner, which soon returned to our ship to take the passengers on shore. The passengers who came out in the *Prince Albert* were on board—namely, the Reverend Mr Gowley, a clergyman of the Church of England, and his lady; and Mr Rob, a sort of catechist, or semi-clerical schoolmaster. They were missionaries bound for Red River Colony; and as I had some prospect of going there myself, I was delighted to have the probable chance of travelling with companions who, from the short survey I had of them while they conversed with the captain and Mr Carles, seemed good-natured and agreeable.

Mr Carles, Mr Wiseacre, and I now bade adieu to the good ship which had been our home for such a length of time (but I must say I did not regret the parting), and followed our baggage on board the schooner, expecting to reach the factory before dusk. "There's many a slip 'twixt the cup and the lip," is a proverb well authenticated and often quoted, and on the present occasion its truth was verified. We had not been long under weigh before the ebb tide began to run so strong against us as to preclude the possibility of our reaching the shore that night. There was no help for it, however; so down went the anchor to the bottom, and down went I to the cabin.

Such a cabin! A good-sized trunk, with a small table in it, and the lid shut down, had about as much right to the name. It was awfully small—even *I* could not stand upright in it, though at the time I had scarcely attained to the altitude

of five feet; yet here were we destined to pass the night—
and a wretched night we did pass. We got over the first part
tolerably, but as it grew late our eyes grew heavy. We yawned,
fidgeted and made superhuman efforts to keep awake and
seem happy; but it would not do. There were only two berths
in the cabin; and, as so many gentlemen were present, Mrs
Gowley would not get into either of them, but declared she
would sit up all night. The gentlemen, on the other hand,
could not be so ungallant as to go to sleep while the only lady
present sat up. The case was desperate, and so I went off to the
hold, intending to lie down on a bale, if I could find one. In
my search I tumbled over something soft, which gave vent to a
frightful howl, and proved to be no less a personage than Mr
Wiseacre, who had anticipated me, and found a convenient
place whereon to lie. My search, however, was less successful.
Not a corner big enough for a cat to sleep in was to be found,
all the goods having been flung hastily into the hold, so that it
was a chaos of box corners, stove legs, edges of kegs and casks,
which presented a surface that put to flight all hope of hori-
zontal repose; so I was obliged to return to the cabin, where
I found the unhappy inmates winking and blinking at each
other like owls in the sunshine.

"You had better make use of one of these berths, my young
friend," said Mr Gowley, with a bland smile, as I entered; "you
seem very much overcome with sleep, and *we* have resolved to
sit up all night."

"Do get in," urged Mrs Gowley, who was a sweet, gentle
creature, and seemed much too delicate and fragile to stand
the rough life that was likely to be the lot of the wife of a missionary to the Red men of the Far North; "I do not intend to
lie down to-night; and besides, it will soon be morning." A

sweet but very sleepy smile flitted across her face as she spoke.

Of course, I protested against this with great vehemence, assuring them that I could not think of anything so ungallant, and that I meant to sit it out manfully with the rest. Mr Rob, who was a comical little Welshman, of about thirty years of age, with a sharp, snub nose, which was decorated with spectacles, sat huddled up in a corner, immersed in sleepiness to such an extent that he would not have smiled for worlds, and spent the weary hours in vain efforts to keep his head on his shoulders—an object, apparently, of some difficulty, seeing that it swayed backwards and forwards and round about like that of a Chinese mandarin! For a few minutes I sat gazing steadfastly at the revolving object before me, when my own head became similarly affected, and fell suddenly back against the bulk-head with a tremendous crash, wakening them all up, and causing Mr Rob to stare at me with an expression of vacant gravity, mingled with surprise, which slowly and gradually faded away again as sleep reasserted its irresistible power.

Flesh and blood could not stand this. I would have lain down on the table, but poor Mrs Gowley's head already covered the greater part of that; or on the floor, but, alas! it was too small. At last I began to reason thus with myself: "Here are two capital beds, with nobody in them; it is the height of folly to permit them to remain empty; but then, what a self-ish-looking thing to leave Mrs Gowley sitting up! After all, she *won't* go to bed. Oh dear! what *is* to be done?" (Bang went the head again.) "You'd better turn in," said Mr Gowley. Again I protested that I could not think of it; but my eyes would not keep open to look him in the face. At last my scruples—I blush to say it—were overcome, and I allowed myself to be half forced into the berth; while Mr Rob, whose self-denial could endure no longer, took advantage of the confusion thus occasioned, and vanished into the other like a harlequin. Poor Mr and Mrs Gowley laid their innocent heads side by side upon the table, and snored in concert.

How long I slept I know not, but long before day a tremendous thumping awoke me, and after I had collected my faculties enough to understand it, I found that the schooner was grounding as the tide receded. "Oh!" thought I; and, being utterly incapable of thinking more, I fell back on the pillow again, sound asleep, and did not awake till long after daybreak.

Next morning was beautiful; but we were still aground, and, from what the skipper said, there appeared to be no prospect of getting ashore till the afternoon. Our patience, however, was not tried so long; for, early in the day, a boat came off from the factory to take us ashore: but the missionaries preferred remaining in the schooner. Mr Carles, young Wiseacre, and I gladly availed ourselves of the opportunity, and were soon sailing with a fair breeze up Hayes River. We approached to within a few yards of the shore; and I formed, at first sight, a very poor opinion of the country which, two years later, I was destined to traverse full many a mile in search of the feathered inhabitants of the marshes.

The Point of Marsh, which was the first land we made, was quite low—only a few feet above the sea—and studded here and there with thick willows, but not a single tree. Long lank grass covered it in every place, affording ducks and geese shelter, in the autumn and spring. In the centre of it stood the ship-beacon—a tall, ungainly-looking pile, which rose upwards like a monster out of the water. Altogether, a more desolate prospect could not well be imagined.

The banks of Hayes River are formed of clay, and they improved a little in verdure as we ascended; but still, wherever the eye turned, the same universal flatness met the gaze. The river was here about two miles wide, and filled with shallows and sandbanks, which render the navigation difficult for vessels above fifty tons.

As we proceeded, a small bark canoe, with an Indian and his wife in it, glided swiftly past us; and this was the first Indian, and the first of these slender craft, I had seen. Afterwards, I became more intimately acquainted with them than was altogether agreeable.

In a short time we reached the wooden wharf, which, owing to the smallness of everything else in the vicinity, had rather an imposing look, and projected a long way into the water; but our boat passed this and made for a small slip, on which two or three gentlemen waited to receive us.

My voyage was ended. The boat's keel grated harshly on the gravel; the next moment my feet once more pressed *terra firma*, and I stood at last on the shores of the New World, a stranger in a strange land.

I do not intend to give a minute description of York Factory here, as a full account of it will be found in a succeeding chapter, and shall, therefore, confine myself to a slight sketch of the establishment, and our proceedings there during a stay of about three weeks.

York Factory is the principal depôt of the Northern department, from whence all the supplies for the trade are issued, and where all the furs of the district are collected and shipped for England. As may be supposed, then, the establishment is a large one. There are always between thirty and forty men resident at the post, (*The word "post," used here and elsewhere throughout the book, signifies an establishment of any kind, small or great, and has no reference whatever to the "post" of epistolary notoriety.*) summer and winter; generally four or five clerks, a postmaster, and a skipper for the small schooners. The whole is under the direction and superintendence of a chief factor, or chief trader.

As the winter is very long (nearly eight months), and the summer very short, all the transport of goods to, and returns from, the interior must necessarily be effected as quickly as possible. The consequence is, that great numbers of men and boats are constantly arriving from the inland posts, and departing again, during the summer; and as each brigade is commanded by a chief factor, trader, or clerk, there is a constant succession of new faces, which, after a long and dreary winter, during which the inhabitants never see a stranger, renders the summer at York Factory the most agreeable part of the year. The arrival of the ship from England, too, delights those inhabitants of the wilderness with letters from *home*, which can only be received twice a year—namely, at the time now alluded to, by the ship; and again in December, when letters and accounts are conveyed throughout the interior by means of sledges drawn by men.

The fort (as all establishments in the Indian country, whether small or great, are sometimes called) is a large square, I should think about six or seven acres, enclosed within high stockades, and planted on the banks of Hayes River, nearly five miles from its mouth. The houses are all of wood, and, of course, have no pretension to architectural beauty; but their clean, white appearance and regularity have a pleasing effect on the eye. Before the front gate stand four large brass field-pieces; but these warlike instruments are only used for the purpose of saluting the ship with blank cartridge on her arrival and departure, the decayed state of the carriages rendering it dangerous to load the guns with a full charge.

The country, as I said before, is flat and swampy, and the only objects that rise very prominently above the rest, and catch the wandering eye, are a lofty "outlook," or scaffolding of wood, painted black, from which to watch for the arrival of the ship; and a flagstaff, from whose peak, on Sundays, the snowy folds of St. George's flag flutter in the breeze.

Such was York Factory in 1841; and as this description is sufficient to give a general idea of the place, I shall conclude it, and proceed with my narrative.

Mr Grave, the chief factor then in charge, received us very kindly, and introduced us to some of the gentlemen standing beside him on the wharf. Mr Carles, being also a chief factor, was taken by him to the *commissioned gentlemen's house*; while Wiseacre and I, being apprentice clerks, were shown the young gentlemen's house—or, as the young gentlemen themselves called it, Bachelors' Hall—and were told to make ourselves at home. To Bachelors' Hall, then, we proceeded, and introduced ourselves. The persons assembled there were—the accountant, five clerks, the postmaster, and one or two others. Some of them were smoking, and some talking; and a pretty considerable noise they made. Bachelors' Hall, indeed, was worthy of its name, being a place that would have killed any woman, so full was it of smoke, noise, and confusion.

After having made ourselves acquainted with everybody, I thought it time to present a letter of introduction I had to Mrs Grave, the wife of the gentleman in charge, who received me very kindly. I was much indebted to this lady for supplying me with several pairs of moccasins for my further voyage, and much useful information, without which I should have been badly off indeed. Had it not been for her kindness, I should in all probability have been allowed to depart very ill provided for the journey to Red River, for which I was desired to hold myself in readiness. Young Wiseacre, on the other hand, learned that he was to remain at York Factory that winter, and was placed in the office the day after our arrival, where he commenced *work* for the first time. We had a long and sage conversation upon the subject the same evening, and I well remember congratulating him, with an extremely grave face, upon his having now begun to *do for himself.* Poor fellow! his subsequent travels in the country were long and perilous.

But let us pause here a while. The reader has been landed in a new country, and it may be well, before describing our voyage to Red River, to make him acquainted with the peculiarities of the service, and the people with whom he will in imagination have to associate.

3

DESCRIPTION OF THE HUDSON BAY COMPANY

*—Description of the Hudson Bay Company—Their Forts and
Establishments—Food—Articles of Trade
and Manner of Trading*

IN THE YEAR 1669, a Company was formed in London, under the direction of Prince Rupert, for the purpose of prosecuting the fur-trade in the regions surrounding Hudson Bay. This Company obtained a charter from Charles the Second, granting to them and their successors, under the name of "The Governor and Company of Adventurers trading into Hudson's Bay," the sole right of trading in all the country watered by rivers flowing into Hudson Bay. The charter also authorised them to build and fit out men-of-war, establish forts, prevent any other company from carrying on trade with the natives in their territories, and required that they should do all in their power to promote Discovery.

Armed with these powers, then, the Hudson Bay Company established a fort near the head of James Bay. Soon afterwards, several others were built in different parts of the country; and before long the Company spread and grew wealthy, and eventually extended their trade far beyond the chartered limits.

With the internal economy of the Company under the superintendence of Prince Rupert, however, I am not acquainted; but as it will be necessary to the reader's forming a correct idea of the peculiarities of the country and service, that he should know something of its character under the direction of Sir George Simpson, I shall give a brief outline of its arrangements.

Reader, you will materially assist me in my description if you will endeavour to draw the following landscape on the retina of your mind's eye.

Imagine an immense extent of country, many hundred miles broad and many hundred miles long, covered with dense forests, expanded lakes, broad rivers, wide prairies, swamps, and mighty mountains: and all in a state of primeval simplicity—undefaced by the axe of civilized man, and untenanted by aught save a few roving hordes of Red Indians and myriads of wild animals. Imagine amid this wilderness a number of small squares, each enclosing half a dozen wooden houses and about a dozen men, and between each of these establishments a space of forest varying from fifty to three hundred miles in length; and you will have a pretty correct idea of the Hudson Bay Company's territories, and of the number of and distance between their forts. The idea, however, may be still more correctly obtained by imagining populous Great Britain converted into a wilderness and planted in the middle of Rupert's Land. The Company, in that case, would build *three* forts in it—one at the Land's End, one in Wales, and one in the Highlands; so that in Britain there would be but three hamlets, with a population of some thirty men, half a dozen women, and a few children! The Company's posts extend, with these intervals between, from the Atlantic to the Pacific Ocean, and from within the Arctic Circle to the northern boundaries of the United States.

Throughout this immense country there are probably not more ladies than would suffice to form half a dozen quadrilles; and these—poor banished creatures!—are chiefly the wives of the principal gentlemen connected with the fur-trade. The rest of the female population consists chiefly of half-breeds and Indians; the latter entirely devoid of education, and the former as much enlightened as can be expected from those whose life is spent in such a country. Even these are not very numerous; and yet without them the men would be in a sad condition, for they are the only tailors and washer-women in the country, and make all the mittens, moccasins, fur caps, deer-skin coats, etcetera, etcetera, worn in the land.

There are one or two favoured spots, however, into which a missionary or two have penetrated; and in Red River Settlement (the only colony in the Company's territories) there are several churches and clergymen, both Protestant and Roman Catholic.

The country is divided into four large departments: the Northern department, which includes all the establishments in the far north and frozen regions; the Southern department, including those to the south and east of this, the post at the head of James Bay, and along the shores of Lake Superior; the Montreal department, including the country in the neighbourhood of Montreal, up the Ottawa River, and along the north shore of the Gulf of St. Lawrence and Esquimaux Bay;

and the Columbia department, which comprehends an immense extent of country to the west of the Rocky Mountains, including the Oregon territory, which, although the Hudson Bay Company still trade in it, now belongs to the Americans.

These departments are divided into a number of districts, each under the direction of an influential officer; and these again are subdivided into numerous establishments, forts, posts, and outposts.

The name of *fort*, as already remarked, is given to all the posts in the country; but some of them certainly do not merit the name—indeed, few of them do. The only two in the country that are real, *bonâ fide* forts, are Fort Garry and the Stone Fort in the colony of Red River, which are surrounded by stone walls with bastions at the corners. The others are merely defended by wooden pickets or stockades; and a few, where the Indians are quiet and harmless, are entirely destitute of defence of any kind. Some of the chief posts have a complement of about thirty or forty men; but most of them have only ten, five, four, and even *two*, besides the gentleman in charge. As in most instances these posts are planted in a wilderness far from men, and the inhabitants have only the society of each other, some idea may be formed of the solitary life led by many of the Company's servants.

The following is a list of the forts in the four different departments, as correctly given as possible; but, owing to the great number in the country, the constant abandoning of old and establishing of new forts, it is difficult to get at a perfectly correct knowledge of their number and names:—

Northern Department

York Fort (the depôt)
Churchill
Severn
Oxford House
Trout Lake House
Norway House
Nelson River House
Berens River House
Red River Colony
Fort Garry
Stone Fort
Manitoba House
Fort Pelly
Cumberland House
Carlton House
Fort Pitt
Edmonton
Rocky Mountain House
Fort Aminaboine
Jasper's House
Henry's House
Fort Chipewyan
Fort Vermilion
Fort Dunvegan
Fort Simpson
Fort Norman
Fort Good Hope
Fort Halkett
Fort Resolution
Peel's River

Fort Alexander
Rat Portage House
Fort Frances
Isle a là Crosse

Southern Department

Moose Factory (the depôt)
Rupert's House
Fort George
Michiskau
Albany
Lac Seul
Kinogomousse
Matawagamingue
Kuckatoosh
New Brunswick
Abitibi
Temiscamingue
Grand Lac
Trout Lake
Matarva
Canasicomica
Lacloche
Sault de Ste. Maria
Fort William
Pic House
Michipicoton
Bachiwino
Nepigon
Washwonaby
Pike Lake

Temagamy
Green Lake
Missisague

Montreal Department
Lachine (the depôt)
Rivière du Moine
Lac des Allumettes
Fort Coulonge
Rivière Desert
Lac des Sables
Lake of Two Mountains
Kikandatch
Weymontachingue
Rat River
Ashabmoushwan
Chicoutimie
Lake St. John's
Tadousac
Isle Jérémie
Port Neuf
Goodbout
Trinity River
Seven Islands
Mingan
Nabisippi
Natoequene
Musquarro
Fort Nasoopie
Mainewan Lake
Sandy Banks

Gull Islands
North-west River
Rigolet
Kiboksk
Eyelick

Columbia Department
Fort Vancouver (the depôt)
Fort George
Nez Percé
Ockanagan
Colville
Fort Hall
Thompson's River
Fort Langley
Cootanies
Flat-head Post
Nisqually
Alexandria
Fort Chilcotin
Fort James
Fort Fluz Cuz
Babine Lake
And an agency in the Sandwich Islands.

There are seven different grades in the service. First, the labourer, who is ready to turn his hand to anything; to become a trapper, fisherman, or rough carpenter at the shortest notice. He is generally employed in cutting firewood for the consumption of the establishment at which he is stationed, shovelling snow from before the doors, mending all sorts of damages to all sorts of things, and, during the summer months, in transporting furs and goods between his post and the nearest depôt. Next in rank is the interpreter. He is, for the most part, an intelligent labourer, of pretty long standing in the service, who, having picked up a smattering of Indian, is consequently very useful in trading with the natives. After the interpreter comes the postmaster; usually a promoted labourer, who, for good behaviour or valuable services, has been put upon a footing with the gentlemen of the service, in the same manner that a private soldier in the army is sometimes raised to the rank of a commissioned officer. At whatever station a postmaster may happen to be placed, he is generally the most useful and active man there. He is often placed in charge of one of the many small stations, or outposts, throughout the country. Next are the apprentice clerks—raw lads, who come out fresh from school, with their mouths agape at the wonders they behold in Hudson Bay. They generally, for the purpose of appearing manly, acquire all the bad habits of the country as quickly as possible, and are stuffed full of what they call fun, with a strong spice of mischief. They become more sensible and sedate before they get through the first five years of their apprenticeship, after which they attain to the rank of clerks. The clerk, after a number of years' service (averaging from thirteen to twenty), becomes a chief trader (or half-share-holder), and in a few years more he attains the highest rank to

CUTTING FIREWOOD IN WINTER.

which any one can rise in the service, that of chief factor (or shareholder).

It is a strange fact that three-fourths of the Company's servants are Scotch Highlanders and Orkneymen. There are very few Irishmen, and still fewer English. A great number, however, are half-breeds and French Canadians, especially among the labourers and *voyageurs*.

From the great extent, and variety of feature, in the country occupied by the fur-traders, they subsist, as may be supposed, on widely different kinds of food. In the prairie, or plain countries, animal food is chiefly used, as there thousands of deer and bisons wander about, while the woods are stocked with game and wild-fowl. In other places, however, where deer are scarce and game not so abundant, fish of various kinds are caught in the rivers and lakes; and in other parts of the country they live partly upon fish and partly upon animal food. Vegetables are very scarce in the more northern posts, owing to the severity of the winter, and consequent shortness of summer. As the Company's servants are liable, on the shortest notice, to be sent from one end of the continent to another, they are quite accustomed to change of diet;—one year rejoicing in buffalo-humps and marrow-bones, in the prairies of the Saskatchewan, and the next devouring hung white-fish and scarce venison, in the sterile regions of Mackenzie River, or varying the meal with a little of that delectable substance often spoken of by Franklin, Back, and Richardson as their only dish—namely, *tripe-de-roche*, a lichen or moss which grows on the most barren rocks, and is only used as food in the absence of all other provisions.

During the first years of the Company, they were much censured for not carrying out the provision contained in the royal charter, that they should prosecute Discovery as much as possible; and it was even alleged that they endeavoured to prevent adventurers, not connected with themselves, from advancing in their researches. There is every reason to believe, however, that this censure was undeserved. A new company, recently formed in a wild country, could not at first be expected to have time or funds to advance the arduous and expensive cause of Discovery. With regard to their having impeded the attempts of others, it is doubtful whether any one in the service ever did so; but even had such been the case, the unauthorised and dishonourable conduct of one or two of their servants does not sanction the condemnation of the whole Company. Besides, the cause of Discovery was effectively advanced in former days by Herne, and in later years by Dease and Simpson, Dr Rae, and others; so that, whatever might have been the case at first, there can be no doubt that the Company have done much for the cause of late years.

The trade carried on by the Company is in peltries of all sorts, oil, dried and salted fish, feathers, quills, etcetera. A list of some of their principal articles of commerce is subjoined:—

Beaver-skins
Bear-skins, Black
Bear-skins, Brown
Bear-skins, White or Polar
Bear-skins, Grizzly
Badger-skins
Buffalo or Bison Robes (see note below)
Castorum, a substance procured from the body of the beaver
Deer-skins, Rein
Deer-skins, Red
Deer-skins, Moose or Elk
Deer-skins, parchment
Feathers of all kinds
Fisher-skins
Fox-skins, Black

Fox-skins, Silver
Fox-skins, Cross
Fox-skins, Red
Fox-skins, White
Fox-skins, Blue
Goose-skins
Ivory (tusks of the Walrus)
Lynx-skins
Marten-skins
Musquash-skins
Otter-skins
Oil, Seal
Oil, Whale
Swan-skins
Salmon, salted
Seal-skins
Wolf-skins
Wolverine-skins

Note. The hide of the bison—or, as it is called by the fur-traders, the buffalo—when dressed on one side and the hair left on the other, is called a robe. Great numbers are sent to Canada, where they are used for sleigh wrappers in winter. In the Indian county they are often used instead of blankets.

The most valuable of the furs mentioned in the above list is that of the *black fox*. This beautiful animal resembles in shape the common fox of England, but it is much larger, and jet-black, with the exception of one or two white hairs along the back-bone and a pure white tuft on the end of the tail. A single skin sometimes brings from twenty-five to thirty guineas in the British market; but, unfortunately, they are very scarce. The *silver fox* differs from the black fox only in the number of white hairs with which its fur is sprinkled; and the more numerous the white hairs, the less valuable does it become. The *cross fox* is a cross between the black or silver and the red fox. The *red fox* bears a much inferior fur to the other kinds; yet it is a good article of trade, as this species is very numerous. These four kinds of foxes are sometimes produced in the same litter, the mother being a red fox. The *white fox* is of less value than the red, and is also very numerous, particularly on the shores of Hudson Bay. The variety termed the *blue fox* is neither numerous nor valuable. It is of a dirty bluish-grey colour, and seldom makes its appearance at the Company's posts.

Beaver, in days of yore, was the staple fur of the country; but, alas! the silk hat has given it its death-blow, and the star of the beaver has now probably set for ever—that is to say, with regard to men; probably the animals themselves fancy that their lucky star has just risen. The most profitable fur in the country is that of the marten. It somewhat resembles the

THE TRADING-STORE.

Russian sable, and generally maintains a steady price. These animals, moreover, are very numerous throughout most part of the Company's territories, particularly in Mackenzie River, whence great numbers are annually sent to England.

All the above animals and a few others are caught in steel

and wooden traps by the natives; while deer, buffaloes, etcetera, are run down, shot, and snared in various ways, the details of which will be found in another part of this volume.

Trade is carried on with the natives by means of a standard valuation, called in some parts of the country a *castor*. This is to obviate the necessity of circulating money, of which there is little or none, excepting in the colony of Red River. Thus, an Indian arrives at a fort with a bundle of furs, with which he proceeds to the Indian trading-room. There the trader separates the furs into different lots, and, valuing each at the standard valuation, adds the amount together, and tells the Indian (who has looked on the while with great interest and anxiety) that he has got fifty or sixty casters; at the same time he hands the Indian fifty or sixty little bits of wood in lieu of cash, so that the latter may know, by returning these in payment of the goods for which he really exchanges his skins, how fast his funds decrease. The Indian then looks round upon the bales of cloth, powder-horns, guns, blankets, knives, etcetera, with which the shop is filled, and after a good while makes up his mind to have a small blanket. This being given him, the trader tells him that the price is six castors; the purchaser hands back six of his little bits of wood, and selects something else. In this way he goes on till all his wooden cash is expended; and then, packing up his goods, departs to show his treasures to his wife, and another Indian takes his place. The value of a castor is from one to two shillings. The natives generally visit the establishments of the Company twice a year—once in October, when they bring in the produce of their autumn hunts; and again in March, when they come in with that of the great winter hunt.

The number of castors that an Indian makes in a winter

hunt varies from fifty to two hundred, according to his perseverance and activity, and the part of the country in which he hunts. The largest amount I ever heard of was made by a man called Piaquata-Kiscum, who brought in furs on one occasion to the value of two hundred and sixty castors. The poor fellow was soon afterwards poisoned by his relatives, who were jealous of his superior abilities as a hunter, and envious of the favour shown him by the white men.

After the furs are collected in spring at all the different outposts, they are packed in conveniently-sized bales, and forwarded, by means of boats and canoes, to the three chief depôts on the sea-coast—namely, Fort Vancouver, at the mouth of the Columbia River, on the shores of the Pacific; York Fort, on the shores of Hudson Bay; and Moose Factory, on the shores of James Bay—whence they are transported in the Company's ships to England. The whole country in summer is, consequently, in commotion with the passing and repassing of brigades of boats laden with bales of merchandise and furs; the still waters of the lakes and rivers are rippled by the paddle and the oar; and the long-silent echoes which have slumbered in the icy embrace of a dreary winter, are now once more awakened by the merry voice and tuneful song of the hardy *voyageur*.

This slight sketch of the Hudson Bay Company and of the territories occupied by them may, for the present, serve to give some idea of the nature of the service and the appearance of the country. We shall now proceed to write of the Indiana inhabiting these wild regions.

(Doubtless the reader is aware that the chartered rights of the Hudson Bay Company now (1875) no longer exist; nevertheless their operations are still conducted in the same manner as of old, so that the above description is applicable in almost all respects to the greater part of the country at the present time.)

4

NORTH AMERICA'S INDIANS

—Their Manners and Customs—Costume, Dwellings,
Implements, etcetera—A Tale of Murder and
Cannibalism—A Night Excursion with an Indian
—A Deer Hunt

THE ABORIGINES OF North America are divided into a great number of nations or tribes, differing not only in outward appearance but also in customs and modes of life, and in some instances entertaining for each other a bitter and implacable hatred.

To describe the leading peculiarities of some of these tribes, particularly those called Crees, will be my object in the present chapter.

Some of the tribes are known by the following names:— Crees, Seauteaux, Stone Indians, Sioux, Blackfeet, Chipewyans, Slave Indians, Crows, Flatheads, etcetera. Of these, the Crees are the quietest and most inoffensive; they inhabit the woody country surrounding Hudson Bay; dwell in tents;

never go to war; and spend their time in trapping, shooting, and fishing. The Seauteaux are similar to the Crees in many respects, and inhabit the country further in the interior. The Stone Indians, Sioux, Blackfeet, Slave Indians, Crows, and Flatheads inhabit the vast plains and forests in the interior of America, on the east and west of the Rocky Mountains, and live chiefly by the produce of the chase. Their country swarms with bisons, and varieties of deer, bears, etcetera, which they hunt, shoot, snare, and kill in various ways. Some of these tribes are well supplied with horses, with which they hunt the buffalo. This is a wild, inspiriting chase, and the natives are very fond of it. They use the gun a good deal, but prefer the bow and arrow (in the use of which they are very expert) for the chase, and reserve the gun for warfare,—many of them being constantly engaged in skirmishing with their enemies. As the Crees were the Indians with whom I had the most in-tercourse, I shall endeavour to describe my old friends more at length.

The personal appearance of the men of this tribe is not bad. Although they have not the bold, daring carriage of the wilder tribes, yet they have active-looking figures, intelligent countenances, and a peculiar brightness in their dark eyes, which, from a constant habit of looking around them while travelling through the woods, are seldom for a moment at rest. Their jet-black hair generally hangs in straight matted locks over their shoulders, sometimes ornamented with beads and pieces of metal, and occasionally with a few partridge feath-ers; but they seldom wear a hat or cap of any kind, except in winter, when they make clumsy imitations of foraging-caps with furs—preferring, if the weather be warm, to go about without any head-dress at all; or, if it be cold, using the large hood of their capotes as a covering. They are thin, wiry men, not generally very muscular in their proportions, but yet capable of enduring great fatigue. Their average height is about five feet five inches; and one rarely meets with individuals varying much from this average, nor with deformed people, among them. The step of a Cree Indian is much longer than that of a European; owing, probably, to his being so much accustomed to walking through swamps and forests, where it is necessary to take long strides. This peculiarity becomes apparent when an Indian arrives at a fort, and walks along the hard ground inside the walls with the trader, whose short, bustling, active step contrasts oddly with the long, solemn, ostrich-like stride of the savage; which, however appropriate in the woods, is certainly strange and ungraceful on a good road.

The summer dress of the Indian is almost entirely provided for him by the Hudson Bay Company. It consists chiefly of a blue or grey cloth, or else a blanket capote reaching below the knee, made much too loose for the figure, and strapped round the waist with a scarlet or crimson worsted belt. A very coarse blue striped cotton shirt is all the underclothing they wear, holding trousers to be quite superfluous; in lieu of which they make leggins of various kinds of cloth, which reach from a few inches above the knee down to the ankle. These leggins are sometimes very tastefully decorated with bead-work, particularly those of the women, and are provided with flaps or wings on either side.

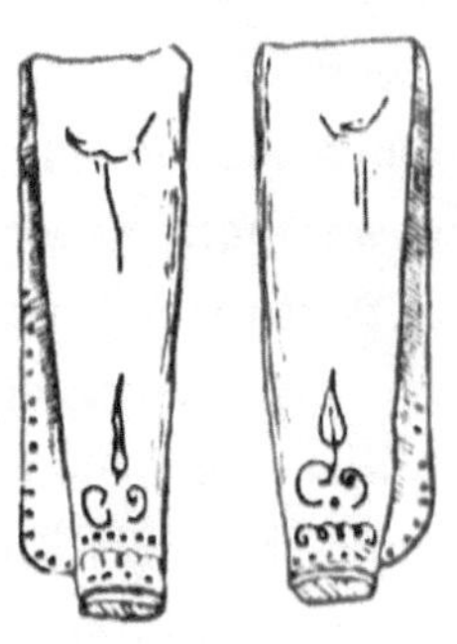

LEGGINS.

The costume, however, is slightly varied in winter. The blanket or cloth

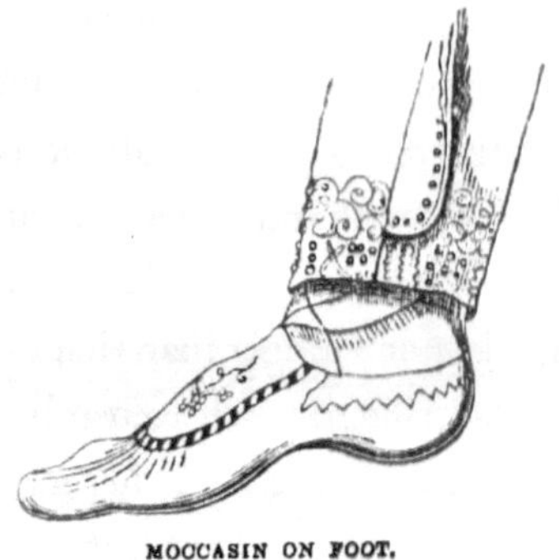

MOCCASIN ON FOOT.

capote is then laid aside for one of smoked red-deer skin, which has very much the appearance of chamois leather. This is lined with flannel, or some other thick, warm substance, and edged with fur (more for ornament, however, than warmth) of different kinds. Fingerless mittens, with a place for the thumb, are also adopted; and shoes or moccasins of the same soft material. The moccasins are very beautiful, fitting the feet as tightly as a glove, and are tastefully ornamented with dyed porcupine quills and silk thread of various colours, at which work the women are particularly *au fait*. As the leather of the moccasin is very thin (see note 1), blanket and flannel socks are worn underneath—one, two, or even four pairs, according to the degree of cold; and in proportion as these socks are increased in number, the moccasin, of course, loses its elegant appearance.

The Indian women are not so good-looking as the men. They have an awkward, slouching gait, and a downcast look—arising, probably, from the rude treatment they experience from their husbands; for the North American Indians, like all other savages, make complete drudges of their women, obliging them to do all the laborious and dirty work, while they reserve the pleasures of the chase for themselves. Their features are sometimes good; but I never saw a really pretty woman among the Crees. Their colour, as well as that of the men, is a dingy brown, which, together with their extreme filthiness, renders them anything but attractive. They are, however, quiet, sweet-tempered, and inoffensive creatures, destitute as well of artificial manners as of *stays*. Their dress is a gown, made without sleeves, and very scanty in the skirt, of coarse blue or green cloth; it reaches down to a little under the knee, below which their limbs are cased in leggins beautifully ornamented. Their whole costume, however, like that of the men, is almost always hid from sight by a thick blanket, without which the Indian seldom ventures abroad. The women usually make the top of the blanket answer the purpose of a head-dress; but when they wish to appear very much to advantage, they put on a cap. It is a square piece of blue cloth, profusely decorated with different-coloured beads, and merely sewed up at the top. They wear their hair in long straggling locks, which have not the slightest tendency to curl, and occasionally in queues or pigtails behind; but in this respect, as in every other, they are very careless of their personal appearance.

These primitive children of the forest live in tents of deer-skin or bark; and sometimes, where skins are scarce, of branches of trees. They are conically shaped, and are constructed thus:— The Indian with his family (probably two wives and three or four children) arrives in his bark canoe at a pretty level spot, sheltered from the north wind, and conveniently situated on the banks of a small stream, where the fish are plentiful, and pine branches (or brush), for the floor of the tent, abundant. Here he runs his canoe ashore, and carries his goods and chattels up the bank. His first business is to cut a

INDIAN WOMAN'S HEAD-DRESS.

number of long poles, and tie three of them at the top, spreading them out in the form of a tripod. He then piles all the other poles round these, at half a foot distance from each other, and thus encloses a circle of between fifteen and twenty feet in diameter. Over the poles (if he is a good hunter, and has plenty of deer-skins) he spreads the skin tent, leaving an opening at the top for the egress of the smoke. If the tent be a birch-bark one, he has it in separate rolls, which are spread over the poles till the whole is covered. A small opening is left facing the river or lake, which serves for a doorway; and this is covered with an old blanket, a piece of deer-skin, or, in some instances, by bison-skin or buffalo robe. The floor is covered with a layer of small pine branches, which serve for carpet and mattress; and in the centre is placed the wood fire, which, when blazing brightly, gives a warmth and comfort to the slight habitation that could scarcely be believed. Here the Indian spends a few days or weeks, according to the amount of game in the vicinity, and then removes to some other place, carrying with him the covering of the tent, but leaving the poles standing, as they would be cumbrous to carry in his small canoe, and thousands may be had at every place where he may wish to land.

The Indian canoe is an exceedingly light and graceful little craft, and well adapted for travelling in through a wild country, where the rivers are obstructed by long rapids, waterfalls, and shallows. It is so light that one man can easily carry it on his shoul-

MAKING A PORTAGE.

ders over the land, when a waterfall obstructs his progress; and as it only sinks about four or six inches in the water, few places are too shallow to float it. The birch bark of which it is made is about a quarter of an inch thick; and the inside is lined with extremely thin flakes of wood, over which a number of light timbers are driven, to give strength and tightness to the machine. In this frail bark, which measures from twelve, fifteen, thirty, to forty feet long, and from two to four feet broad in the middle, a whole Indian family of eight or ten souls will travel hundreds of miles, over rivers and lakes innumerable; now floating swiftly down a foaming rapid, and anon gliding over the surface of a quiet lake, or *making a portage* overland when a rapid is too dangerous to descend; and, while the elders of the family assist in carrying the canoe, the youngsters run about plucking berries, and the shaggy little curs (one or two of which are possessed by every Indian family) search for food, or bask in the sun at the foot of the baby's cradle, which stands bolt upright against a tree, while the child gazes upon all these operations with serene indifference.

Not less elegant and useful than the canoe is the snowshoe, without which the Indian would be badly off indeed. It is not, as many suppose, used as a kind of *skate*, with which to *slide* over the snow, but as a machine to prevent, by its size and breadth, the wearer from sinking into the snow; which is so deep that, without the assistance of the snowshoe, no one could walk a quarter of a mile through the

INDIAN CHILD AND CRADLE

woods in winter without being utterly exhausted.

It is formed of two thin pieces of light wood, tied at both ends, and spread out near the middle, thus making a kind of long oval, the interior of which is filled up with network of deer-skin threads. Strength is given to the frame by placing wooden bars across; and it is fastened *loosely* to the foot by a slight line going over the toe. In case, however, it may be supposed that by a shoe I mean an article something the size of a man's foot, it may be as well to state that snow-shoes measure from *four* to *six feet* long, and from thirteen to twenty inches wide. Notwithstanding their great size, the extreme lightness of their materials prevents them being cumbrous; and, after a little practice, a traveller forgets that he has them on, if the weather be good for such walking. Frosty weather is the best for snow-shoe travelling, as the snow is fine and dust-like, and falls through the net-work. If the weather be warm, the wet snow renders the shoe heavy, and the lines soon begin to gall the feet. On these shoes an Indian will travel between twenty and thirty miles a day; and they often accomplish from thirty to forty when hard pressed.

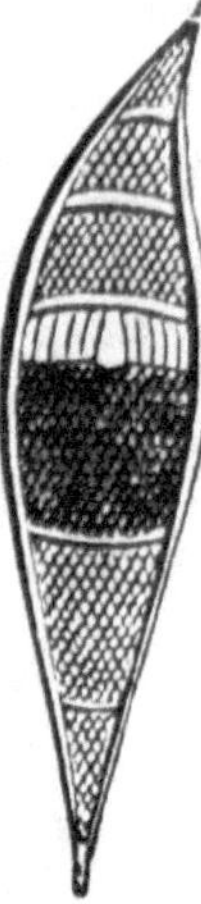

Fig. 1.

The food of the Indian varies according to circumstances. Sometimes he luxuriates on deer, partridges, and fat beaver; whilst at others he is obliged to live almost entirely on fish, and not unfrequently on *tripe-de-roche*. This

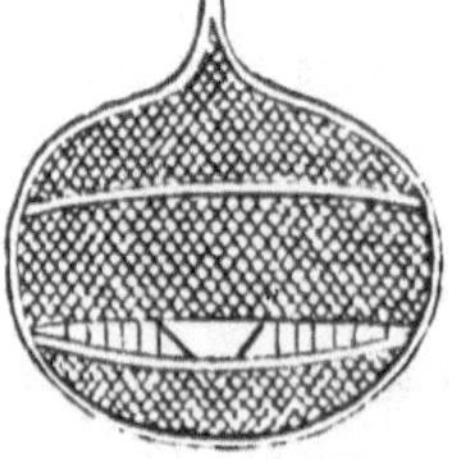

Fig. 2.

substance, however, does no more than retard his ultimate destruction by starvation; and unless he meets with something more nourishing, it cannot prevent it. When starving, the Indian will not hesitate to appease the cravings of hunger by resorting to cannibalism; and there were some old dames with whom I was myself acquainted, who had at different periods eaten several of their children. Indeed, some of them, it was said, had also eaten their husbands!

The following anecdote, related to me by my friend Carles, who spent many years of his life among the North American Indians, depicts one of the worst of these cases of cannibalism.

It was in the spring of 18 hundred and something that Mr Carles stood in the Indian Hall of one of the far-distant posts in Athabasca, conversing with a party of Chipewyan Indians, who had just arrived with furs from their winter hunting-grounds. The large fires of wood, sparkling and blazing cheerfully up the wide chimney, cast a bright light round the room, and shone upon the dusky countenances of the Chipewyans, as they sat gravely on the floor, smoking their spwagans in silence. A dark shade lowered upon every face, as if thoughts of an unpleasant nature disturbed their minds; and so it was. A deed of the most revolting description had been perpetrated by an Indian of the Cree tribe, and they were about to relate the story to Mr Carles.

After a short silence, an old Indian removed his pipe, and, looking round upon the others, as if to ask their consent to his becoming spokesman, related the particulars of the story, the substance of which I now give.

Towards the middle of winter, Wisagun, a Cree Indian, removed his encampment to another part of the country, as game was scarce in the place where he had been residing. His family consisted of a wife, a son of eight or nine years of age, and two or three children, besides several of his relations; in all, ten souls, including himself. In a few days they arrived at their new encamping ground, after having suffered a great deal of misery by the way from starvation. They were all much exhausted and worn out, but hoped, having heard of buffaloes in the vicinity, that their sufferings would soon be relieved.

Here they remained several days without finding any game, and were reduced to the necessity of devouring their moccasins and leathern coats, rendered eatable by being singed over the fire. Soon this wretched resource was also gone, and they were reduced to the greatest extremity, when a herd of buffaloes was descried far away in the prairie, on the edge of which they were encamped. All were instantly on the *qui vive*. Guns were loaded, snow-shoes put on, and in ten minutes the males of the hungry party set off after the herd, leaving Wisagun's wife and children with another girl in the tent. It was not long, however, before the famished party began to grow tired. Some of the weakest dropped behind; while Wisagun, with his son Natappe, gave up the chase, and returned to the encampment. They soon arrived at it, and Wisagun, peeping in between the chinks of the tent to see what the women were doing, saw his wife engaged in cutting up one of her own children, preparatory to cooking it. In a transport of passion, the Indian rushed forward and stabbed her, and also the other woman; and then, fearing the wrath of the other Indians, he fled to the woods. It may be conceived what were the feelings of the remainder of the party when they returned and found their relatives murdered. They were so much exhausted, however, by previous suffering, that they could only sit down and gaze on the mutilated bodies in despair. During the night,

Wisagun and Natappe returned stealthily to the tent, and, under cover of the darkness, murdered the whole party as they lay asleep. Soon after this the two Indians were met by another party of savages, in *good condition*, although, from the scarcity of game, the others were starving. The former accounted for this, however, by saying that they had fallen in with a deer not long ago; but that, before this had happened, all the rest of the family had died of starvation.

It was the party who had met the two Indians wandering in the plains that now sat round the fire relating the story to Mr Carles.

The tale was still telling when the hall door slowly opened, and Wisagun, gaunt and cadaverous, the very impersonation of famine, slunk into the room, along with Natappe, and seated himself in a corner near the fire. Mr Carles soon obtained from his own lips confirmation of the horrible deed, which he excused by saying that *most* of his relations had died before he ate them.

In a few days after this, the party of Indians took their departure from the house, to proceed to their village in the forest; and shortly after Wisagun and Natappe also left, to rejoin their tribe. The news of their deeds, however, had preceded them, so they were received very coldly; and soon after Wisagun pitched his tent, the other Indians removed, with one accord, to another place, as though it were impossible to live happily under the shadow of the same trees. This exasperated Wisagun so much that he packed up his tent and goods, launched his canoe, and then, before starting, went up to the village, and told them it was true he had killed all his relatives; and that he was a conjurer, and had both power and inclination to conjure them to death too. He then strode down to the banks of the river, and, embarking with his son, shot out into the stream. The unhappy man had acted rashly in his wrath. There is nothing more dangerous than to threaten to kill a savage, as he will certainly endeavour to kill the person who threatens him, in order to render the execution of his purpose impossible. Wisagun and his son had no sooner departed than two men coolly took up their guns, entered a canoe, and followed them. Upon arriving at a secluded spot, one of them raised his gun and fired at Wisagun, who fell over the side of the canoe, and sank to rise no more. With the rapidity of thought, Natappe seized his father's gun, sprang ashore, and bounded up the bank; a shot was fired which went through the fleshy part of his arm, and the next moment he was behind a tree. Here he called out to the Indians, who were reloading their guns, not to kill him, and he would tell them all. After a little consideration, they agreed to spare him; he embarked with them, and was taken afterwards to the fort, where he remained many years in the Company's service.

Although instances of cannibalism are not unusual among the Indian tribes, they do not resort to it from choice, but only when urged by the irrepressible cravings of hunger.

All the Indian tribes are fond of spirits; and in former times, when the distribution of rum to the natives was found necessary to compete with other companies, the use of the "fire-water" was carried to a fearful extent. Since Sir George Simpson became governor, however, the distribution of spirits has been almost entirely given up; and this has proved a most beneficial measure for the poor Indians.

Tobacco also is consumed by them in great quantities; indeed, the pipe is seldom out of the Indian's mouth. If he is not hunting, sleeping, or eating, he is sure to be smoking. A peculiar kind of shrub is much used by them, mixed with tobacco—partly for the purpose of making it go far, and partly because they can smoke more of it at a time with impunity.

The Indian is generally very lazy, but can endure, when requisite, great fatigue and much privation. He can go longer without eating than a European, and, from the frequent fasts he has to sustain, he becomes accustomed, without injury, to eat more at a meal than would kill a white man. The Indian children exhibit this power in a very extraordinary degree, looking sometimes wretchedly thin and miserable, and an hour or two afterwards waddling about with their little stomachs swollen almost to bursting!

When an Indian wants a wife, he goes to the *fair* one's father, and asks his consent. This being obtained, he informs the young lady of the circumstance, and then returns to his wigwam, whither the bride follows him, and installs herself as mistress of the house without further ceremony. Generally speaking, Indians content themselves with one wife, but it is looked upon as neither unusual nor improper to take two, or even three wives. The great point to settle is the husband's ability to support them. Thus, a bad hunter can only afford one wife, whilst a good one may have three or four.

If an old man or woman of the tribe becomes infirm, and unable to proceed with the rest when travelling, he or she, as the case may be, is left behind in a small tent made of willows, in which are placed a little firewood, some provisions, and a vessel of water. Here the unhappy wretch remains in solitude till the fuel and provisions are exhausted, and then dies. Should the tribe be in their encampment when an Indian dies, the deceased is buried, sometimes in the ground, and sometimes in a rough wooden coffin raised a few feet above it. They do not now bury guns, knives, etcetera, with their dead, as they once did, probably owing to their intercourse with white men.

The Supreme Being among the Indians is called Manitou; but He can scarcely be said to be worshipped by them, and the few ideas they have of His attributes are imperfect and erroneous. Indeed, no religious rites exist among them, unless the unmeaning mummery of the medicine tent can be looked upon as such. Of late years, however, missionaries, both of the Church of England and the Wesleyans, have exerted themselves to spread the Christian religion among these tribes, than whom few savages can be more unenlightened or morally degraded; and there is reason to believe that the light of the gospel is now beginning to shine upon them with beneficial influence.

There is no music in the soul of a Cree, and the only time they attempt it is when gambling—of which they are passionately fond—when they sing a kind of monotonous chant, accompanied with a noisy rattling on a tin kettle. The celebrated war-dance is now no longer in existence among this tribe. They have wisely renounced both war and its horrors long ago. Among the wilder inhabitants of the prairies, however, it is still in vogue, with all the dismal accompaniments of killing, scalping, roasting, and torturing that distinguished American warfare a hundred years ago.

The different methods by which the Indian succeeds in snaring and trapping animals are numerous. A good idea of these may be had by following an Indian in his rounds.

Suppose yourself, gentle reader, standing at the gate of one of the forts in Hudson Bay, watching a savage arranging his snow-shoes, preparatory to entering the gloomy forest. Let us walk with this Indian on a visit to his traps.

The night is very dark, as the moon is hid by thick clouds, yet it occasionally breaks out sufficiently to illumine our path to Stemaw's wigwam, and to throw the shadows of the neighbouring trees upon the pale snow, which *crunches* under our feet as we advance, owing to the intense cold. No wind breaks the stillness of the night, or shakes the lumps of snow off the branches of the neighbouring pines or willows; and nothing is heard save the occasional crackling of the trees as the severe frost acts upon their branches. The tent, at which we soon arrive, is pitched at the foot of an immense tree, which stands in a little hollow where the willows and pines are luxuriant enough to afford a shelter from the north wind. Just in front, a small path leads to the river, of which an extensive view is had through the opening, showing the long fantastic shadows of huge blocks and mounds of ice cast upon the white snow by the flickering moonlight. A huge chasm, filled with fallen trees and mounds of snow, yawns on the left of the tent; and the ruddy sparks of fire which issue from a hole in its top throw this and the surrounding forest into deeper gloom. The effect of this wintry scene upon the mind is melancholy in the extreme—causing it to speed across the bleak and frozen plains, and visit again the warm fireside and happy faces in a far-distant home; and yet there is a strange romantic attraction in the wild woods that gradually brings it back again, and makes us impatient to begin our walk with the Indian. Suddenly the deer-skin robe that covers the aperture of the wigwam is raised, and a bright stream of warm light gushes out, tipping the dark-green points of the opposite trees, and mingling strangely with the paler light of the moon—and Stemaw stands erect in front of his solitary home, to gaze

STEMAW MEDITATES A NIGHT MARCH.

a few moments on the sky and judge of the weather, as he intends to take a long walk before laying his head upon his capote for the night. He is in the usual costume of the Cree Indians: a large leathern coat, very much overlapped in front, and fastened round his waist with a scarlet belt, protects his body from the cold. A small rat-skin cap covers his head, and his legs are cased in the ordinary blue cloth leggins. Large moccasins, with two or three pair of blanket socks, clothe his feet; and fingerless mittens, made of deer-skin, complete his costume. After a few minutes passed in contemplation of the heavens, the Indian prepares himself for the walk. First he sticks a small axe in his belt, serving as a counterpoise to a large hunting-knife and fire-bag which depend from the other side. He then slips his feet through the lines of his snow-shoes, and throws the line of a small hand-sledge over his shoulder. The hand-sledge is a thin, flat slip or plank of wood, from five to six feet long by one foot broad, and is turned up at one end. It is extremely light, and Indians invariably use it when visiting their traps, for the purpose of dragging home the animals or game they may have caught. Having attached this sledge to his back, he stoops to receive his gun from his faithful *squaw* (see note 2), who has been watching his operations through a hole in the tent; and throwing it on his shoulder, strides off, without uttering a word, across the moonlit space in front of the tent, turns into a narrow track that leads down the dark ravine, and disappears in the shades of the forest. Soon he reaches the termination of the track (made for the purpose of reaching some good dry trees for firewood), and stepping into the deep snow with the long, regular, firm tread of one accustomed to snow-shoe walking, he winds his way rapidly through the thick stems of the surrounding trees, and turns aside the smaller branches of the bushes.

The forest is now almost dark, the foliage overhead having become so dense that the moon only penetrates through it in a few places, causing the spots on which it falls to shine with a strange phosphoric light, and rendering the surrounding masses darker by contrast. The faint outline, of an old snow-shoe track, at first discernible, is now quite invisible; but still Stemaw moves forward with rapid, noiseless step, as sure of his way as if a broad beaten track lay before him. In this manner he moves on for nearly two miles, sometimes stooping to examine closely the newly-made track of some wild animal, and occasionally giving a glance at the sky through the openings in the leafy canopy above him, when a faint sound in the bushes ahead brings him to a full stop. He listens attentively, and a noise, like the rattling of a chain, is heard proceeding from the recesses of a dark, wild-looking hollow a few paces in front. Another moment, and the rattle is again distinctly heard; a slight smile of satisfaction crosses Stemaw's dark visage, for one of his traps is set in that place, and he knows that something is caught. Quickly descending the slope, he enters the bushes whence the sound proceeds, and pauses when within a yard or two of his trap, to peer through the gloom. A cloud passes off the moon, and a faint ray reveals, it may be, a beautiful black fox caught in the snare. A slight blow on the snout from Stemaw's axe-handle kills the unfortunate animal; in ten minutes more it is tied to his sledge, the trap is reset and again covered over with snow, so that it is almost impossible to tell that anything is there; and the Indian pursues his way.

FOX IN A TRAP.

The steel-trap used by the Indians is almost similar to the ordinary rat-trap of England, with this difference, that it is a little larger, is destitute of teeth, and has two springs in place of one. A chain is attached to one spring for the purpose of fixing a weight to the trap, so that the animal caught may not be able to drag it far from the place where it was set. The track in the snow enables the hunter to find his trap again. It is generally set so that the jaws, when spread out flat, are exactly on a level with the snow. The chain and weight are both hid, and a thin layer of snow spread on top of the trap. The bait (which generally consists of chips of a frozen partridge, rabbit, or fish) is then scattered around in every direction; and, with the exception of this, nothing distinguishes the spot. Foxes, beavers, wolves, lynx, and other animals are caught in this way, sometimes by a fore leg, sometimes by a hind leg, and some-times by two legs at once, and occasionally by the nose. Of all these ways the Indians prefer catching by two legs, as there is then not the slightest possibility of the animal escaping. When foxes are caught by one leg, they often *eat it off* close to the trap, and escape on the other three. I have frequently seen this happen; and I once saw a fox caught which had evidently escaped in this way, as one of its legs was gone, and the stump healed up and covered again with hair. When they are caught by the nose they are almost sure to escape, unless taken out of the trap very soon after being caught, as their snouts are so sharp or wedge-like that they can pull them from between the jaws of the trap without much difficulty.

Having now described the way of using this machine, we will rejoin Stemaw, whom we left on his way to the next trap. There he goes, moving swiftly over the snow mile after mile, as if he could not feel fatigue, turning aside now and then to visit a trap, and giving a short grunt when nothing is in it, or killing the animal when caught, and tying it on the sledge. Towards midnight, however, he begins to walk more cautiously, examines the priming of his gun, and moves the axe in his belt, as if he expected to meet some enemy suddenly. The fact is, that close to where he now stands are two traps which he set in the morning close to each other for the purpose of catching one of the formidable coast wolves. These animals are so sagacious that they will scrape all round a trap, let it be ever so well set, and after eating all the bait, walk away unhurt. Indians consequently endeavour in every possible way to catch them—and, among others, by setting *two* traps close together; so that, while the wolf scrapes at one, he may perhaps put his foot in the other. It is in this way that Stemaw's traps are set, and he now proceeds cautiously towards them, his gun in the hollow of his left arm. Slowly he advances, peering through the bushes, but nothing is visible; suddenly a branch crashes under his snow-shoe, and with a savage growl a large wolf bounds towards him, landing almost at his feet. A single glance, however, shows the Indian that both traps are on his legs, and that the chains prevent his further advance. He places his gun against a tree, draws his axe from the belt, and advances to kill the animal. It is an undertaking, however, of some difficulty. The fierce brute, which is larger than a Newfoundland dog, strains every nerve and sinew to break its chains; while its eyes glisten in the uncertain light, and foam curls from its blood-red mouth. Now it retreats as the Indian advances, grinning horribly as it goes; and anon, as the chains check its further retreat, it springs with fearful growl towards Stemaw, who slightly wounds it with his axe, as he jumps backward just in time to save himself from the infuriated

STEMAW SHOULDERS THE WOLF.

animal, which catches in its fangs the flap of his leggin, and tears it from his limb. Again Stemaw advances, and the wolf retreats and again springs on him, but without success. At last, as the wolf glances for a moment to one side—apparently to see if there is no way of escape—quick as lightning the axe descends with stunning violence on its head; another blow follows; and in five minutes more Stemaw heaves the huge brute across his shoulders, and carries it to his sledge.

This, however, has turned out a more exhausting business than Stemaw expected; so he determines to encamp and rest for a few hours. Selecting a large pine, whose spreading branches cover a patch of ground free from underwood, he scrapes away the snow with his snow-shoe. Silently but busily he labours for a quarter of an hour; and then, having cleared a space seven or eight feet in diameter, and nearly four feet deep, he cuts down a number of small branches, which he strews at the bottom of the hollow, till all the snow is covered. This done, he fells two or three of the nearest trees, cuts them up into lengths of about five feet long, and piles them at the root of the tree. A light is soon applied to the pile, and up glances the ruddy flame, crackling among the branches overhead, and sending thousands of bright sparks into the air. No one who has not seen it can have the least idea of the change that takes place in the appearance of the woods at night when a large fire is suddenly lighted. Before, all was cold, silent, chilling, gloomy, and desolate, and the pale snow looked unearthly in the dark. Now, a bright ruddy glow falls upon the thick stems of the trees, and penetrates through the branches overhead, tipping those nearest the fire with a ruby tinge, the mere sight of which warms one. The white snow changes to a beautiful pink, whilst the stems of the trees, bright and clearly visible near at hand, become more and more indistinct in the distance, till they are lost in the black background. The darkness, however, need not be seen from the encampment; for, when the Indian lies down, he will be surrounded by the snow walls, which sparkle in the firelight as if set with diamonds. These do not melt, as might be expected. The frost is much too intense for that, and nothing melts except the snow quite close to the fire. Stemaw has now concluded his arrangements: a small piece of dried deer's meat warms before the blaze; and, meanwhile, he spreads his green blanket on the ground, and fills a stone calumet (or pipe with a wooden stem) with tobacco, mixed with a kind of weed prepared by himself. The white smoke from this soon mingles with the thicker volumes from the fire, which curl up through the branches into the sky, now shrouding him in their wreaths, and then, as the bright flame obtains the mastery, leaving his dark face and coal-black eyes shining in the warm light. No one enjoys a pipe more than an Indian; and Stemaw's tranquil visage, wreathed in tobacco smoke, as he reclines at full length under the spreading branches of the pine, and allows the white vapour to pass slowly out of his mouth *and nose*, certainly gives one an excellent idea of savage enjoyment.

Leaving him here, then, to solace himself with a pipe preparatory to resting his wearied limbs for the night, we will change the hour, and conduct the reader to a different scene.

It is now day. The upper edge of the sun has just risen, red and frosty-looking, in the east, and countless myriads of icy particles glitter on every tree and bush in its red rays; while the white tops of the snow-drifts, which dot the surface of the small lake at which we have just arrived, are tipped with the same rosy hue. The lake is of considerable breadth, and the woods on its opposite shore are barely visible. An unbroken coat of pure white snow covers its entire surface, whilst here and there a small islet, covered with luxuriant evergreens, attracts the eye, and breaks the sameness of the scene. At the extreme left of the lake, where the points of a few bulrushes and sedgy plants appear above the snow, are seen a number of small earthy mounds, in the immediate vicinity of which the trees and bushes are cut and barked in many places, while some of them are nearly cut down. This is a colony of beavers. In the warm months of summer and autumn, this spot is a lively, stirring place, as the beavers are then employed *nibbling* down trees and bushes, for the purpose of repairing their dams, and

BEAVERS.

supplying their storehouses with food. The bark of willows is their chief food, and all the bushes in the vicinity are more or less cut through by these persevering little animals. Their dams, however (which are made for the purpose of securing to themselves a constant sufficiency of water), are made with large trees; and stumps will be found, if you choose to look for them, as thick as a man's leg, which the beavers have entirely nibbled through, and dragged by their united efforts many yards from where they grew.

Now, however, no sign of animal life is to be seen, as the beavers keep within doors all winter; yet I venture to state that there are many now asleep under the snow before us. It is not, reader, merely for the purpose of showing you the outside of a beaver-lodge that I have brought you such a distance from human habitations. Be patient, and you shall soon see more. Do you observe that small black speck moving over the white surface of the lake, far away on the horizon? It looks like a crow, but the forward motion is much too steady and constant for that. As it approaches, it assumes the form of a man; and at last the figure of Stemaw, dragging his empty sleigh behind him (for he has left his wolf and foxes in the last night's encampment, to be taken up when returning home), becomes clearly distinguishable through the dreamy haze of the cold wintry morning. He arrives at the beaver-lodges, and, I warrant, will soon play havoc among the inmates.

His first proceeding is to cut down several stakes, which he points at the ends. These are driven, after he has cut away a good deal of ice from around the beaver-lodge, into the ground between it and the shore. This is to prevent the beaver from running along the passage they always have from their lodges to the shore, where their storehouse is kept, which would make it necessary to excavate the whole passage. The beaver, if there are any, being thus imprisoned in the lodge, the hunter next stakes up the opening into the storehouse on shore, and so imprisons those that may have fled there for shelter on hearing the noise of his axe at the other house. Things being thus arranged to his entire satisfaction, he takes an instrument called an ice-chisel—which is a bit of steel about a foot long by one inch broad, fastened to the end of a stout pole—wherewith he proceeds to dig through the lodge. This is by no means an easy operation; and although he covers the snow around him with great quantities of frozen mud and sticks, yet his work is not half finished. At last, however, the interior of the hut is laid bare; and the Indian, stooping down, gives a great pull, when out comes a large, fat, sleepy beaver, which he flings sprawling on the snow. Being thus unceremoniously awakened from its winter nap, the shivering animal looks languidly around, and even goes the length of grinning at Stemaw, by way of showing its teeth, for which it is rewarded with a blow on the head from the pole of the ice-chisel, which puts an end to it. In this way several more are killed, and packed on the sleigh. Stemaw then turns his face towards his encampment, where he collects the game left there; and away he goes at a tremendous pace, dashing the snow in clouds from his snow-shoes, as he hurries over the trackless wilderness to his forest home.

Near his tent, he makes a détour to visit a marten trap; where, however, he finds nothing. This trap is of the simplest construction, being composed of two logs, the one of which is supported over the other by means of a small stick, in such a manner that when the marten creeps between the two and pulls the bait, the support is removed, and the upper log falls on and crushes it to death.

In half an hour the Indian arrives at his tent, where the dark eyes of his wife are seen gazing through a chink in the covering, with an expression that denotes immense joy at the prospect of gorging for many days on fat beaver, and having wherewithal to purchase beads and a variety of ornaments from the white men, upon the occasion of her husband and herself visiting the posts of the fur-traders in the following spring.

But some of the tribes have a more sociable as well as a more productive way of conducting business, at least as regards venison; for they catch the deer in a "pound."

"Their mode of accomplishing this is to select a well-frequented deer-path, and enclose with a strong fence of twisted trees and brushwood a space about a mile in circumference, and sometimes more. The entrance of the pound is not larger than a common gate, and its inside is crowded with innumerable small hedges, in the openings of which are fixed snares of strong well-twisted thongs. One end is generally fastened to a growing tree; and as all the wood and jungle within the enclosure is left standing, its interior forms a complete labyrinth. On each side of the door a line of small trees, stuck up in the snow fifteen or twenty yards apart, form two sides of an acute angle, widening gradually from the entrance, from which they sometimes extend two or three miles. Between these rows of brushwood runs the path frequented by the deer. When all things are prepared, the Indians take their station on some eminence commanding a prospect of this path, and the moment any deer are seen going that way, the whole encampment—men, women, and children—steal under cover of the woods till they get behind them. They then show themselves in the open ground, and, drawing up in the form of a crescent, advance with shouts. The deer finding themselves pursued, and at the same time imagining the rows of brushy poles to be people stationed to prevent their passing on either side, run straight forward till they get into the pound. The Indians instantly close in, block up the entrance, and whilst the women and children run round the outside to prevent them from breaking or leaping the fence, the men enter with their spears and bows, and speedily dispatch such as are caught in the snares or are running loose." (see "Hearne's Journey." pages 78 to 80).

"McLean, a gentleman who spent twenty-five years in the Hudson Bay territories, assures us that on one occasion he and a party of men entrapped and slaughtered in this way a herd of three hundred deer in two hours."

I must crave the reader's pardon for this long digression, and beg him to recollect that at the end of the second chapter I left myself awaiting orders to depart for Red River, to which settlement we will now proceed.

Note 1: Many people at home have asked me how such *thin things* can keep out the wet of the snow. The reader must bear in mind that the snow, for nearly seven months, is not even *damp* for five minutes, so constant is the frost. When it becomes wet in spring, Europeans adopt ordinary English shoes, and Indians do not mind the wet.

Note 2: *Squeiaw* is the Indian for a woman. *Squaw* is the English corruption of the word, and is used to signify a wife.

DEER-HUNTING.

5

VOYAGE FROM YORK FACTORY TO RED RIVER

*—Voyage Begun—Our Manner of Travelling
—Encamping in the Woods—Portaging and Shooting
Wildfowl—Whisky-jacks—A Storm—Lake Winnipeg
—Arrival at Red River Settlement*

SOMEWHERE ABOUT the beginning of September, Mr Carles, Mr and Mrs Gowley, Mr Rob, and myself set out with the *Portage La Loche* brigade, for the distant colony of Red River. The Portage la Loche brigade usually numbers six or seven boats, adapted for inland travelling where the navigation is obstructed by rapids, waterfalls, and cataracts, to surmount which, boats and cargo are carried overland by the crews. These carrying places are called *portages*; and between York Factory and Red River there are upwards of thirty-six, of various lengths. Besides these, there are innumerable rapids, up which the boats have to be pushed inch by inch with poles, for miles together; so that we had to look forward to a long and tedious voyage.

The brigade with which we left York Factory usually leaves Red River about the end of May, and proceeds to Norway House, where it receives Athabasca and Mackenzie River outfits. It then sets out for the interior; and upon arriving at Portage la Loche, the different boats land their cargoes, while the Mackenzie River boats, which came to meet them, exchange their furs for the outfits. The brigade then begins to retrace its way, and returns to Norway House, whence it proceeds to York Factory, where it arrives about the commencement of September, lands the furs, and receives part of the Red River outfit, with which it sets out for that place as soon as possible.

With this brigade, then, we started from York Factory, with a cheering song from the men in full chorus. They were in good spirits, being about to finish the long voyage, and return to their families at Red River, after an absence of nearly five months, during which time they had encountered and overcome difficulties that would have cooled the most sanguine temperament; but these hardy Canadians and half-breeds are accustomed to such voyages from the age of fifteen or sixteen, and think no more of them than other men do of ordinary work.

Mr Carles and I travelled together in the guide's boat; Mr and Mrs Gowley in another; and Mr Rob in a third by himself. We took the lead, and the others followed as they best could. Such was the order of march in which we commenced the ascent of Hayes River.

It may not be uninteresting here to describe the *matériel* of our voyage.

Our boat, which was the counterpart of the rest, was long, broad, and shallow, capable of carrying forty hundredweight, and nine men, besides three or four passengers, with provi-

STARTING OF THE PORTAGE BRIGADE.

sions for themselves and the crew. It did not, I suppose, draw more than three feet of water when loaded, perhaps less, and was, moreover, very light for its size. The cargo consisted of bales, being the goods intended for the Red River sale-room and trading-shop. A rude mast and tattered sail lay along the seats, ready for use, should a favourable breeze spring up; but this seldom occurred, the oars being our chief dependence during the greater part of the voyage.

The provisions of the men consisted of pemmican and flour; while the passengers revelled in the enjoyment of a ham, several cured buffalo-tongues, tea, sugar, butter, and biscuit, and a little brandy and wine, wherewith to warm us in cold weather, and to cheer the crew with a dram after a day of unusual exertion. All our provisions were snugly packed in a case and basket, made expressly for the purpose.

Pemmican being a kind of food with which people in the civilized world are not generally acquainted, I may as well describe it here.

It is made by the buffalo-hunters of the Red River, Swan River, and Saskatchewan prairies; more particularly by those of Red River, where many of the colonists spend a great part of the year in pursuit of the buffalo. They make it thus: Having shot a buffalo (or bison), they cut off lumps of his flesh, and slitting it up into flakes or layers, hang it up in the sun to dry. In this state it is often made up into packs, and sent about the country to be consumed as dried meat; but when *pemmican* is wanted, it has to go through another process. When dry, the meat is pounded between two stones till it is broken into small pieces; these are put into a bag made of the animal's hide, with the hair on the outside, and well mixed with melted grease; the top of the bag is then sewn up, and the pemmican allowed to cool. In this state it may be eaten uncooked; but the *voyageurs*, who subsist on it when travelling, mix it with a little flour and water, and then boil it; in which state it is known throughout the country by the elegant name of *robbiboo*. Pemmican is good wholesome food, will keep fresh for a great length of time, and were it not for its unprepossessing appearance, and a good many buffalo hairs mixed with it, through the carelessness of the hunters, would be very palatable. After a time, however, one becomes accustomed to those little peculiarities.

It was late in the afternoon when we left York Factory; and after travelling a few miles up Hayes River, put ashore for the night.

We encamped upon a rough, gravelly piece of ground, as there was no better in the neighbourhood; so that my first night in the woods did not hold out the prospect of being a very agreeable one. The huge log fires, however, soon blazed cheerily up, casting a ruddy glow upon the surrounding foliage and the wild uncouth figures of the *voyageurs*, who, with their long dark hair hanging in luxuriant masses over their bronzed faces, sat or reclined round the fires, smoking their pipes, and chatting with as much carelessness and good-humour as if the long and arduous journey before them never once entered their minds. The tents were pitched on the most convenient spot we could find; and when supper was spread out, and a candle lighted (which, by the way, the strong blaze of our camp-fire rendered quite unnecessary), and Mr Carles, seating himself upon a pile of cloaks, blankets, and cushions, looked up with a broad grin on his cheerful, good-humoured countenance, and called me to supper, I began to think that if all travelling in Hudson Bay were like this, a voyage of discovery to the North Pole would be a mere pleasure trip! Alas! in after-years I found it was not always thus.

Supper was soon disposed of, and having warmed ourselves at the fire, and ventured a few rash prophecies on the probable weather of the morrow, we spread our blankets over an oiled cloth, and lay lovingly down together; Mr Carles to snore vociferously, and I to dream of home.

At the first blush of day I was awakened by the loud halloo of the guide, who, with a voice of a Stentor, gave vent to a "*Lève! Lève! lève!*" that roused the whole camp in less than two minutes. Five minutes more sufficed to finish our toilet (for, be it known, Mr Carles and I had only taken off our coats), tie up our blankets, and embark. In ten minutes we were once more pulling slowly up the current of Hayes River.

The missionaries turned out to be capital travellers, and never delayed the boats a moment; which is saying a good deal for them, considering the short space of time allowed for dressing. As for the hardy *voyageurs*, they slept in the same clothes in which they had wrought during the day, each with a single blanket round him, in the most convenient spot he could find. A few slept in pairs, but all reposed under the wide canopy of heaven.

Early morning is always the most disagreeable part of the traveller's day. The cold dews of the past night render the air chilly, and the gloom of departing night tends greatly to depress the spirits. As I became acquainted with this mode of travelling, I became more knowing; and, when there was not much probability of being interrupted by portages, I used to spread out my blanket in the stern of the boat, and snooze till breakfast-time. The hour for breakfast used to vary, according as we arrived late or early at an eligible spot. It was seldom earlier than seven, or later than nine o'clock.

Upon the occasion of our first breakfast in the woods, we were fortunate. The sun shone brightly on the surrounding trees and bushes; the fires blazed and crackled; pots boiled, and cooks worked busily on a green spot, at the side of a small bay or creek, in which the boats quietly floated, scarce rippling the surface of the limpid water. A little apart from the men, two white napkins marked our breakfast-place, and the busy appearance of our cook gave hopes that our fast was nearly over. The whole scene was indescribably romantic and picturesque, and worthy of delineation by a more experienced pencil than mine. Breakfast was a repetition of the supper of the preceding night; the only difference being, that we ate it by daylight, in the open air, instead of by candlelight, under the folds of our canvas tent. After it was over, we again embarked, and proceeded on our way.

The men used to row for a space of time denominated a *pipe*; so called from the circumstance of their taking a smoke at the end of it. Each *spell* lasted for nearly two hours, during which time they rowed without intermission. The *smoke* usually occupied five or ten minutes, after which they pulled again for two hours more; and so on. While travelling in boats, it is only allowable to put ashore for breakfast; so, about noon, we had a cold dinner in the boat: and, with appetites sharpened by exposure to the fresh air, we enjoyed it pretty well.

In a couple of days we branched off into Steel River, and began its ascent. The current here was more rapid than in Hayes River; so rapid, indeed, that, our oars being useless, we were obliged to send the men ashore with the tracking-line. Tracking, as it is called, is dreadfully harassing work. Half of the crew go ashore, and drag the boat slowly along, while the other half go to sleep. After an hour's walk, the others then take their turn; and so on, alternately, during the whole day.

The banks of the river were high, and very precipitous; so that the poor fellows had to scramble along, sometimes close to the water's edge, and sometimes high up the bank, on ledges so narrow that they could scarcely find a footing, and where they looked like flies on a wall. The banks, too, being composed of clay or mud, were very soft, rendering the work disagreeable and tiresome; but the light-hearted *voya-*

geurs seemed to be quite in their element, and laughed and joked while they toiled along, playing tricks with each other, and plunging occasionally up to the middle in mud, or to the neck in water, with as much nonchalance as if they were jumping into bed.

On the fifth day after leaving York Factory, we arrived at the Rock Portage. This is the first on the route, and it is a very short one. A perpendicular waterfall, eight or ten feet high, forms an effectual barrier to the upward progress of the boats by water; so that the only way to overcome the difficulty is to carry everything across the flat rock, from which the portage derives its name, and reload at the upper end.

Upon arriving, a novel and animating scene took place. Some of the men, jumping ashore, ran briskly to and fro with enormous burdens on their backs; whilst others hauled and pulled the heavy boats slowly up the cataract, hallooing and shouting all the time, as if they wished to drown the thundering noise of the water, which boiled and hissed furiously around the rocks on which we stood. In about an hour our boat, and one or two others, had passed the falls; and we proceeded merrily on our way, with spirits elevated in proportion to the elevation of our bodies.

It was here that I killed my first duck; and well do I remember the feeling of pride with which I contemplated the achievement. That I had shot her sitting about five yards from the muzzle of my gun, which was loaded with an enormous charge of shot, is undeniable; but this did not lessen my exultation a whit. The sparrows I used to kill in days of yore, with inexpressible delight, grew "small by degrees" and comically less before the plump inhabitant of the marshes, till they dwindled into nothing; and the joy and fuss with which I hailed

TRACKING ON STEEL RIVER.

the destruction of the unfortunate bird can only be compared to, and equalled by, the crowing and flurry with which a hen is accustomed to announce the production of her first egg.

During the voyage, we often disturbed large flocks of geese, and sometimes shot a few. When we chanced to come within sight of them before they saw us, the boats all put ashore; and L'Esperance, our guide, went round through the bushes, to the place where they were, and seldom failed in rendering at least one of the flock *hors de combat*. At first I would as soon have volunteered to shoot a lion in Africa, with a Bushman beside me, as have presumed to attempt to kill geese while L'Esperance was present—so poor an opinion had I of my skill as a marksman; but, as I became more accustomed to seeing them killed, I waxed bolder; and at last, one day, having come in sight of a flock, I begged to be allowed to try my hand. The request was granted; L'Esperance lent me his gun, and away I went cautiously through the bushes. After a short walk, I came close to where they were swimming about in the water; and cocking my gun, I rushed furiously down the bank, breaking everything before me, and tumbling over half a dozen fallen trees in my haste, till I cleared the bushes; and then, scarcely taking time to raise the gun to my shoulder, banged right into the middle of the flock, just as they were taking wing. All rose; but they had not gone far when one began to waver a little, and finally sat down in the water again—a sure sign of being badly wounded. Before the boats came up, however, he had swam to the opposite bank, and hid himself among the bushes; so that, much to my disappointment, I had not the pleasure of handling this new trophy of my prowess.

Upon one occasion, while sauntering along the banks of the river in search of ducks and geese, while the boats were slowly ascending against the strong current, I happened to cast my eyes across the stream, and there, to my amazement, beheld a large black bear bounding over the rocks with the ease and agility of a cat. He was not within shot, however, and I was obliged to content myself with seeing him run before me for a quarter of a mile, and then turn off into the forest.

This was truly the happiest time I ever spent in the Nor'-West. Everything was full of novelty and excitement. Rapid succeeded rapid, and portage followed portage in endless succession—giving me abundance of opportunities to range about in search of ducks and geese, which were very numerous, while the men were dragging the boats, and carrying the goods over the portages. The weather was beautiful, and it was just the season of the year when the slight frost in the mornings and evenings renders the blazing camp-fire agreeable, and destroys those little wretches, the mosquitoes. My friend Mr Carles was a kind and indulgent companion, bearing good-naturedly with my boyish pranks, and cautioning me, of course ineffectually, against running into danger. I had just left home and the restraint of school, and was now entering upon a wild and romantic career. In short, every thing combined to render this a most agreeable and interesting voyage. I have spent many a day of amusement and excitement in the country, but on none can I look back with so much pleasure as on the time spent in this journey to Red River.

The scenery through which we passed was pretty and romantic, but there was nothing grand about it. The country generally was low and swampy; the highest ground being the banks of the river, which sometimes rose to from sixty to seventy feet. Our progress in Hill River was slow and tedious, owing to the number of rapids encountered on the way. The hill from which the river derives its name is a small, insignificant mound, and owes its importance to the flatness of the surrounding country.

Besides the larger wild-fowl, small birds of many kinds were very numerous. The most curious, and at the same time the most impudent, among the latter were the whisky-jacks. They always hovered round us at breakfast, ready to snap up anything that came within their reach—advancing sometimes to within a yard or two of our feet, and looking at us with a very comical expression of countenance. One of the men told me that he had often caught them in his hand, with a piece of pemmican for a bait; so one morning after breakfast I went a little to one side of our camp, and covering my face with leaves, extended my hand with a few crumbs in the open palm. In five minutes a whisky-jack jumped upon a branch over my head, and after reconnoitring a minute or so, lit upon my hand, and began to breakfast forthwith. You may be sure the *trap* was not long in going off; and the screeching that Mr Jack set up on finding my fingers firmly closed upon his toes was tremendous. I never saw a more passionate little creature in my life: it screamed, struggled, and bit unceasingly, until I let it go; and even then it lighted on a tree close by, and looked at me as impudently as ever. The same day I observed that when the men were ashore the whisky-jacks used to eat out of the pemmican bags left in the boats; so I lay down close to one, under cover of a buffalo-skin, and in three minutes had made prisoner of another of these little inhabitants of the forest. They are of a bluish-grey colour, and nearly the size of a blackbird; but they are such a bundle of feathers that when plucked they do not look much larger than a sparrow. They live apparently on animal food (at least, they are very fond of it), and are not considered very agreeable eating.

We advanced very slowly up Hill River. Sometimes, after a day of the most toilsome exertions, during which the men were constantly pushing the boats up long rapids, with poles, at a very slow pace, we found ourselves only four or five miles ahead of the last night's encampment. As we ascended higher up the country, however, travelling became more easy. Sometimes small lakes and tranquil rivers allowed us to use the oars—and even the sails, when a puff of fair wind arose. Occasionally we were sweeping rapidly across the placid water; anon buffeting with, and advancing against, the foaming current of a powerful river, whose raging torrent seemed to bid defiance to our further progress: now dragging boats and cargoes over rocks, and through the deep shades of the forest, when a waterfall checked us on our way; and again dashing across a lake with favouring breeze; and sometimes, though rarely, were wind-bound on a small islet or point of land.

Our progress was slow, but full of interest, novelty, and amusement. My fellow-travellers seemed to enjoy the voyage very much; and even Mrs Gowley, to whom hardships were new, liked it exceedingly.

On our way we passed Oxford House—a small outpost of York Factory district. It is built on the brow of a grassy hill, which rises gradually from the margin of Oxford Lake. Like most of the posts in the country, it is composed of a collection of wooden houses, built in the form of a square, and surrounded by tall stockades, pointed at the tops. These, however, are more for ornament than defence. A small flag-staff towers above the buildings; from which, upon the occasion of an arrival, a little red Hudson Bay Company's flag waves its folds in the gentle current of an evening breeze. There were only two or three men at the place; and not a human being, save one or two wandering Indians, was to be found within hundreds of miles of this desolate spot. After a stay here of about half an hour, we proceeded on our way.

Few things are more beautiful or delightful than crossing a lake in the woods on a lovely morning at sunrise. The brilliant sun, rising in a flood of light, pierces through the thin haze of morning, converting the countless myriads of dew-drops that hang on tree and bush into sparkling diamonds, and burnishing the motionless flood of water, till a new and mighty firmament is reflected in the wave; as if Nature, rising early from her couch, paused to gaze with admiration on her resplendent image reflected in the depths of her own matchless mirror. The profound stillness, too, broken only by the measured sweep of the oars, fills the soul with awe; whilst a tranquil but unbounded happiness steals over the heart of the traveller as he gazes out upon the distant horizon, broken here and there by small verdant islets, floating as it were in air. He wanders back in thought to far-distant climes; or wishes, mayhap, that it were possible to dwell in scenes like this with those he loves for ever.

As the day advances, the scene, though slightly changed, is still most beautiful. The increasing heat, dispelling the mists, reveals in all its beauty the deep blue sky speckled with thin fleecy clouds, and, imparting a genial warmth to the body, creates a sympathetic glow in the soul. Flocks of snow-white gulls sail in graceful evolutions round the boats, dipping lightly in the water as if to kiss their reflected images; and, rising suddenly in long rapid flights, mount in circles up high above the tranquil world into the azure sky, till small white specks alone are visible in the distance. Up, up they rise on sportive wing, till the straining eye can no longer distinguish them, and they are gone! Ducks, too, whir past in rapid flight, steering wide of the boats, and again bending in long graceful curves into their course. The sweet, plaintive cry of the whip-poor-will rings along the shore; and the faint answer of his mate floats over the lake, mellowed by distance to a long tiny note. The air is motionless as the water; and the enraptured eye gazes in dreamy enjoyment on all that is lovely and peaceful in nature.

These are the *pleasures* of travelling in the wilderness. Let us change the picture.

The sun no longer shines upon the tranquil scene. Dark, heavy clouds obscure the sky; a suffocating heat depresses the spirits and enervates the frame; sharp, short gusts of wind now ruffle the inky waters, and the floating islands sink into insignificance as the deceptive haze which elevated them flies before the approaching storm. The ducks are gone, and the plaintive notes of the whip-poor-will are hushed as the increasing breeze rustles the leafy drapery of the forest. The gulls wheel round still, but in more rapid and uncertain flight, accompanying their motions with shrill and mournful cries, like the dismal wailings of the spirit of the storm. A few drops of rain patter on the boats, or plump like stones into the water, and the distant melancholy growl of thunder swells upon the coming gale. Uneasy glances are cast, ever and anon, towards clouds and shore, and grumbling sentences are uttered by the men. Suddenly a hissing sound is heard, a loud clap of thunder growls overhead, and the gale, dashing the white spray wildly before it, rushes down upon the boats.

"*A terre! à terre!*" shout the men. The boats are turned towards the shore, and the bending oars creak and groan as they pull swiftly on. Hiss! whir! the gale bursts forth, dashing clouds of spray into the air, twisting and curling the foaming water in its fury. The thunder crashes with fearful noise, and the lightning gleams in fitful lurid streaks across the inky sky. Presently the shore is gained, amid a deluge of rain which saturates everything with water in a few minutes. The tents are pitched, but the fires will scarcely burn, and are at last allowed to go out. The men seek shelter under the oiled cloths of the boats; while the travellers, rolled up in damp blankets, with the rain oozing through the tents upon their couches, gaze mournfully upon the dismal scene, and ponder sadly on the shortness of the step between happiness and misery.

Nearly eighteen days after we left York Factory we arrived in safety at the depôt of Norway House. This fort is built at the mouth of a small and sluggish stream, known by the name of Jack River. The houses are ranged in the form of a square; none of them exceed one story in height, and most of them are whitewashed. The ground on which it stands is rocky; and a small garden, composed chiefly of sand, juts out from the stockades like a strange excrescence. A large, rugged mass of

NORWAY HOUSE.

rocks rises up between the fort and Playgreen Lake, which stretches out to the horizon on the other side of them. On the top of these rocks stands a flagstaff, as a beacon to guide the traveller; for Norway House is so ingeniously hid in a hollow that it cannot be seen from the lake till the boat almost touches the wharf. On the left side of the building extends a flat grassy park or green, upon which during the summer months there is often a picturesque and interesting scene. Spread out to dry in the sun may be seen the snowy tent of the chief factor, lately arrived. A little further off, on the rising ground, stands a dark and almost imperceptible wigwam, the small wreath of white smoke issuing from the top proving that it is inhabited. On the river bank three or four boats and a north canoe are hauled up; and just above them a number of sunburned *voyageurs* and a few Indians amuse themselves with various games, or recline upon the grass, basking in the sunshine. Behind the fort stretches the thick forest, its outline broken here and there by cuttings of firewood or small clearings for farming.

Such was Norway House in 1841. The rocks were crowded when we arrived, and we received a hearty welcome from Mr Russ—the chief factor in charge—and his amiable family.

As it was too late to proceed any further that day, we determined to remain here all night.

From the rocks before mentioned, on which the flagstaff stands, we had a fine view of Playgreen Lake. There was nothing striking or bold in the scene, the country being low and swampy, and no hills rose on the horizon or cast their shadows on the lake; but it was pleasing and tranquil, and enlivened by one or two boats sailing about on the water.

We spent an agreeable evening; and early on the following morning started again on our journey, having received an agreeable addition to our party in the person of Miss Jessie Russ, second daughter of Mr Russ, from whom we had just parted.

On the evening of the first day after our departure from Norway House, we encamped on the shores of Lake Winnipeg. This immense body of fresh water is about three hundred miles long by about fifty broad. The shores are generally flat and uninteresting, and the water shallow; yet here and there a few pretty spots may be seen at the head of a small bay or inlet, where the ground is a little more elevated and fertile.

Nothing particular occurred during our voyage along the shores of the lake, except that we hoisted our sails oftener to a favourable breeze, and had a good deal more night travelling than heretofore. In about five days after leaving Norway House we arrived at the mouth of Red River; and a very swampy, sedgy, flat-looking mouth it was, covered with tall bulrushes and swarming with water-fowl. The banks, too, were low and swampy; but as we ascended they gradually became more woody and elevated, till we arrived at the Stone Fort—twenty miles up the river—where they were tolerably high.

A few miles below this we passed an Indian settlement, the cultivated fields and white houses of which, with the church spire in the midst, quite refreshed our eyes, after being so long accustomed to the shades of the primeval forest.

The Stone Fort is a substantial fortification, surrounded by high walls and flanked with bastions, and has a fine appearance from the river.

Here my friend and fellow-traveller, Mr Carles, hearing of his wife's illness, left us, and proceeded up the settlement on horseback. The missionaries also disembarked, and I was left alone, to be rowed slowly to Fort Garry, nearly twenty miles further up the river.

The river banks were lined all the way along with the houses and farms of the colonists, which had a thriving, cleanly appearance; and from the quantity of live stock in the farmyards, the number of pigs along the banks, and the healthy appearance of the children who ran out of the cottages to gaze upon us as we passed, I inferred that the settlers generally were well-to-do in the world. The houses of some of the more wealthy inhabitants were very handsome-looking buildings, particularly that of Mr McAllum, where in a few hours I landed. This gentleman was the superintendent of the Red River Academy, where the children of the wealthier colonists and those of the gentlemen belonging to the Hudson Bay Company are instructed in the various branches of English literature, and made to comprehend how the world was convulsed in days of yore by the mighty deeds of the heroes of ancient Greece and Rome.

Here I was hospitably treated to an excellent breakfast, and then proceeded on foot with Mr Carles—who rejoined me here—to Fort Garry, which lay about two miles distant.

Upon arriving I was introduced to Mr Finlayson, the chief factor in charge, who received me very kindly, and introduced me to my fellow-clerks in the office. Thus terminated my first inland journey.

6

RED RIVER SETTLEMENT

*—Origin of the Colony—Opposition Times and Anecdotes
—The Flood of 1826—Climate—Being Broken-in
—Mr Simpson, the Arctic Discoverer
—The Mackenzie River Brigade*

RED RIVER SETTLEMENT is, to use a high-flown expression, an oasis in the desert, and may be likened to a spot upon the moon or a solitary ship upon the ocean. In plain English, it is an isolated settlement on the borders of one of the vast prairies of North America. It is situated partly on the banks of Red River, and partly on the banks of a smaller stream called the Assinaboine, in latitude 50 degrees, and extends upwards of fifty miles along the banks of these two streams. The country around it is a vast treeless prairie, upon which scarcely a shrub is to be seen; but a thick coat of grass covers it throughout its entire extent, with the exception of a few spots where the hollowness of the ground has collected a little moisture, or the meandering of some small stream or rivulet enriches the soil, and covers its banks with verdant shrubs and trees.

The banks of the Red and Assinaboine Rivers are covered with a thick belt of woodland—which does not, however, extend far back into the plains. It is composed of oak, poplar, willows, etcetera, the first of which is much used for fire-wood by the settlers. The larger timber in the adjacent woods is thus being rapidly thinned.

The settlers are a mixture of French Canadians, Scotch-men, and Indians. The first of these occupy the upper part of the settlement, the second live near the middle, and the Indians inhabit a village at its lower extremity.

There are four Protestant churches: the upper, middle, and lower churches, and one at the Indian settlement. There are also two Roman Catholic chapels, some priests, and a Roman Catholic bishop resident in the colony, besides one or two schools; the principal being, as before mentioned, under the superintendence of Mr McAllum, who has since been ordained by the Bishop of Montreal, during that prelate's visit to Red River (see note 1).

For the preservation of the peace, and the punishment of evil-doers, a Recorder and body of magistrates are provided, who assemble every quarter at Fort Garry, the seat of the court-house, for the purpose of redressing wrongs, punishing crimes, giving good advice, and eating an excellent dinner at the Company's table. There was once, also, a body of policemen; but, strange to say, they were chosen from among the most turbulent of the settlers, and were never expected to be on duty except when a riot took place: the policemen themselves generally being the ringleaders on those occasions, it may be supposed they did not materially assist in quelling disturbances.

The Scotch and Indian settlers cultivate wheat, barley,

and Indian corn in abundance; for which the only market is that afforded by the Company, the more wealthy settlers, and retired chief factors. This market, however, is a poor one, and in years of plenty the settlers find it difficult to dispose of their surplus produce. Wild fruits of various descriptions are abundant, and the gardens are well stocked with vegetables. The settlers have plenty of sheep, pigs, poultry, and horned cattle; and there is scarcely a man in the place who does not drive to church on Sundays in his own cariole.

Red River is a populous settlement; the census taken in 1843 proved it to contain upwards of 5,000 souls, and since then it has been rapidly increasing.

There is a paper currency in the settlement, which obviates the necessity of having coin afloat. English pence and halfpence, however, are plentiful. The lowest paper note is one shilling sterling, the next five shillings, and the highest twenty shillings. The Canadian settlers and half-breeds are employed, during the greater part of the year, in travelling with the Company's boats and in buffalo-hunting. The Scotch settlers are chiefly farmers, tradesmen, and merchants.

The rivers, which are crossed in wooden canoes, in the absence of bridges, are well stocked with fish, the principal kinds being goldeyes, sturgeon, and catfish. Of these, I think the goldeyes the best; at any rate, they are the most numerous. The wild animals inhabiting the woods and prairies are much the same as in the other parts of North America—namely, wolves, foxes, brown and black bears, martens, minks, musquash, rabbits, etcetera; while the woods are filled with game, the marshes and ponds with ducks, geese, swans, cranes, and a host of other water-fowl.

Red River was first settled upon by the fur-traders, who

established a trading-post many years ago on its banks; but it did not assume the character of a colony till 1811, when Lord Selkirk sent out a number of emigrants to form a settlement in the wild regions of the North-West. Norwegians, Danes, Scotch, and Irish composed the motley crew; but the great bulk of the colonists then, as at the present time, consisted of Scotchmen and Canadians. Unlike other settlements in a wild country inhabited by Indians, the infant colony had few difficulties to contend with at the outset. The Indians were friendly, and had become accustomed to white men, from their previous contact for many years with the servants of the Hudson Bay Company; so, with the exception of one or two broils among themselves and other fur-traders, the colonists plodded peacefully along. On one occasion, however, the Hudson Bay Company and the North-West Company, who were long at enmity with each other, had a sharp skirmish, in which Mr Semple, then Governor of the Hudson Bay Company, was killed, and a number of his men were killed and wounded.

The whole affair originated very foolishly. A body of men had been observed from the walls of Fort Garry, travelling past the fort; and as Governor Semple wished to ascertain their intentions, he sallied forth with a few men to intercept them, and demand their object. The North-West party, on seeing a body of men coming towards them from the fort, halted till they came up; and Cuthbert Grant, who was in command, asked what they wanted. Governor Semple required to know where they were going. Being answered in a surly manner, an altercation took place between the two parties (of which the North-West was the stronger); in the middle of which a shot was unfortunately fired by one of the Hudson Bay party. It was never known who fired this shot, and many believe that it was discharged accidentally; at any rate, no one was injured by it. The moment the report was heard, a volley was fired by the North-Westers upon the Hudson Bay party, which killed a few, and wounded many; among the latter was Governor Semple. Cuthbert Grant did his utmost to keep back the fierce half-castes under his command, but without avail; and at last, seeing that this was impossible, he stood over the wounded Semple, and endeavoured to defend him. In this he succeeded for some time; but a shot from behind at last took effect in the unfortunate governor's body, and killed him. After this, the remainder of his party fled to the fort, and the victorious half-breeds pursued their way.

During the time that these two companies opposed each other, the country was in a state of constant turmoil and excitement. Personal conflicts with fists between the men—and, not unfrequently, the gentlemen—of the opposing parties were of the commonest occurrence, and frequently more deadly weapons were resorted to. Spirits were distributed among the wretched natives to a dreadful extent, and the scenes that sometimes ensued were disgusting in the extreme. Amid all this, however, stratagem was more frequently resorted to than open violence by the two companies, in their endeavours to prevent each other from procuring furs from the Indians. Men were constantly kept on the lookout for parties of natives returning from hunting expeditions; and those who could arrive first at the encampment always carried off the furs. The Indians did not care which company got them—"first come, first served," was the order of the day; and both were equally welcome, provided they brought plenty of *fire-water*.

Although the individuals of the two companies were thus almost always at enmity, at the forts, strange to say, they often acted in the most friendly manner to each other; and (except when furs were in question) more agreeable or friendly neighbours seldom came together than the Hudson Bay and North-West Companies, when they planted their forts (which they often did) within two hundred yards of each other in the wilds of North America. The clerks and labourers of the opposing establishments constantly visited each other; and during the Christmas and New-Year's holidays parties and balls were given without number. Dances, however, were not confined entirely to the holidays; but whenever one was given at an unusual time, it was generally for the purpose of drawing the attention of the entertained party from some movement of their entertainers.

Thus, upon one occasion the Hudson Bay Company's lookout reported that he had discovered the tracks of Indians in the snow, and that he thought they had just returned from a hunting expedition. No sooner was this heard than a grand ball was given to the North-West Company, Great preparations were made; the men, dressed in their newest capotes and gaudiest hat-cords, visited each other, and nothing was thought of or talked of but the ball. The evening came, and with it the guests; and soon might be heard within the fort sounds of merriment and revelry, as they danced, in lively measures, to a Scottish reel, played by some native fiddler upon a violin of his own construction. Without the gates, however, a very different scene met the eye. Down in a hollow, where the lofty trees and dense underwood threw a shadow on the ground, a knot of men might be seen, muffled in their leathern coats and fur caps, hurrying to and fro with bundles on their backs and snow-shoes under their arms; packing and tying them firmly on trains of dog-sledges, which stood, with the dogs ready harnessed, in the shadow of the bushes. The men whispered eagerly and hurriedly to each other as they packed their goods, while others held the dogs, and patted them to keep them quiet; evidently showing that, whatever was their object, expedition and secrecy were necessary. Soon all was in readiness: the bells, which usually tinkled on the dogs' necks, were unhooked and packed in the sledges; an active-looking man sprang forward and set off at a round trot over the snow, and a single crack of the whip sent four sledges, each with a train of four or five dogs, after him, while two other men brought up the rear. For a time the muffled sound of the sledges was heard as they slid over the snow, while now and then the whine of a dog broke upon the ear, as the impatient drivers urged them along. Gradually these sounds died away, and nothing was heard but the faint echoes of music and mirth, which floated on the frosty night-wind, giving token that the revellers still kept up the dance, and were ignorant of the departure of the trains.

Late on the following day the Nor'-West scouts reported the party of Indians, and soon a set of sleighs departed from the fort with loudly-ringing bells. After a long day's march of forty miles, they reached the encampment, where they found all the Indians dead drunk, and not a skin, not even the remnant of a musquash, left to repay them for their trouble! Then it was that they discovered the *ruse* of the ball, and vowed to have their revenge.

Opportunity was not long wanting. Soon after this occurrence, one of their parties met a Hudson Bay train on its way to trade with the Indians, of whom they also were in search. They exchanged compliments with each other, and, as the day was very cold, proposed lighting a fire and taking a dram together. Soon five or six goodly trees yielded to their vigorous blows, and fell crashing to the ground; and in a few minutes one of the party, lighting a sulphur match with his flint and steel, set fire to a huge pile of logs, which crackled and burned furiously, sending up clouds of sparks into the wintry sky, and casting a warm tinge upon the anew and the surrounding trees. The canteen was quickly produced, and they told their stories and adventures while the liquor mounted to their brains. The Nor'-Westers, however, after a little time, spilled their grog on the snow, unperceived by the others, so that they kept tolerably sober, while their rivals became very much elevated; and at last they began boasting of their superior powers of drinking, and, as a proof, each of them swallowed a large bumper. The Hudson Bay party, who were nearly dead drunk by this time, of course followed their example, and almost instantly fell in a heavy sleep on the snow. In ten minutes more they were tied firmly upon their sledges, and the dogs being turned homewards, away they went straight for the Hudson Bay Fort, where they soon after arrived, the men still sound asleep; while the Nor'-Westers started for the Indian camp, and this time, at least, had the furs all to themselves.

Such were the scenes that took place thirty years ago in the northern wildernesses of America. Since then, the two companies have joined, retaining the name of the richer and more powerful of the two—the "Hudson Bay Company." Spirits were still imported after the junction; but of late years they have been dispensed with throughout the country, except at the colony of Red River, and the few posts where opposition is carried on by the American fur-companies; so that now the poor savage no longer grovels in the dust of his native wilderness under the influence of the white man's fire-water, and the stranger who travels through those wild romantic regions no longer beholds the humiliating scenes or hears of the frightful crimes which were seen and heard of too often in former days, and which always have been, and always must be, prevalent wherever spirituous liquors, the great curse of mankind, are plentiful, and particularly where, as in that country, the wild inhabitants fear no laws, human or divine.

In the year 1826, Red River overflowed its banks, and flooded the whole settlement, obliging the settlers to forsake their houses, and drive their horses and cattle to the trifling eminences in the immediate vicinity. These eminences wore few and very small, so that during the flood they presented a curious appearance, being crowded with men, women, and children, horses, cattle, sheep, and poultry. The houses, being made of wood, and only built on the ground, not sunk into it, were carried away by dozens, and great numbers of horses and cattle were drowned. During the time it lasted, the settlers sailed and paddled among their houses in boats and canoes; and they now point out, among the waving grass and verdant bushes, the spot where they dwelt in their tents, or paddled about the deep waters in their canoes, in the "year of the flood." This way of speaking has a strangely antediluvian sound. The hale, middle-aged colonist will tell you, with a ludicrously grave countenance, that his house stood on such a spot, or such and such an event happened, "*a year before the flood.*"

Fort Garry, the principal establishment of the Hudson Bay Company, stands on the banks of the Assinaboine River, about two hundred yards from its junction with Red River. It is a square stone building, with bastions pierced for cannon at the corners. The principal dwelling-houses, stores, and offices are built within the walls, and the stables at a small distance from the fort. The situation is pretty and quiet; but the surrounding country is too flat for the lover of the grand and picturesque. Just in front of the gate runs, or rather glides, the peaceful Assinaboine, where, on a fine day in autumn, may be seen thousands of goldeyes playing in its limpid waters.

On the left extends the woodland fringing the river, with here and there a clump of smaller trees and willows surrounding the swamps formed by the melting snows of spring, where flocks of wild-ducks and noisy plover give animation to the scene, while through the openings in the forest are seen glimpses of the rolling prairie. Down in the hollow, where the stables stand, are always to be seen a few horses and cows, feeding or lazily chewing their cud in the rich pasturage, giving an air of repose to the scene, which contrasts forcibly with the view of the wide plains that roll out like a vast green sea from the back of the fort, studded here and there with little islets and hillocks, around which may be seen hovering a watchful hawk or solitary raven.

The climate of Red River is salubrious and agreeable. Winter commences about the month of November, and spring generally begins in April. Although the winter is very long, and extremely cold (the thermometer usually varying between ten and thirty degrees below *zero)*, yet, from its being always *dry* frost, it is much more agreeable than people accustomed to the damp thawy weather of Great Britain might suppose.

Winter is here the liveliest season of the year. It is then that the wild, demi-savage colonist leads the blushing half-breed girl to the altar, and the country about his house rings with the music of the sleigh bells, as his friends assemble to congratulate the happy pair, and dance for three successive days. It is at this season the hardy *voyageurs* rest from their toils, and, circling round the blazing fire, recount many a tale of danger, and paint many a wild romantic scene of their long and tedious voyages among the lakes and rapids of the interior; while their wives and children gaze with breathless interest upon their swarthy, sunburned faces, lighted up with animation as they recall the scenes of other days, or, with low and solemn voice, relate the death of a friend and fellow *voyageur* who perished among the foaming cataracts of the wilderness.

During the summer months there are often very severe thunderstorms, accompanied with tremendous showers of hail, which do great mischief to the crops and houses. The hailstones are of an enormous size—upwards of an inch in diameter; and on two or three occasions they broke all the windows in Fort Garry that were exposed to the storm.

Generally speaking, however, the weather is serene and calm, particularly in autumn, and during the delicious season peculiar to America called the Indian summer, which precedes the commencement of winter.

The scenery of Red River, as I said before, is neither grand nor picturesque; yet, when the sun shines brightly on the waving grass and glitters on the silver stream, and when the distant and varied cries of wild-fowl break in plaintive cadence on the ear, one experiences a sweet exulting happiness, akin to the feelings of the sailor when he gazes forth at early morning on the polished surface of the sleeping sea.

Such is Red River, and such the scenes on which I gazed in wonder, as I rode by the side of my friend and fellow-clerk, McKenny, on the evening of my arrival at my new home. Mr McKenny was mounted on his handsome horse "Colonel," while I cantered by his side on a horse that afterwards bore me over many a mile of prairie land. It is not every day that one has an opportunity of describing a horse like the one I then rode, so the reader will be pleased to have a little patience while I draw his portrait. In the first place, then, his name was "Taureau." He was of a moderate height, of a brown colour, and had the general outlines of a horse, when viewed as that animal might be supposed to appear if reflected from the depths of a bad looking-glass. His chief peculiarity was the great height of his hind-quarters, In youth they had outgrown the fore-quarters, so that, upon a level road, you had all the advantages of riding down-hill. He cantered delightfully, trotted badly, walked slowly, and upon all and every occasion evinced a resolute pig-headedness, and a strong disinclination to accommodate his will to that of his rider. He was decidedly porcine in his disposition, very plebeian in his manners, and doubtless also in his sentiments.

Such was the Bucephalus upon which I took my first ride over the Red River prairie; now swaying to and fro on his back as we galloped over the ground; anon *stotting*, in the manner of a recruit in a cavalry regiment as yet unaccustomed to the saddle, when he trotted on the beaten track; and occasionally, to the immense delight of McKenny, seizing tight hold of the saddle, as an uncertain waver in my body reminded me of Sir Isaac Newton's law of gravitation, and that any rash departure on my part from my *understanding* would infallibly lay me prostrate on the ground.

Soon after my arrival I underwent the operation which my horse had undergone before me—namely, that of being broken-in—the only difference being that he was broken-in to the saddle and I to the desk. It is needless to describe the agonies I endured while sitting, hour after hour, on a long-legged stool, my limbs quivering for want of their accustomed exercise, while the twittering of birds, barking of dogs, lowing of cows, and neighing of horses seemed to invite me to join them in the woods. Often, as my weary pen scratched slowly over the paper, their voices seemed to change to hoarse derisive laughter, as if they thought the little misshapen frogs croaking and whistling in the marshes freer far than their proud masters, who coop themselves up in smoky houses the livelong day, and call themselves the free, unshackled "lords of the creation."

I soon became accustomed to these minor miseries of human life, and ere long could sit:—

From morn till night
To scratch and write
Upon a three-legged stool;
Nor mourn the joys
Of truant boys
Who stay away from school.

There is a proverb which says, "It is a poor heart that never rejoices." Now, taking it for granted that the proverb speaks truth, and not wishing by our disregard of it to be thought poor-hearted, we—that is, McKenny and I—were in the habit of rejoicing our spirits occasionally—not in the usual way, by drinking brandy and water (though we did sometimes, when nobody knew it, indulge in a glass of beer, with the red-hot poker thrust into it), but by shouldering our guns and sallying forth to shoot the partridges, or rather grouse, which abound in the woods of Red River. On these occasions McKenny and I used to range the forest in company, enlivening our walk with converse, sometimes light and cheerful, often philosophically deep, or thinking of the "light of other days." We seldom went out without bringing home a few brace of grey grouse, which were exceedingly tame—so tame, indeed, that sometimes they did not take wing until two or three shots had been fired. On one occasion, after walking about for half an hour without getting a shot, we started a covey of seven, which alighted upon a tree close at hand. We instantly fired at the two lowest, and brought them down, while the others only stretched out their long necks, as if to see what had happened to their comrades, but did not fly away. Two more were soon shot; and while we were reloading our guns, the other three flew off to a neighbouring tree. In a few minutes more they followed their companions, and we had bagged the whole seven. This is by no means an uncommon exploit when the birds are tame; and though poor *sport*, yet it helps to fill your larder with somewhat better fare than it would often contain without such assistance. The only thing that we had to avoid was, aiming at the birds on the higher branches, as the noise they make in falling frightens those below. The experienced sportsman always begins with the lowest bird; and if they sit after the first shot, he is almost sure of the rest.

Shooting, however, was not our only amusement. Sometimes, on a fine evening, we used to saddle our horses and canter over the prairie till Red River and the fort were scarcely visible in the horizon; or, following the cart road along the settlement, we called upon our friends and acquaintances, returning the polite "*Bonjour*" of the French settler as he trotted past us on his shaggy pony, or smiling at the pretty half-caste girls as they passed along the road. These same girls, by the way, are generally very pretty; they make excellent wives, and are uncommonly thrifty. With beads, and brightly-coloured porcupines' quills, and silk, they work the most beautiful devices on the moccasins, leggins, and leathern coats worn by the inhabitants; and during the long winter months they spin and weave an excellent kind of cloth from the wool produced by the sheep of the settlement, mixed with that of the buffalo, brought from the prairies by the hunters.

About the middle of autumn the body of Mr Thomas Simpson, the unfortunate discoverer, who, in company with Mr Dease, attempted to discover the Nor'-West Passage, was brought to the settlement for burial. Poor Mr Simpson had set out with a party of Red River half-breeds, for the purpose of crossing the plains to St. Louis, and proceeding thence through the United States to England. Soon after his departure, however, several of the party returned to the settlement, stating that Mr Simpson had, in a fit of insanity, killed two of his men, and then shot himself, and that they had buried him on the spot where he fell. This story, of course, created a great sensation in the colony; and as all the party gave the same account of the affair upon investigation, it was believed by many that he had committed suicide. A few, however, thought that he had been murdered, and had shot the two men in self-defence. In the autumn of 1841 the matter was ordered to be further inquired into; and, accordingly, Dr Bunn was sent to the place where Mr Simpson's body had been interred, for the purpose of raising and examining it. Decomposition, however, had proceeded too far; so the body was conveyed to the colony for burial, and Dr Bunn returned without having discovered anything that could throw light on the melancholy subject.

I did not know Mr Simpson personally, but, from the report of those who did, it appears that, though a clever and honourable man, he was of rather a haughty disposition, and in consequence was very much disliked by the half-breeds of Red River. I therefore think, with many of Mr Simpson's friends and former companions, that he did *not* kill himself, and that this was only a false report of his murderers. Besides, it is not probable that a man who had just succeeded in making important additions to our geographical knowledge, and who might reasonably expect honour and remuneration upon returning to his native land, would, without any known or apparent cause, first commit murder and then suicide. By his melancholy death the Hudson Bay Company lost a faithful servant, and the world an intelligent and enterprising man.

Winter, according to its ancient custom, passed away; and spring, not with its genial gales and scented flowers, but with burning sun and melting snow, changed the face of nature, and broke the icy covering of Red River. Duffle coats vanished, and a few of the half-breed settlers doffed their fur caps and donned the "bonnet rouge," while the more hardy and savage contented themselves with the bonnet *noir*, in the shape of their own thick black hair. Carioles still continued to run, but it was merely from the force of habit, and it was evident they would soon give up in despair. Sportsmen began to think of ducks and geese, farmers of ploughs and wheat, and *voyageurs* to dream of rapid streams and waterfalls, and of distant voyages in light canoes.

Immediately upon the ice in the lakes and rivers breaking up, we made arrangements for dispatching the Mackenzie River brigade—which is always the first that leaves the colony—for the purpose of conveying goods to Mackenzie River, and carrying furs to the sea-coast.

Choosing the men for this long and arduous voyage was an interesting scene. L'Esperance, the old guide, who had many a day guided this brigade through the lakes and rivers of the interior, made his appearance at the fort a day or two before the time fixed for starting; and at his heels followed a large band of wild, careless, happy-looking half-breeds. Having collected in front of the office door, Mr McKenny went out with a book and pencil in his hand, and told L'Esperance to begin. The guide went a little apart from the rest, accompanied by the steersmen of the boats (seven or eight in number), and then, scanning the group of dark athletic men who stood smiling before him, called out, "Pierre!" A tall, Herculean man answered to the call, and, stepping out from among the rest, stood beside his friend the guide. After this one of the steersmen chose another man; and so on, till the crews of all the boats were completed. Their names were then marked down in a book, and they all proceeded to the trading-room, for the purpose of taking "advances," in the shape of shirts, trousers, bonnets, caps, tobacco, knives, capotes, and all the other things necessary for a long, rough journey.

On the day appointed for starting, the boats, to the number of six or seven, were loaded with goods for the interior; and the *voyageurs*, dressed in their new clothes, embarked, after shaking hands with, and in many cases embracing, their comrades on the land; and then, shipping their oars, they shot from the bank and rowed swiftly down Red River, singing one of their beautiful boat-songs, which was every now and then interrupted by several of the number hallooing a loud farewell, as they passed here and there the cottages of friends.

With this brigade I also bade adieu to Red River, and, after a pleasant voyage of a few days, landed at Norway House, while the boats pursued their way.

Red River Settlement is now (1875) very much changed, as, no doubt, the reader is aware, and the foregoing description is in many respects inapplicable.

Note 1: The reader must bear in remembrance that this chapter was written in 1847.

7

NORWAY HOUSE

—Adventure with a Bear—Indian Feast—The Portage Brigade—The Clerks' House—Catching a Buffalo—Goldeye Fishing—Rasping a Rock

Norway House, as we have before mentioned, is built upon the shores of Playgreen Lake, close to Jack River, and distant about twenty miles from Lake Winnipeg. At its right-hand corner rises a huge abrupt rock, from whose summit, where stands a flagstaff, a fine view of Playgreen Lake and the surrounding country is obtained. On this rock a number of people were assembled to witness our arrival, and among them Mr Russ, who sauntered down to the wharf to meet us as we stepped ashore.

A few days after my arrival, the Council "resolved" that I should winter at Norway House; so next day, in accordance with the resolution of that august assembly, I took up my quarters in the clerks' room, and took possession of the books and papers.

It is an author's privilege, I believe, to jump from place

to place and annihilate time at pleasure. I avail myself of it to pass over the autumn—during which I hunted, fished, and paddled in canoes to the Indian village at Rossville a hundred times—and jump at once into the middle of winter.

Norway House no longer boasts the bustle and excitement of the summer season. No boats arrive, no groups of ladies and gentlemen assemble on the rocks to gaze at the sparkling waters. A placid stillness reigns around, except in the immediate vicinity of the fort, where a few axe-men chop the winter firewood, or start with trains of dog-sledges for the lakes, to bring home loads of white-fish and venison. Mr Russ is reading the "Penny Cyclopaedia" in the Hall (as the winter mess-room is called), and I am writing in the dingy little office in the shade, which looks pigstyish in appearance without, but is warm and snug within. Alongside of me sits Mr Cumming, a tall, bald-headed, sweet-tempered man of forty-five, who has spent the greater part of his life among the bears and Indians of Hudson Bay, and is now on a Christmas visit at Norway House. He has just arrived from his post a few hundred miles off, whence he walked on snowshoes, and is now engaged in taking off his moccasins and blanket socks, which he spreads out carefully below the stove to dry.

We do not continue long, however, at our different occupations. Mr Evans, the Wesleyan missionary, is to give a feast to the Indians at Rossville, and afterwards to examine the little children who attend the village school. To this feast we are invited; so in the afternoon Mr Cumming and I put on our moose-skin coats and snow-shoes, and set off for the village, about two miles distant from the fort.

By the way Mr Cumming related an adventure he had had while travelling through the country; and as it may serve to show the dangers sometimes encountered by those who wander through the wilds of North America, I will give it here in his own words.

Mr Cumming's Adventure with a Bear:

"It was about the beginning of winter," said he, "that I set off on snow-shoes, accompanied by an Indian, to a small lake to fetch fish caught in the autumn, and which then lay frozen in a little house built of logs, to protect them for winter use. The lake was about ten miles off; and as the road was pretty level and not much covered with underwood, we took a train of dogs with us, and set off before daybreak, intending to return again before dark; and as the day was clear and cold, we went cheerily along without interruption, except an occasional fall when a branch caught our snow-shoes, or a stoppage to clear the traces when the dogs got entangled among the trees. We had proceeded about six miles, and the first grey streaks of day lit up the eastern horizon, when the Indian who walked in advance paused, and appeared to examine some footprints in the snow. After a few minutes of close observation he rose, and said that a bear had passed not long before, and could not be far off, and asked permission to follow it. I told him he might do so, and said I would drive the dogs in his track, as the bear had gone in the direction of the fish-house. The Indian threw his gun over his shoulder, and was soon lost in the forest. For a quarter of an hour I plodded on behind the dogs, now urging them along, as they flagged and panted in the deep snow, and occasionally listening for a shot from my Indian's gun. At last he fired, and almost immediately after fired again; for you must know that some Indians can load so fast that two shots from their single barrel sound almost like the discharge in succession of the two shots from a double-barrelled gun. Shortly after, I heard another shot; and then, as all became silent, I concluded he had killed the bear, and that I should soon find him cutting it up. Just as I thought this, a fierce growl alarmed me; so, seizing a pistol which I always carried with me, I hastened forward. As I came nearer, I heard a man's voice mingled with the growls of a bear; and upon arriving at the foot of a small mound, my Indian's voice, apostrophising death, became distinctly audible. 'Come, Death!' said he, in a contemptuous tone; 'you have got me at last, but the Indian does not fear you!' A loud angry growl from the bear, as he saw me rushing up the hill, stopped him; and the unfortunate man turned his eyes upon me with an imploring look. He was lying on his back, while the bear (a black one) stood over him, holding one of his arms in its mouth. In rushing up the mound I unfortunately stumbled, and filled my pistol with snow; so that when the bear left the Indian and rushed towards me it missed fire, and I had only left me the poor, almost hopeless, chance, of stunning the savage animal with a blow of the butt-end. Just as he was rearing on his hind legs, my eye fell upon the Indian's axe, which fortunately lay at my feet; and seizing it, I brought it down with all my strength on the bear's head, just at the moment that he fell upon me, and we rolled down the hill together. Upon recovering myself, I found that the blow of the axe had killed him instantly, and that I was uninjured. Not so the Indian: the whole calf of his left leg was bitten off, and his body lacerated dreadfully in various places. He was quite sensible, however, though very faint, and spoke to me when I stooped to examine his wounds. In a short time I had tied them up; and placing him on the sledge with part of the bear's carcass, which I intended to dine upon, we returned immediately to the fort. The poor Indian got better slowly, but he never recovered the perfect use of his leg, and now hobbles about the fort, cutting firewood, or paddling about the lake in search of ducks and geese in his bark canoe."

Mr Cumming concluded his story just as we arrived at the little bay, at the edge of which the Indian village of Rossville is built. From the spot where we stood the body of the village did not appear to much advantage; but the parsonage and church, which stood on a small mound, their white walls in strong contrast to the background of dark trees, had a fine picturesque effect. There were about twenty houses in the village, inhabited entirely by Indians, most of whom were young and middle-aged men. They spend their time in farming during the summer, and are successful in raising potatoes and a few other vegetables for their own use. In winter they go into the woods to hunt fur-bearing animals, and also deer; but they never remain long absent from their homes. Mr Evans resided among them, and taught them and their children writing and arithmetic, besides instructing them in the principles of Christianity. They often assembled in the school-house for prayer and sacred music, and attended divine service regularly in the church every Sunday. Mr Evans, who was a good musician, had taught them to sing in parts; and it has a wonderfully pleasing effect upon a stranger to hear these dingy sons and daughters of the wilderness raising their melodious voices in harmony in praise of the Christian's God.

Upon our arrival at the village, we were ushered into Mr Evans' neat cottage, from the windows of which is a fine view of Playgreen Lake, studded with small islands, stretching out to the horizon on the right, and a boundless wilderness of trees on the left. Here were collected the ladies and gentlemen of Norway House, and a number of indescribable personages, apparently engaged in mystic preparations for the approaching feast. It was with something like awe that I entered the schoolroom, and beheld two long rows of tables covered with puddings, pies, tarts, stews, hashes, and vegetables of all shapes, sizes, and descriptions, smoking thereon. I feared for the Indians, although they can stand a great deal in the way of repletion; moderation being, of course, out of the question, with such abundance of good things placed before them. A large shell was sounded after the manner of a bugle, and all the Indians of the village walked into the room and seated themselves, the women on one side of the long tables, and the men on the other. Mr Evans stood at the head, and asked a blessing; and then commenced a work of demolition, the like of which has not been seen since the foundation of the world! The pies had strong crusts, but the knives were stronger; the paste was hard and the interior tough, but Indian teeth were harder and Indian jaws tougher; the dishes were gigantic, but the stomachs were capacious, so that ere long numerous skeletons and empty dishes alone graced the board. One old woman, of a dark-brown complexion, with glittering black eyes and awfully long teeth, set up in the wholesale line, and demolished the viands so rapidly, that those who sat beside her, fearing a dearth in the land, began to look angry. Fortunately, however, she gave in suddenly, while in the middle of a venison pasty, and reclining languidly backward, with a sweetly contented expression of countenance, while her breath came thickly through her half-opened mouth, she gently fell asleep—and thereby, much to her chagrin, lost the tea and cakes which were served out soon afterwards by way of dessert. When the seniors had finished, the juveniles were admitted *en masse*, and they soon cleared away the remnants of the dinner.

The dress of the Indians upon this occasion was generally blue cloth capotes with hoods, scarlet or blue cloth leggins, quill-worked moccasins, and no caps. Some of them were dressed very funnily; and one or two of the oldest appeared in blue surtouts, which were very ill made, and much too large for the wearers. The ladies had short gowns without plaits, cloth leggins of various colours highly ornamented with beads, cotton handkerchiefs on their necks, and sometimes also on their heads. The boys and girls were just their seniors in miniature.

After the youngsters had finished dinner, the schoolroom was cleared by the guests; benches were ranged along the entire room, excepting the upper end, where a table, with two large candlesticks at either end, served as a stage for the young actors. When all was arranged, the elder Indians seated themselves on the benches, while the boys and girls ranged themselves along the wall behind the table. Mr Evans then began by causing a little boy about four years old to recite a long comical piece of prose in English. Having been well drilled for weeks beforehand, he did it in the most laughable style. Then came forward four little girls, who kept up an animated philosophical discussion as to the difference of the days in the moon and on the earth. Then a bigger boy made a long speech in the Seauteaux language, at which the Indians laughed immensely, and with which the white people present (who did not understand a word of it) appeared to be greatly delighted, and laughed loudly too. Then the whole of the little band, upon a sign being given by Mr Evans, burst at once into a really beautiful hymn, which was quite unexpected, and consequently all the more gratifying. This concluded the examination, if I may so call it; and after a short prayer the Indians departed to their homes, highly delighted with their entertainment. Such was the Christmas feast at Rossville, and many a laugh it afforded us that night as we returned home across the frozen lake by the pale moonlight.

Norway House is perhaps one of the best posts in the Indian country. The climate is dry and salubrious; and although (like nearly all the other parts of the country) extremely cold in winter, it is very different from the damp, chilling cold of that season in Great Britain. The country around is swampy and rocky, and covered with dense forests. Many of the Company's posts are but ill provided with the necessaries of life, and entirely destitute of luxuries. Norway house, however, is favoured in this respect. We always had fresh meat of some kind or other; sometimes beef, mutton, or venison, and occasionally buffalo meat, was sent us from the Swan River district. Of tea, sugar, butter, and bread we had more than enough; and besides the produce of our garden in the way of vegetables, the river and lake contributed white-fish, sturgeon, and pike, or jack-fish, in abundance. The pike is not a delicate fish, and the sturgeon is extremely coarse, but the white-fish is the most delicate and delicious I ever ate. I am not aware of their existence in any part of the Old World, but the North American lakes abound with them. It is generally the size of a good salmon trout, of a bright silvery colour, and tastes a little like salmon. Many hundreds of fur-traders live almost entirely on white-fish, particularly at those far northern posts where flour, sugar, and tea cannot be had in great quantities, and where deer are scarce. At these posts the Indians are sometimes reduced to cannibalism, and the Company's people have, on more than one occasion, been obliged to eat their beaver-skins! The beaver-skin is thick and oily, so that, when the fur is burned off, and the skin well boiled, it makes a kind of soup that will at least keep one alive. Starvation is quite common among the Indians of those distant regions; and the scraped rocks, divested of their covering of *tripe-de-roche* (which resembles dried-up seaweed), have a sad meaning and melancholy appearance to the traveller who journeys through the wilds and solitudes of Rupert's Land.

Norway House is also an agreeable and interesting place, from its being in a manner the gate to the only route to Hudson Bay, so that during the spring and summer months all the brigades of boats and canoes from every part of the northern department must necessarily pass it on their way to York Factory with furs: and as they all return in the autumn, and some of the gentlemen leave their wives and families for a few weeks till they return to the interior, it is at this sunny season of the year quite gay and bustling; and the clerks' house, in which I lived, was often filled with a strange and noisy collection of human beings, who rested here a while ere they started for the shores of Hudson Bay, for the distant region of Mackenzie River, or the still more distant land of Oregon.

During winter our principal amusement was white-partridge shooting. This bird is a species of ptarmigan, and is pure white, with the exception of the tips of the wings and tail. They were very numerous during the winter, and formed an agreeable dish at our mess-table. I also enjoyed a little skating at the beginning of the winter; but the falling snow soon put an end to this amusement.

Spring, beautiful spring! returned again to cheer us in our solitude, and to open into life the waters and streams of Hudson Bay. Great will be the difference between the reader's idea of that season in that place and the reality. Spring, with its fresh green leaves and opening flowers, its emerald fields and shady groves, filled with sounds of melody! No, reader; that is not the spring we depict: not quite so beautiful, though far more prized by those who spend a monotonous winter of more than six months in solitude. The sun shines brightly in a cloudless sky, lighting up the pure white fields and plains with dazzling brilliancy. The gushing waters of a thousand rills, formed by the melting snow, break sweetly on the ear, like the well-remembered voice of a long-absent friend. The whistling wings of wild-fowl, as they ever and anon desert the pools of water now open in the lake and hurry over the forest-trees, accord well with the shrill cry of the yellow-leg and curlew, and with the general wildness of the scene; while the reviving frogs chirrup gladly in the swamps to see the breaking up of winter and welcome back the spring. This is the spring I write of; and to have a correct idea of the beauties and the sweetness of *this* spring, you must first spend a winter in Hudson Bay.

As I said, then, spring returned. The ice melted, floated off, and vanished. Jack River flowed gently on its way, as if it had never gone to sleep; and the lake rolled and tumbled on its shores, as if to congratulate them on the happy change. Soon the boats began to arrive. First came the "Portage Brigade," in charge of L'Esperance. There were seven or eight boats; and ere long as many fires burned on the green beside the fort, with a merry, careless band of wild-looking Canadian and half-breed *voyageurs* round each. And a more picturesque set of fellows I never saw. They were all dressed out in new light-blue capotes and corduroy trousers, which they tied at the knee with beadwork garters. Moose-skin moccasins cased their feet, and their brawny, sunburned necks were bare. A scarlet belt encircled the waist of each; and while some wore hats with gaudy feathers, others had their heads adorned with caps and bonnets, surrounded with gold and silver tinsel hat-cords. A few, however, despising coats, travelled in blue and white striped shirts, and trusted to their thickly-matted hair to guard them from the rain and sun. They were truly a wild yet handsome set of men; and no one, when gazing on their happy faces as they lay or stood in careless attitudes round the fires, puffing clouds of smoke from their ever-burning pipes, would have believed that these men had left their wives and families but the week before, to start on a five months' voyage of the most harassing description, fraught with the dangers of the boiling cataracts and foaming rapids of the interior.

They stopped at Norway House on their way, to receive the outfit of goods for the Indian trade of Athabasca (one of the interior districts); and were then to start for Portage la Loche, a place where the whole cargoes are carried on the men's shoulders overland for twelve miles to the head-waters of another river, where the traders from the northern posts come to meet them, and, taking the goods, give in exchange the "returns" in furs of the district.

Next came old Mr Mottle, with his brigade of five boats from Isle à la Crosse, one of the interior districts; and soon another set of camp-fires burned on the green, and the clerks' house received another occupant. After them came the Red River brigades in quick succession: careful, funny, uproarious Mr Mott, on his way to York for goods expected by the ship (for you must know Mr Mott keeps a store in Red River, and is a man of some importance in the colony); and grasping, comical, close-fisted Mr Macdear; and quiet Mr Sink—all passing onwards to the sea, rendering Norway House quite lively for a time, and then leaving it silent. But not for long, as the Saskatchewan brigade, under the charge of chief trader Harrit and young Mr Polly, suddenly arrived, and filled the whole country with noise and uproar. The Saskatchewan brigade is the largest and most noisy that halts at Norway House. It generally numbers from fifteen to twenty boats, filled with the wildest men in the service. They come from the prairies and Rocky Mountains, and are consequently brimful of stories of the buffalo hunt, attacks upon grizzly bears, and wild Indians—some of them interesting and true enough, but most of them either tremendous exaggerations, or altogether inventions of their own wild fancies. Soon after, the light canoes arrived from Canada, and in them an assortment of raw material for the service in the shape of four or five green young men.

The clerks' house now became crammed. The quiet, elderly folks, who had continued to fret at its noisy occupants, fled in despair to another house, and thereby left room for the newcomers—or greenhorns, as they were elegantly styled by their more knowing fellow-clerks. Now, indeed, the corner of the fort in which we lived was avoided by all quiet people as if it were smitten with the plague; while the loud laugh, uproarious song, and sounds of the screeching flute or scraping fiddle, issued from the open doors and windows, frightening away the very mosquitoes, and making roof and rafters ring. Suddenly a dead silence would ensue; and then it was conjectured by the knowing ones of the place that Mr Polly was *coming out strong* for the benefit of the new arrivals. Mr Polly had a pleasant way of getting the green ones round him, and, by detailing some of the wild scenes and incidents of his voyages in the Saskatchewan, of leading them on from truth to exaggeration, and from that to fanciful composition, wherein he would detail, with painful minuteness, all the horrors of Indian warfare, and the improbability of any one who entered those dreadful regions ever returning alive.

Norway House was now indeed in full blow, and many a happy hour did I spend upon one of the clerks' beds—every inch of which was generally occupied—listening to the story or the song. The young men there assembled had arrived from the distant quarters of America, and some of them even from England. Some were in the prime of manhood, and had spent many years in the Indian country; some were beginning to scrape the down from their still soft chins; while others were boys of fourteen, who had just left home, and were listening for the first time, open-mouthed, to their seniors' description of life in the wilderness.

Alas, how soon were those happy, careless young fellows to separate, and how little probability was there of their ever meeting again! A sort of friendship had sprung up among three of us. Many a happy hour had we spent in rambling among the groves and woods of Norway House: now ranging about in search of wild pigeons, anon splashing and tumbling in the clear waters of the lake, or rowing over its surface in a light canoe; while our inexperienced voices filled the woods with snatches of the wild yet plaintive songs of the *voyageurs*, which we had just begun to learn. Often had we lain on our little pallet in Bachelors' Hall, recounting to each other our adventures in the wild woods, or recalling the days of our childhood, and making promises of keeping up a steady correspondence through all our separations, difficulties, and dangers.

A year passed away, and at last I got a letter from one of my friends, dated from the Arctic regions, near the mouth of Mackenzie River; the other wrote to me from among the snow-clad caps of the Rocky Mountains; while I addressed them from the swampy, ice-begirt shores of Hudson Bay.

In the Saskatchewan brigade two young bisons were conveyed to York Factory for the purpose of being shipped for England in the *Prince Rupert*. They were a couple of the wild-

BUFFALO-HUNTING.

est little wretches I ever saw, and were a source of great annoyance to the men during the voyage. The way they were taken was odd enough, and I shall here describe it.

In the Saskatchewan the chief food both of white men and Indians is buffalo meat, so that parties are constantly sent out to hunt the buffalo. They generally chase them on horseback—the country being mostly prairie land—and when they get close enough, shoot them with guns. The Indians, however, shoot them oftener with the bow and arrow, as they prefer keeping their powder and shot for warfare. They are very expert with the bow, which is short and strong, and can easily send an arrow quite through a buffalo at twenty yards off. One of these parties, then, was ordered to procure two calves alive, if possible, and lead them to the Company's establishment. This they succeeded in doing in the following manner. Upon meeting with a herd, they all set off full gallop in chase. Away went the startled animals at a round trot, which soon increased to a gallop as the horse men neared them, and a shot or two told that they were coming within range. Soon the shots became more numerous, and here and there a black spot on the prairie told where a buffalo had fallen. No slackening of the pace occurred, however, as each hunter, upon killing an animal, merely threw down his cap or mitten to mark it as his own, and continued in pursuit of the herd, loading his gun as he galloped along. The buffalo-hunters, by the way, are very expert at loading and firing quickly while going at full gallop. They carry two or three bullets in their mouths, which they spit into the muzzles of their guns after dropping in a little powder, and instead of ramming it down with a rod, merely hit the butt-end of the gun on the pommel of their saddles; and in this way fire a great many shots in quick succession.

This, however, is a dangerous mode of shooting, as the ball sometimes sticks half-way down the barrel and bursts the gun, carrying away a finger, and occasionally a hand.

In this way they soon killed as many buffaloes as they could carry in their carts, and one of the hunters set off in chase of a calf. In a short time he edged one away from the rest, and then, getting between it and the herd, ran straight against it with his horse and knocked it down. The frightened little animal jumped up again and set off with redoubled speed; but another butt from the horse again sent it sprawling. Again it rose, and was again knocked down, and in this way was at last fairly tired out; when the hunter, jumping suddenly from his horse, threw a rope round its neck, and drove it before him to the encampment, and soon after brought it to the fort. It was as wild as ever when I saw it at Norway House, and seemed to have as much distaste to its thraldom as the day it was taken.

As the summer advanced the heat increased, and the mosquitoes became perfectly insupportable. Nothing could save one from the attacks of these little torments. Almost all other insects went to rest with the sun: sand-flies, which bite viciously during the day, went to sleep at night; the large *bull-dog*, whose bite is terrible, slumbered in the evening; but the mosquito, the long-legged, determined, vicious, persevering mosquito, whose ceaseless hum dwells for ever on the ear, *never* went to sleep. Day and night the painful, tender little pimples on our necks and behind our ears were being constantly retouched by these villainous flies, it was useless killing thousands of them—millions supplied their place. The only thing, in fact, that can protect one during the night (*nothing* can during the day) is a net of gauze hung over the bed; but as this was looked upon by the young men as somewhat effeminate, it was seldom resorted to. The best thing for their destruction, we found, was to fill our rooms with smoke, either by burning damp moss or by letting off large puffs of gunpowder, and then throwing the doors and windows open to allow them to fly out. This, however, did not put them all out; so we generally spent an hour or so before going to bed in hunting them with candles. Even this did not entirely destroy them; and often might our friends, by looking telescopically through the keyhole, have seen us wandering during the late hours of the night in our shirts looking for mosquitoes, like unhappy ghosts doomed to search perpetually for something they can never find. The intense, suffocating heat also added greatly to our discomfort.

In fine weather I used to visit my friend Mr Evans at Rossville, where I had always a hearty welcome. I remember on one occasion being obliged to beg the loan of a canoe from an Indian, and having a romantic paddle across part of Playgreen Lake. I had been offered a passage in a boat which was going to Rossville, but was not to return. Having nothing particular to do, however, at the time, I determined to take my chance of finding a return conveyance of some kind or other. In due time I arrived at the parsonage, where I spent a pleasant afternoon in sauntering about the village, and in admiring the rapidity and ease with which the Indian children could read and write the Indian language by means of a syllable alphabet invented by their clergyman. The same gentleman afterwards made a set of leaden types with no other instrument than a penknife, and printed a great many hymns in the Indian language.

In the evening I began to think of returning to the fort; but no boat or canoe could be found small enough to be paddled by one man, and as no one seemed inclined to go with me, I began to fear that I should have to remain all night. At last a young Indian told me he had a hunting canoe, which I might have if I chose to venture across the lake in it, but it was very small. I instantly accepted his offer; and, bidding adieu to my friends at the parsonage, followed him down to a small creek overshaded by tall trees, where, concealed among the reeds and bushes, lay the canoe. It could not, I should think, have measured more than three yards in length, by eighteen inches in breadth at the middle, whence it tapered at either end to a thin edge. It was made of birch bark scarcely a quarter of an inch thick; and its weight may be imagined when I say

SMALL HUNTING CANOE.

that the Indian lifted it from the ground with one hand and placed it in the water, at the same time handing me a small light paddle. I stepped in with great care, and the frail bark trembled with my weight as I seated myself, and pushed out into the lake. The sun had just set, and his expiring rays cast a glare upon the overhanging clouds in the west, whilst the shades of night gathered thickly over the eastern horizon. Not a breath of wind disturbed the glassy smoothness of the water, in which every golden-tinted cloud was mirrored with a fidelity that rendered it difficult to say which was image and which reality. The little bark darted through the water with the greatest ease, and as I passed among the deepening shadows of the lofty pines, and across the gilded waters of the bay, a wild enthusiasm seized me; I strained with all my strength upon the paddle, and the sparkling drops flew in showers behind me as the little canoe flew over the water more like a phantom than a reality—when suddenly I missed my stroke; my whole weight was thrown on one side, the water gurgled over the gunwale of the canoe, and my heart leaped to my mouth, as I looked for an instant into the dark water. It was only for a moment; in another instant the canoe righted, and I paddled the remainder of the way in a much more gentle manner—enthusiasm gone, and a most wholesome degree of timidity pervading my entire frame. It was dark when I reached the fort, and upon landing I took the canoe under my arm and carried it up the bank with nearly as much ease as if it had been a camp-stool.

When the day was warm and the sun bright—when the sky was clear and the water blue—when the air was motionless, and the noise of arrivals and departures had ceased—when work was at a stand, and we enjoyed the felicity of having nothing to do, Mr Russ and I used to saunter down to the water's edge to have an hour or two's fishing. The fish we fished for were goldeyes, and the manner of our fishing was this:—

Pausing occasionally as we walked along, one of us might be observed to bend in a watchful manner over the grass, and, gradually assuming the position of a quadruped, fall plump upon his hands and knees. Having achieved this feat, he would rise with a grasshopper between his finger and thumb; a tin box being then held open by the other, the unlucky insect was carefully introduced to the interior, and the lid closed sharply—some such remark attending each capture as that "*That* one was safe," or, "There went another;" and the mystery of the whole proceeding being explained by the fact that these same incarcerated grasshoppers were intended to form the bait with which we trusted to beguile the unwary goldeyes to their fate.

Having arrived at the edge of the place where we usually fished, each drew from a cleft in the rock a stout branch of a tree, around the end of which was wound a bit of twine with a large hook attached to it. This we unwound quickly, and after impaling a live grasshopper upon the barbs of our respective hooks, dropped them into the water, and gazed intently at the lines. Mr Russ, who was a great lover of angling, now began to get excited, and made several violent pulls at the line, under the impression that something had *bitten*. Suddenly his rod, stout as it was, bent with the immense muscular force applied to it, and a small goldeye, about three or four inches long, flashed like an electric spark from the water, and fell with bursting force on the rocks behind, at the very feet of a small Indian boy, who sat, nearly in a state of nature, watching our movements from among the bushes. The little captive was of a bright silvery colour, with a golden eye, and is an excellent fish

AN UNLUCKY CAST.

for breakfast. The truth of the proverb, "It never rains but it pours," was soon verified by the immense number of goldeyes of every size, from one foot to four inches, which we showered into the bushes behind us. Two or three dozen were caught in a few minutes, and at last we began to get quite exhausted; and Mr Russ proposed going up to the house for his new fly-rod, by way of diversifying the sport, and rendering it more scientific.

Down he came again in a few minutes, with a splendidly varnished, extremely slim rod, with an invisible line and an aërial fly. This instrument was soon put up; and Mr Russ, letting out six fathoms of line, stood erect, and making a splendid heave, caught the Indian boy by the hair! This was an embarrassing commencement; but being an easy, good-natured man, he only frowned the boy out of countenance, and shortened his line. The next cast was more successful; the line swept gracefully through the air, and fell in a series of elegant circles within a few feet of the rock on which he stood. Goldeyes, however, are not particular; and ere he could draw the line straight, a very large one darted at the fly, and swallowed it. The rod bent into a beautiful oval as Mr Russ made a futile attempt to whip the fish over his head, according to custom, and the line straightened with fearful rigidity as the fish began to pull for its life. The fisher became energetic, and the fish impatient, but there was no prospect of its ever being landed; till at last, having got his rod inextricably entangled among the neighbouring bushes, he let it fall, and most unscientifically hauled the fish out by the line, exclaiming, in the bitterness of his heart, "that rods were contemptible childish things, and that a stout branch of a tree was the rod for him." This last essay seemed to have frightened all the rest away, for not another bite did we get after that.

Towards the beginning of June 1843, orders arrived from headquarters, appointing me to spend the approaching winter at York Factory, the place where I had first pressed American soil. It is impossible to describe the joy with which I received the news. Whether it was my extreme fondness for travelling, or the mere love of change, I cannot tell, but it had certainly the effect of affording me immense delight, and I set about making preparation for the journey immediately. The arrival of the canoes from Canada was to be the signal for my departure, and I looked forward to their appearance with great impatience.

In a few days the canoes arrived; and on the 4th of June, 1843, I started, in company with several other gentlemen, in two north canoes. These light, graceful craft were about thirty-six feet long, by from five to six broad, and were capable of containing eight men and three passengers. They were made entirely of birch bark, and gaudily painted on the bow and stern. In these fairy-like boats, then, we swept swiftly over Playgreen Lake, the bright vermilion paddles glancing in the sunshine, and the woods echoing to the lively tune of *A la claire fontaine*, sung by the two crews in full chorus. We soon left Norway House far behind us, and ere long were rapidly descending the streams that flow through the forests of the interior into Hudson Bay.

While running one of the numerous rapids with which these rivers abound, our canoe struck upon a rock, which tore a large hole in its side. Fortunately the accident happened close to the shore, and nearly at the usual breakfasting hour; so that while some of the men repaired the damages, which they did in half an hour, we employed ourselves agreeably in demolishing a huge ham, several slices of bread, and a cup or two of strong tea.

This was the only event worth relating that happened to us during the voyage; and as canoe-travelling is enlarged upon in another chapter, we will jump at once to the termination of our journey.

8

YORK FACTORY

—Winter Amusements—Intense Cold—The Seasons
—"Skylarking"—Sporting in the Woods and Marshes
—Trading with Indians—Christmas Doings
—Breaking-up of the Ice in Spring

ARE YOU AMBITIOUS, reader, of dwelling in a "pleasant cot in a tranquil spot, with a distant view of the changing sea?" If so, do not go to York Factory. Not that it is such an unpleasant place—for I spent two years very happily there—but simply (to give a poetical reason, and explain its character in one sentence) because it is a monstrous blot on a swampy spot, with a partial view of the frozen sea!

First impressions are generally incorrect; and I have little doubt that *your* first impression is, that a "monstrous blot on a swampy spot" cannot by any possibility be an agreeable place. To dispel this impression, and at the same time to enlighten you with regard to a variety of facts with which you are probably unacquainted, I shall describe York Factory as graphically as may be. An outline of its general appearance has been already

145

given in a former chapter, so I will now proceed to particularise the buildings. The principal edifice is the "general store," where the goods, to the amount of two years' outfit for the whole northern department, are stored. On each side of this is a long, low whitewashed house, with green edgings, in one of which visitors and temporary residents during the summer are quartered. The other is the summer mess-room. Four roomy fur-stores stand at right angles to these houses, thus forming three sides of the front square. Behind these stands a row of smaller buildings for the labourers and tradesmen; and on the right hand is the dwelling-house of the gentleman in charge, and adjoining it the clerks' house; while on the left are the provision-store and Indian trading-shop. A few insignificant buildings, such as the oil-store and lumber-house, intrude themselves here and there; and on the right a tall ungainly outlook rises in the air, affording the inhabitants an extensive view of their wild domains; and just beside it stands the ice-house. This latter building is filled every spring with blocks of solid ice of about three feet square, which do not melt during the short but intensely hot summer. The inhabitants are thus enabled to lay up a store of fresh meat for summer use, which lasts them till about the commencement of winter. The lower stratum of ice in this house never melts; nor, indeed, does the soil of the surrounding country, which only thaws to the depth of a few feet, the subsoil being perpetually frozen.

The climate of York Factory is very bad in the warm months of the year, but during the winter the intensity of the cold renders it healthy. Summer is very short; and the whole three seasons of spring, summer, and autumn are included in the months of June, July, August, and September—the rest being winter.

During part of summer the heat is extreme, and millions of flies, mosquitoes, etcetera, render the country unbearable. Fortunately, however, the cold soon extirpates them. Scarcely anything in the way of vegetables can be raised in the small spot of ground called by courtesy a garden. Potatoes one year, for a wonder, attained the size of walnuts; and sometimes a cabbage and a turnip are prevailed upon to grow. Yet the woods are filled with a great variety of wild berries, among which the cranberry and swampberry are considered the best. Black and red currants, as well as gooseberries, are plentiful; but the first are bitter, and the last small. The swampberry is in shape something like the raspberry, of a light yellow colour, and grows on a low bush, almost close to the ground. They make excellent preserves, and, together with cranberries, are made into tarts for the mess during winter.

In the month of September there are generally a couple of weeks or so of extremely fine weather, which is called the Indian summer; after which winter, with frost, cold, and snow, sets in with rapidity. For a few weeks in October there is sometimes a little warm weather (or rather, I should say, a little *thawy*, weather); but after that, until the following April, the thermometer seldom rises to the freezing-point. In the depth of winter it falls from 30 to 40, 45, and even 50 degrees *below zero* of Fahrenheit. This intense cold, however, is not so much felt as one might suppose, as during its continuance the air is perfectly calm. Were the slightest breath of wind to arise when the thermometer stands so low, no man could show his face to it for a moment. Forty degrees below zero, and quite calm, is infinitely preferable to fifteen degrees below, or thereabouts, with a strong breeze of wind. Spirit of wine is, of course, the only liquid that can be used in the thermometers, as mercury, were it exposed to such cold, would remain frozen nearly half the winter. Spirit never froze in any cold ever experienced at York Factory, unless when very much adulterated with water; and even then the spirit would remain liquid in the centre of the mass (see note 1).

To resist this intense cold the inhabitants dress, not in furs, as is generally supposed, but in coats and trousers made of smoked deer-skins; the only piece of fur in their costume being the cap. The houses are built of wood, with double windows and doors. They are heated by means of large iron stoves, fed with wood; yet so intense is the cold, that I have seen the stove in places *red-hot*, and a basin of water in the room *frozen* nearly solid. The average cold, I should think, is about 15 or 16 degrees below zero, or 48 degrees of frost. The country around is a complete swamp, but the extreme shortness of the warm weather, and the consequent length of winter, fortunately prevent the rapid decomposition of vegetable matter. Another cause of the unhealthiness of the climate during summer is the prevalence of dense fogs, which come off the bay and enshroud the country; and also the liability of the weather to sudden and extreme changes.

Summer may be said to commence in July, the preceding month being a fight between summer and winter, which cannot claim the slightest title to the name of spring. As August advances the heat becomes great; but about the commencement of September Nature wears a more pleasing aspect, which lasts till the middle of October. It is then clear and beautiful, just cold enough to kill all the mosquitoes, and render brisk exercise agreeable. About this time, too, the young ducks begin to fly south, affording excellent sport among the marshes. A week or so after this winter commences, with light falls of snow occasionally, and hard frost during the night. Flocks of snow-birds (the harbingers of cold in autumn, and heat in spring) begin to appear, and soon the whirring wings of the white partridge may be heard among the snow-encompassed willows. The first thaw generally takes place in April; and May is characterised by melting snow, disruption of ice, and the arrival of the first flocks of wild-fowl.

The country around the fort is one immense level swamp, thickly covered with willows, and dotted here and there with a few clumps of pine-trees. The only large timber in the vicinity grows on the banks of Hayes and Nelson Rivers, and consists chiefly of spruce fir. The swampy nature of the ground has rendered it necessary to raise the houses in the fort several feet in the air upon blocks of wood; and the squares are intersected by elevated wooden platforms, which form the only promenade the inhabitants have during the summer, as no one can venture fifty yards beyond the gates without wetting his feet. Nothing bearing the most distant resemblance to a hillock exists in the land. Nelson River is a broad stream, which discharges itself into Hudson Bay, near the mouth of Hayes River, between which lies a belt of swamp and willows, known by the name of the Point of Marsh. Here may be found, during the spring and autumn, millions of ducks, geese, and plover, and during the summer billions of mosquitoes. There are a great many strange plants and shrubs in this marsh, which forms a wide field of research and pleasure to the botanist and the sportsman; but the lover of beautiful scenery and the florist will find little to please the eye or imagination, as Nature has here put on her plainest garb, and flowers there are none.

Of the feathered tribes there are the large and small grey Canada goose, the laughing goose (so called from the resemblance of its cry to laughter), and the wavie or white goose. The latter are not very numerous. There are great numbers of wild ducks, pintails, widgeons, divers, sawbills, black ducks, and teal; but the prince of ducks (the canvas-back) is not there. In spring and autumn the whole country becomes musical with the wild cries and shrill whistle of immense hosts of plover of all kinds—long legs, short legs, black legs, and yellow legs—sandpipers and snipe, which are assisted in their noisy concerts by myriads of frogs. The latter are really the best songsters in Hudson Bay (see note 2). Bitterns are also found in the marshes; and sometimes, though rarely, a solitary crane finds its way to the coast. In the woods, and among the dry places around, there are a few grey grouse and wood partridges, a great many hawks, and owls of all sizes—from the gigantic white owl, which measures five feet across the back and wings, to the small grey owl, not much bigger than a man's hand.

In winter the woods and frozen swamps are filled with ptarmigan—or, as they are called by the trappers, white partridges. They are not very palatable; but, nevertheless, they form a pretty constant dish at the winter mess-table of York Factory, and afford excellent sport to the inhabitants. There are also great varieties of small birds, among which the most interesting are the snow-birds, or snow-flakes, which pay the country a flying visit at the commencement and termination of winter.

Such is York Fort, the great depôt and gate to the wild regions surrounding Hudson Bay. Having described its appearance and general characteristics, I shall proceed to introduce the reader to my future companions, and describe our amusements and sports among the marshes.

Bachelors' Hall:

On the — of June, 1843, I landed the second time on the wharf of York Fort, and betook myself to Bachelors' Hall, where Mr Grave, whom I met by the way, told me to take up my quarters. As I approached the door of the well-remembered house, the most tremendous uproar that ever was heard proceeded from within its dingy walls; so I jumped the paling that stood in front of the windows, and took a peep at the interior before introducing myself.

The scene that met my eye was ludicrous in the extreme. Mounted on a chair, behind a bedroom door, stood my friend Crusty, with a large pail of water in his arms, which he raised cautiously to the top of the door, for the purpose of tilting it over upon two fellow-clerks who stood below, engaged in a wrestling match, little dreaming of the cataract that was soon to fall on their devoted heads; at the door of a room opposite stood the doctor, grinning from ear to ear at the thought of sending a thick stream of water in Crusty's face from a large syringe which he held in his hands; while near the stove sat the jolly skipper, looking as grave as possible under the circumstances.

The practical joke was just approaching to a climax when I looked in. The combatants neared the door behind which Crusty was ensconced. The pail was raised, and the syringe pointed, when the hall door opened, and Mr Grave walked in! The sudden change that ensued could not have been more rapidly effected had Mr Grave been a magician. The doctor thrust the syringe into his pocket, into which a great deal of the water escaped and dripped from the skirts of his coat as he walked slowly across the room and began to examine, with a wonderful degree of earnestness, the edge of an amputating knife that lay upon his dressing-table. The two wrestlers sprang with one accord into their own room, where they hid their flushed faces behind the door. Certain smothered sounds near the stove proclaimed the skipper to be revelling in an excruciating fit of suppressed laughter; while poor Crusty, who slipped his foot in rapidly descending from his chair, lay sprawling in an ocean of water, which he had upset upon himself in his fall.

Mr Grave merely went to Mr Wilson's room to ask a few questions, and then departed as if he had seen nothing; but a peculiar twist in the corners of his mouth, and a comical twinkle in his eye, showed that, although he said nothing, he had a pretty good guess that his "young men" had been engaged in mischief!

Such were the companions to whom I introduced myself shortly after; and, while they went off to the office, I amused myself in looking round the rooms in which I was to spend the approaching winter.

The house was only one story high, and the greater part of the interior formed a large hall, from which several doors led into the sleeping apartments of the clerks. The whole was built of wood; and few houses could be found wherein so little attention was paid to ornament or luxury. The walls were originally painted white, but this, from long exposure to the influence of a large stove, had changed to a dirty yellow. No carpet covered the floor; nevertheless, its yellow planks had a cheerful appearance; and gazing at the numerous knots with which it was covered often afforded me a dreamy kind of amusement when I had nothing better to do. A large oblong iron box, on four crooked legs, with a funnel running from it through the roof, stood exactly in the middle of the room; this was a stove, but the empty wood-box in the corner showed that its services were not required at that time. And truly they were not; for it was the height of summer, and the whole room was filled with mosquitoes and bull-dog flies, which kept up a perpetual hum night and day. The only furniture that graced the room consisted of two small unpainted deal tables without tablecloths, five whole wooden chairs, and a broken one—which latter, being light and handy, was occasionally used as a missile by the young men when they happened to quarrel. Several guns and fishing-rods stood in the corners of the hall, but their dirty appearance proclaimed that sporting, at that time, was not the order of the day. The tables were covered with a miscellaneous collection of articles; and from a number of pipes reposing on little odoriferous heaps of cut tobacco, I inferred that my future companions were great smokers. Two or three books, a pair of broken foils, a battered mask, and several surgical instruments, over which a huge mortar and pestle presided, completed the catalogue.

The different sleeping apartments around were not only interesting to contemplate, but also extremely characteristic of the pursuits of their different tenants. The first I entered was very small—just large enough to contain a bed, a table, and a chest, leaving little room for the occupant to move about in; and yet, from the appearance of things, he did move about in it to some purpose, as the table was strewn with a number of saws, files, bits of ivory and wood, and in a corner a small vice held the head of a cane in its iron jaws. These were mixed with a number of Indian account-books and an inkstand, so that I concluded I had stumbled on the bedroom of my friend Mr Wilson, the postmaster.

The quadrant-case and sea-chest in the next room proved it to be the skipper's, without the additional testimony of the oiled-cloth coat and sou'-wester hanging from a peg in the wall.

The doctor's room was filled with dreadful-looking instruments, suggestive of operations, amputations, bleeding wounds, and human agony; while the accountant's was equally characterised by methodical neatness, and the junior clerks' by utter and chaotic confusion. None of these bedrooms were carpeted; none of them boasted of a chair—the trunks and boxes of the persons to whom they belonged answering instead; and none of the beds were graced with curtains. Notwithstanding this emptiness, however, they had a somewhat furnished appearance, from the number of greatcoats, leather capotes, fur caps, worsted sashes, guns, rifles, shot-belts, snow-shoes, and powder-horns with which the walls were profusely decorated. The ceilings of the rooms, moreover, were very low—so much that by standing on tiptoe I could touch them with my hand; and the window in each was only about three feet high by two and a half broad, so that, upon the whole, the house was rather snug than otherwise.

Such was the habitation in which I dwelt; such were the companions with whom I associated at York Factory.

As the season advanced the days became shorter, the nights more frosty, and soon a few flakes of snow fell, indicating the approach of winter. About the beginning of October the cold, damp, snowy weather that usually precedes winter set in; and shortly afterwards Hayes River was full of drifting ice, and the whole country covered with snow. A week or so after this the river was completely frozen over; and Hudson Bay itself, as far as the eye could reach, was covered with a coat of ice. We now settled down into our winter habits. Double windows were fitted in, and double doors also. Extra blankets were put upon the beds; the iron stove kept constantly alight; and, in fact, every preparation was made to mitigate the severity of the winter.

The water froze every night in our basins, although the stove was kept at nearly a red heat all day, and pretty warm all night; and our out-of-door costume was changed from jackets and shooting-coats to thick leather capotes, fur caps, duffle socks, and moccasins.

Soon after this, white partridges showed themselves; and one fine clear, frosty morning, after breakfast, I made my first essay to kill some, in company with my fellow-clerk and room-mate Crusty, and the worthy skipper.

The manner of dressing ourselves to resist the cold was curious. I will describe Crusty, as a type of the rest. After donning a pair of deer-skin trousers, he proceeded to put on three pair of blanket socks, and over these a pair of moose-skin moccasins. Then a pair of blue cloth leggins were hauled over his trousers, partly to keep the snow from sticking to them, and partly for warmth. After this he put on a leather capote edged with fur. This coat was very warm, being lined with flannel, and overlapped very much in front. It was fastened with a scarlet worsted belt round the waist, and with a loop at the throat. A pair of thick mittens made of deer-skin hung round his shoulders by a worsted cord; and his neck was wrapped in a huge shawl, above whose mighty folds his good-humoured visage beamed like the sun on the edge of a fog-bank. A fur cap with ear-pieces completed his costume. Having finished his toilet, and tucked a pair of snow-shoes, five feet long, under one arm, and a double-barrelled fowling-piece under the other, Crusty waxed extremely impatient, and proceeded systematically to aggravate the unfortunate skipper (who was always very slow, poor man, except on board ship), addressing sundry remarks to the stove upon the slowness of seafaring men in general, and skippers in particular. In a few minutes the skipper appeared in a similar costume, with a monstrously long gun over his shoulder, and under his arm a pair of snow-shoes gaudily painted by himself; which snow-shoes he used to admire amazingly, and often gave it as his opinion that they were "slap-up, tossed-off-to-the-nines" snow-shoes!

In this guise, then, we departed on our ramble. The sun shone brightly in the cold blue sky, giving a warm appearance to the scene, although no sensible warmth proceeded from it, so cold was the air. Countless millions of icy particles covered every bush and tree, glittering tremulously in its rays like diamonds—psha! that hackneyed simile: diamonds of the purest water never shone like these evanescent little gems of nature. The air was biting cold, obliging us to walk briskly along to keep our blood in circulation; and the breath flew thick and white from our mouths and nostrils, like clouds of steam, and, condensing on our hair and the breasts of our coats, gave us the appearance of being powdered with fine snow. Crusty's red countenance assumed a redder hue by contrast, and he cut a very comical figure when his bushy whiskers changed from their natural auburn hue to a pure white, under the influence of this icy covering. The skipper, who all this while had been floundering slowly among the deep snow, through which his short legs were but ill cal-culated to carry him, sud-denly wheeled round, and presented to our view the phenomenon of a very red, warm face, and an extreme-

ly livid cold nose thereunto affixed. We instantly apprised him of the fact that his nose was frozen, which he would scarcely believe for some time; however, he was soon convinced, and after a few minutes' hard rubbing it was restored to its usual temperature.

We had hitherto been walking through the thick woods near the river's bank; but finding no white partridges there, we stretched out into the frozen swamps, which now presented large fields and plains of compact snow, studded here and there with clumps and thickets of willows. Among these we soon discovered fresh tracks of birds in the snow, whereat the skipper became excited (the sport being quite new to him), and expressed his belief, in a hoarse whisper, that they were not far off. He even went the length of endeavouring to walk on tiptoe, but being unable, from the weight of his snow-shoes, to accomplish this, he only tripped himself, and falling with a stunning crash through a large dried-up bush, buried his head, shoulders, and gun in the snow. Whir-r-r! went the alarmed birds—crack! bang! went Crusty's gun, and down came two partridges; while the unfortunate skipper, scarce taking time to clear his eyes from snow, in his anxiety to get a shot, started up, aimed at the birds, and blew the top of a willow, which stood a couple of feet before him, into a thousand atoms. The partridges were very tame, and only flew to a neighbouring clump of bushes, where they alighted. Meanwhile Crusty picked up his birds, and while reloading his gun complimented the skipper upon the beautiful manner in which he *pointed*. To this he answered not, but raising his gun, let drive at a solitary bird which, either from fear or astonishment, had remained behind the rest, and escaped detection until now, owing to its resemblance to the surround-

ing snow. He fortunately succeeded in hitting this time, and bagged it with great exultation. Our next essay was even more successful. The skipper fired at one which he saw sitting near him, killed it,—and also two more which he had not seen, but which had happened to be in a line with the shot; and Crusty and I killed a brace each when they took wing.

During the whole day we wandered about the woods, sometimes killing a few ptarmigan, and occasionally a kind of grouse, which are called by the people of the country wood-partridges. Whilst sauntering slowly along in the afternoon, a rabbit darted across our path; the skipper fired at it without even putting the gun to his shoulder, and to his utter astonishment killed it. After this we turned to retrace our steps, thinking that, as our game bags were pretty nearly full, we had done enough for one day. Our sport was not done, however; we came suddenly upon a large flock of ptarmigan, so tame that they would not fly, but merely ran from us a little way at the noise of each shot. The firing that now commenced was quite terrific. Crusty fired till both barrels of his gun were stopped up; the skipper fired till his powder and shot were done; and I fired till—*I skinned my tongue*! Lest any one should feel surprised at the last statement, I may as well explain *how* this happened. The cold had become so intense, and my hands so benumbed with loading, that the thumb at last obstinately refused to open the spring of my powder-flask. A partridge was sitting impudently before me, so that, in the fear of losing the shot, I thought of trying to open it with my teeth. In the execution of this plan, I put the brass handle to my mouth, and my tongue happening to come in contact with it, stuck fast thereto—or, in other words, was frozen to it. Upon discovering this, I instantly pulled the flask away, and with it a piece of skin about the size of a sixpence. Having achieved this little feat, we once more bent our steps homeward.

During our walk the day had darkened, and the sky insensibly become overcast. Solitary flakes of snow fell here and there around us, and a low moaning sound, as of distant wind, came mournfully down through the sombre trees, and, eddying round their trunks in little gusts, gently moved the branches, and died away in the distance. With an uneasy glance at these undoubted signs of an approaching storm, we hastened towards the fort as fast as our loads permitted us, but had little hope of reaching it before the first burst of the gale. Nature had laid aside her sparkling jewels, and was now dressed in her simple robe of white. Dark leaden clouds rose on the northern horizon, and the distant howling of the cold, cold wind struck mournfully on our ears, as it rushed fresh and bitterly piercing from the Arctic seas, tearing madly over the frozen plains, and driving clouds of hail and snow before it. Whew! how it dashed along—scouring wildly over the ground, as if maddened by the slight resistance offered to it by the swaying bushes, and hurrying impetuously forward to seek a more worthy object on which to spend its bitter fury! Whew! how it curled around our limbs, catching up mountains of snow into the air, and dashing them into impalpable dust against our wretched faces. Oh! it was bitterly, bitterly cold. Notwithstanding our thick wrappings, we felt as if clothed in gauze; while our faces seemed to collapse and wrinkle up as we turned them from the wind and hid them in our mittens. One or two flocks of ptarmigan, scared by the storm, flew swiftly past us, and sought shelter in the neighbouring forest. We quickly followed their example, and availing ourselves of the partial shelter of the trees, made the best of our way back to the fort, where we arrived just as it was getting dark, and entered the warm precincts of Bachelors' Hall like three animated marble statues, so completely were we covered from head to foot with snow.

It was curious to observe the change that took place in the appearance of our guns after we entered the warm room. The barrels, and every bit of metal upon them, instantly became white, like ground glass! This phenomenon was caused by the condensation and freezing of the moist atmosphere of the room upon the cold iron. Any piece of metal, when brought suddenly out of such intense cold into a warm room, will in this way become covered with a pure white coating of hoar-frost. It does not remain long in this state, however, as the warmth of the room soon heats the metal and melts the ice. Thus, in about ten minutes our guns assumed three different appearances: when we entered the house, they were clear, polished, and dry; in five minutes they were white as snow; and in five more, dripping wet!

On the following morning a small party of Indians arrived with furs, and Mr Wilson went with them to the trading-room, whither I accompanied him.

The trading-room—or, as it is frequently called, the Indian-shop—was much like what is called a store in the United States. It contained every imaginable commodity likely to be needed by Indians. On various shelves were piled bales of cloth of all colours, capotes, blankets, caps, etcetera; and in smaller divisions were placed files, scalping-knives, gun-screws, flints, balls of twine, fire-steels, canoe-awls, and glass beads of all colours, sizes, and descriptions. Drawers in the counter contained needles, pins, scissors, thimbles, fish-hooks, and vermilion for painting canoes and faces. The floor was strewn with a variety of copper and tin kettles, from half a pint to a gallon; and on a stand in the furthest corner of the room stood about a dozen trading guns, and beside them a keg of powder and a box of shot.

Upon our entrance into this room trade began. First of all, an old Indian laid a pack of furs upon the counter, which Mr Wilson counted and valued. Having done this, he marked the amount opposite the old man's name in his "Indian book," and then handed him a number of small pieces of wood. The use of these pieces of wood is explained in the third chapter.

The Indian then began to look about him, opening his eyes gradually, as he endeavoured to find out which of the many things before him he would like to have. Sympathising with his eyes, his mouth slowly opened also; and having remained in this state for some time, the former looked at Mr Wilson, and the latter pronounced *ahcoup* (blanket). Having received the blanket, he paid the requisite number of bits of wood for it, and became abstracted again. In this way he bought a gun, several yards of cloth, a few beads, etcetera, till all his sticks were gone, and he made way for another. The Indians were uncommonly slow, however, and Mr Wilson and I returned to the house in a couple of hours, with very cold toes and fingers, and exceedingly blue noses.

During winter we breakfasted usually at nine o'clock; then sat down to the desk till one, when we dined. After dinner we resumed our pens till six, when we had tea; and then wrote again till eight; after which we either amused ourselves with books (of which we had a few), kicked up a row, or, putting on our snow-shoes, went off to pay a moonlight visit to our traps. On Wednesdays and Saturdays, however, we did no work, and generally spent these days in shooting.

It is only at the few principal establishments of the Company, where the accounts of the country are collected annually, to be forwarded to the Hudson Bay House in London, that so much writing is necessary.

As the Christmas holidays approached, we prepared for the amusements of that joyous season. On the morning before Christmas, a gentleman, who had spent the first part of the winter all alone at his outpost, arrived to pass the holidays at York Factory. We were greatly delighted to have a new face to look at, having seen no one but ourselves since the ship left for

England, nearly four months before.

Our visitor had travelled in a dog cariole. This machine is very narrow, just broad enough to admit one person. It is a wooden frame covered with deer-skin parchment, painted gaudily, and is generally drawn by four Esquimaux dogs (see note 3). Dogs are invaluable in the Arctic regions, where horses are utterly useless, owing to the depth of snow which covers the earth for so large a portion of the year. The comparatively light weight of the dogs enables them to walk without sinking much; and even when the snow is so soft as to be incapable of supporting them, they are still able to sprawl along more easily than any other species of quadruped could do. Four are usually attached to a sledge, which they haul with great vigour; being followed by a driver on snow-shoes, whose severe lash is brought to bear so powerfully on the backs of the poor animals, should any of them be observed to slacken their pace, that they are continually regarding him with deprecatory glances as they run along. Should the lash give a flourish, there is generally a short yelp from the pack; and should it descend amongst them with a vigorous crack, the vociferous yelling that results is perfectly terrific. These drivers are sometimes very cruel; and when a pack of dogs have had a fight, and got their traces hopelessly ravelled (as is often the case), they have been known to fall on their knees in their passion, seize one of the poor dogs by the nose with their teeth, and almost bite it off. Dogs are also used for dragging carioles, which vehicles are used by gentlemen in the Company's service who are either too old or too lazy to walk on snow-shoes. The cariole is in form not unlike a slipper bath, both in shape and size. It is lined with buffalo robes, in the midst of a bundle of which the occupant reclines luxuriously, while the dogs drag him slowly through the soft snow, and among the trees and bushes of the forest, or scamper with him over the hard-beaten surface of a lake or river; while the machine is prevented from capsizing by a *voyageur* who walks behind on snow-shoes, holding on to a line attached to the back part of the cariole. The weather during winter is so cold that it is often a matter of the greatest difficulty for the traveller to keep his toes from freezing, despite the buffalo robes; and sometimes, when the dogs start fresh in the morning, with a good breakfast, a bright, clear, frosty day, and a long expanse of comparatively open country before them, where the snow from exposure has become quite hard, away they go with a loud yelp, upsetting the driver in the bolt, who rises to heap undeserved and very improper epithets upon the poor brutes, who, careering over the ground at the rate of eleven miles an hour, swing the miserable cariole over the snow, tear it through the bushes, bang it first on one side, then on the other, against stumps and trees, yelling all the while, partly with frantic glee at the thought of having bolted, and partly with fearful anticipation of the tremendous welting that is to come; until at last the cariole gets jammed hard and fast among the trees of the forest, or plunges down the steep bank of a river head over heels till they reach the foot—a horrible and struggling compound of dogs, traveller, traces, parchment, buffalo robes, blankets, and snow!

Christmas morning dawned, and I opened my eyes to behold the sun flashing brightly on the window, in its endeavours to make a forcible entry into my room, through the thick hoar-frost which covered the panes. Presently I became aware of a gentle breathing near me, and, turning my eyes slowly round, I beheld my companion Crusty standing on tiptoe, with a tremendous grin on his countenance, and a huge pillow

INCIDENT IN CARIOLE TRAVELLING.

in his hands, which was in the very act of descending upon my devoted head. To collapse into the smallest possible compass, and present the most invulnerable part of my body to the blow, was the work of an instant, when down came the pillow, bang! "Hooroo! hurroo! hurroo! a merry Christmas to you, you rascal!" shouted Crusty. Bang! bang! went the pillow. "Turn out of that, you lazy lump of plethoric somnolescence," whack!—and, twirling the ill-used pillow round his head, my facetious friend rushed from the room, to bestow upon the other occupants of the hall a similar salutation. Upon recovering from the effects of my pommelling, I sprang from bed and donned my clothes with all speed, and then went to pay my friend Mr Wilson the compliments of the season. In passing through the hall for this purpose, I discovered Crusty struggling in the arms of the skipper, who, having wrested the pillow from him, was now endeavouring to throttle him partially. I gently shut and fastened the door of their room, purposing to detain them there till *very nearly* too late for breakfast, and then sat down with Mr Wilson to discuss our intended proceedings during the day. These were—firstly, that we should go and pay a ceremonious visit to the men; secondly, that we should breakfast; thirdly, that we should go out to shoot partridges; fourthly, that we should return to dinner at five; and fifthly, that we should give a ball in Bachelors' Hall in the evening, to which were to be invited all the men at the fort, and *all* the Indians, men, women, and children, inhabiting the country for thirty miles round. As the latter, however, did not amount to above twenty, we did not fear that more would come than our hall was calculated to accommodate. In pursuance, then, of these resolutions, I cleaned my gun, freed my prisoners just as the breakfast-bell was ringing, and shortly afterwards went out to shoot. I will not drag the reader after me, but merely say that we all returned about dusk, with game-bags full, and appetites ravenous.

Our Christmas dinner was a good one, in a substantial point of view; and a very pleasant one, in a social point of view. We ate it in the winter mess-room; and really (for Hudson Bay) this was quite a snug and highly decorated apartment. True, there was no carpet on the floor, and the chairs were home-made; but then the table was mahogany, and the walls were hung round with several large engravings in bird's-eye maple frames. The stove, too, was brightly polished with black lead, and the painting of the room had been executed with a view to striking dumb those innocent individuals who had spent the greater part of their lives at outposts, and were, consequently, accustomed to domiciles and furniture of the simplest and most unornamental description. On the present grand occasion the mess-room was illuminated by an argand lamp, and the table covered with a snow-white cloth, whereon reposed a platter containing a beautiful, fat, plump wild-goose, which had a sort of come-eat-me-up-quick-else-I'll-melt expression about it that was painfully delicious. Opposite to this smoked a huge roast of beef, to procure which one of our most useless draught oxen had been sacrificed. This, with a dozen of white partridges, and a large piece of salt pork, composed our dinner. But the greatest rarities on the board were two large decanters of port wine, and two smaller ones of Madeira. These were flanked by tumblers and glasses; and truly, upon the whole, our dinner made a goodly show.

"Come away, gentlemen," said Mr Grave, as we entered the room and approached the stove where he stood, smiling with that benign expression of countenance peculiar to stout, good-natured gentlemen at this season, and at this particular hour. "Your walk must have sharpened your appetites; sit down, sit down. This way, doctor—sit near me; find a place, Mr Ballantyne, beside your friend Crusty there; take the foot, Mr Wilson;" and amid a shower of such phrases we seated ourselves and began.

At the top of the table sat Mr Grave, indistinctly visible through the steam that rose from the wild-goose before him. On his right and left sat the doctor and the accountant; and down from them sat the skipper, four clerks, and Mr Wilson, whose honest face beamed with philanthropic smiles at the foot of the table. Loud were the mirth and fun that reigned on this eventful day within the walls of the highly decorated room at York Factory. Bland was the expression of Mr Grave's face when he asked each of the young clerks to drink wine with him in succession; and great was the confidence which thereby inspired the said clerks, prompting them to the perpetration of several rash and unparalleled pieces of presumption—such as drinking wine with each other (an act of free-will on their part almost unprecedented), and indulging in sundry sly pieces of covert humour, such as handing the vinegar to each other when the salt was requested, and becoming profusely apologetic upon discovering their mistake. But the wildest storm is often succeeded by the greatest calm, and the most hilarious mirth by the most solemn gravity. In the midst of our fun Mr Grave proposed a toast. Each filled a bumper, and silence reigned around while he raised his glass and said, "Let us drink to absent friends." We each whispered, "Absent friends," and set our glasses down in silence, while our minds flew back to the scenes of former days, and we mingled again in spirit with our dear, dear friends at home. How different the mirth of the loved ones there, circling round the winter hearth, from that of the *men* seated round the Christmas table in the Nor'-West wilderness I question very much if this toast was ever drunk with a more thorough appreciation of its melancholy import than upon the present memorable occasion. Our sad feelings, however, were speedily put to flight, and our gravity routed, when the skipper, with characteristic modesty, proposed, "The ladies;" which toast we drank with a hearty good-will, although, indeed, the former included them, inasmuch as they also were *absent* friends—the only one within two hundred and fifty miles of us being Mr Grave's wife.

What a magical effect ladies have upon the male sex, to be sure! Although hundreds of miles distant from an unmarried specimen of the species, upon the mere mention of their name there was instantly a perceptible alteration for the better in the looks of the whole party. Mr Wilson unconsciously arranged his hair a little more becomingly, as if his ladye-love were actually looking at him; and the skipper afterwards confessed that his heart had bounded suddenly out of his breast, across the snowy billows of the Atlantic, and come smash down on the wharf at Plymouth Dock, where he had seen the last wave of Nancy's checked cotton neckerchief as he left the shores of Old England.

Just as we had reached the above climax, the sound of a fiddle struck upon our ears, and reminded us that our guests who had been invited to the ball were ready; so, emptying our glasses, we left the dining-room, and adjourned to the hall.

Here a scene of the oddest description presented itself. The room was lit up by means of a number of tallow candles, stuck in tin sconces round the walls. On benches and chairs sat the Orkneymen and Canadian half-breeds of the establishment, in their Sunday jackets and capotes; while here and there the dark visage of an Indian peered out from among their white ones. But round the stove—which had been removed to one side to leave space for the dancers—the strangest group was collected. Squatting down on the floor, in every ungraceful attitude imaginable, sat about a dozen Indian women, dressed in printed calico gowns, the chief peculiarity of which was the immense size of the balloon-shaped sleeves, and the extreme scantiness, both in length and width, of the skirts. Coloured handkerchiefs covered their heads, and ornamented moccasins decorated their feet; besides which, each one wore a blanket in the form of a shawl, which they put off before standing up to dance. They were chatting and talking to each other with great volubility, occasionally casting a glance behind them, where at least half a dozen infants stood bolt upright in their tight-laced cradles. On a chair, in a corner near the stove, sat a young, good-looking Indian, with a fiddle of his own making beside him. This was our Paganini; and beside him sat an Indian boy with a kettle-drum, on which he tapped occasionally, as if anxious that the ball should begin.

All this flashed upon our eyes; but we had not much time for contemplating it, as, the moment we entered, the women simultaneously rose, and coming modestly forward to Mr Wilson, who was the senior of the party, saluted him, one after another! I had been told that this was a custom of the *ladies* on Christmas Day, and was consequently not quite unprepared to go through the ordeal. But when I looked at the superhuman ugliness of some of the old ones—when I gazed at the immense, and in some cases toothless, chasms that were pressed to my senior's lips, and that gradually, like a hideous nightmare, approached towards me—and when

I reflected that these same mouths might have, in former days, demolished a few children—my courage forsook me, and I entertained for a moment the idea of bolting. The doctor seemed to labour under the same disinclination as myself; for when they advanced to him, he refused to bend his head, and, being upwards of six feet high, they of course were obliged to pass him. They looked, however, so much disappointed at this, and withal so very modest, that I really felt for them, and prepared to submit to my fate with the best grace possible. A horrible old hag advanced towards me, the perfect embodiment of a nightmare, with a fearful grin on her countenance. I shut my eyes. Suddenly a bright idea flashed across my mind: I stooped down, with apparent goodwill, to salute her; but just as our lips were about to meet, I slightly jerked up my head, and she kissed my *chin*. Oh, happy thought! They were all quite satisfied, and attributed the accident, no doubt, to their own clumsiness—or to mine!

This ceremony over, we each chose partners, the fiddle struck up, and the ball began. Scotch reels were the only dances known by the majority of the guests, so we confined ourselves entirely to them.

The Indian women afforded us a good deal of amusement during the evening. Of all ungraceful beings, they are the most ungraceful; and of all accomplishments, dancing is the one in which they shine least. There is no rapid motion of the feet, no lively expression of the countenance; but with a slow, regular, up-and-down motion, they stalk through the figure with extreme gravity. They seemed to enjoy it amazingly, however, and scarcely allowed the poor fiddler a moment's rest during the whole evening.

Between eleven and twelve o'clock our two tables were put

CHRISTMAS BALL IN BACHELORS' HALL.

together, and spread with several towels; thus forming a pretty respectable supper-table, which would have been perfect, had not the one part been three inches higher than the other. On it was placed a huge dish of cold venison, and a monstrous iron kettle of tea. This, with sugar, bread, and a lump of salt butter, completed the entertainment to which the Indians sat down. They enjoyed it very much—at least, so I judged from the rapid manner in which the viands disappeared, and the incessant chattering and giggling kept up at intervals. After all were satisfied, the guests departed in a state of great happiness; particularly the ladies, who tied up the remnants of their supper in their handkerchiefs, and carried them away.

Before concluding the description of our Christmas doings, I may as well mention a circumstance which resulted from the effects of the ball, as it shows in a curious manner the severity of the climate at York Factory. In consequence of the breathing of so many people in so small a room for such a length of time, the walls had become quite damp, and ere the guests departed moisture was trickling down in many places. During the night this moisture was frozen, and on rising the following morning I found, to my astonishment, that Bachelors' Hall was apparently converted into a palace of crystal. The walls and ceiling were thickly coated with beautiful minute crystalline flowers, not sticking flat upon them, but projecting outwards in various directions, thus giving the whole apartment a cheerful, light appearance, quite indescribable. The moment our stove was heated, however, the crystals became fluid, and ere long evaporated, leaving the walls exposed in all their original dinginess.

Winter passed away; but not slowly, or by degrees. A winter of so long duration could not be expected to give up its dominion without a struggle. In October it began, and in November its empire was established. During December, January, February, March, and April it reigned unmolested, in steadfast bitterness; enclosing in its icy bands, and retaining in torpid frigidity, the whole inanimate and vegetable creation. But in May its powerful enemy, caloric, made a decided attack upon the empire, and dealt hoary Winter a stunning blow.

About the beginning of April a slight thaw occurred, the first that had taken place since the commencement of winter; but this was speedily succeeded by hard frost, which continued till the second week in May, when thaw set in so steadily that in a few days the appearance of the country entirely changed.

On the 12th of May, Hayes River, which had been covered for nearly eight months with a coat of ice upwards of six feet thick, gave way before the floods occasioned by the melting snow; and all the inmates of the fort rushed out to the banks upon hearing the news that the river was going. On reaching the gate, the sublimity of the spectacle that met our gaze can scarcely be imagined. The noble river, here nearly two miles broad, was entirely covered with huge blocks and jagged lumps of ice, rolling and dashing against each other in chaotic confusion, as the swelling floods heaved them up and swept them with irresistible force towards Hudson Bay. In one place, where the masses were too closely packed to admit of violent collision, they ground against each other with a slow but powerful motion that curled their hard edges up like paper, till the smaller lumps, unable to bear the pressure, were ground to powder, and with a loud crash the rest hurried on to renew the struggle elsewhere, while the ice above, whirling swiftly round in the clear space thus formed, as if delighted at its sudden release, hurried onwards. In another place, where it was not so closely packed, a huge lump suddenly grounded on a shallow; and in a moment the rolling masses, which were hurrying towards the sea with the velocity of a cataract, were precipitated against it with a noise like thunder, and the tremendous pressure from above forcing block upon block with a loud hissing noise, raised, as if by magic, an icy castle in the air, which, ere its pinnacles had pointed for a second to the sky, fell with stunning violence into the boiling flood from whence it rose. In a short time afterwards the mouth of the river became so full of ice that it stuck there, and in less than an hour the water rose ten or fifteen feet, nearly to a level with the top of the bank. In this state it continued for a week; and then, about the end of May, the whole floated quietly out to sea, and the cheerful river gurgled along its bed with many a curling eddy and watery dimple rippling its placid face, as if it smiled to think of having overcome its powerful enemy, and at length burst its prison walls.

Although the river was free, many a sign of winter yet remained around our forest home. The islands in the middle of the stream were covered with masses of ice, many of which were piled up to a height of twenty or thirty feet. All along the banks, too, it was strewn thickly; while in the woods snow still lay in many places several feet deep. In time, however, these last evidences of the mighty power of winter gave way before the warm embraces of spring. Bushes and trees began to bud, gushing rills to flow, frogs to whistle in the swamp, and ducks to sport upon the river, while the hoarse cry of the wild-goose, the whistling wings of teal, and all the other sounds and cries of the long-absent inhabitants of the marshes, gave life and animation to the scene.

Often has nature been described as falling asleep in the arms of winter, and awaking at the touch of spring; but nowhere is this simile so strikingly illustrated as in these hyperborean climes, where, for eight long, silent months, nature falls into a slumber so deep and unbroken that death seems a fitter simile than sleep, and then bursts into a life so bright, so joyous, so teeming with animal and vegetable vitality, and, especially when contrasted with her previous torpidity, so noisy, that awakening from sleep gives no adequate idea of the change.

Now was the time that our guns were cleaned with peculiar care, and regarded with a sort of brotherly affection. Not that we despised the sports of winter, but we infinitely preferred those of spring.

Young Crusty and I were inseparable companions; we had slept in the same room, hunted over the same ground, and scribbled at the same desk during the whole winter, and now we purchased a small hunting canoe from an Indian, for the purpose of roaming about together in spring. Our excursions were always amusing; and, as a description of one of them may perhaps prove interesting to the reader, I shall narrate:—

A Canoe Excursion on the Shores of Hudson Bay:

It is needless to say that the day we chose was fine; that the sun shone brightly; that the curling eddies of the river smiled sweetly; that the jagged pinnacles of the blocks of ice along shore which had not yet melted sparkled brilliantly; that the fresh green foliage of the trees contrasted oddly with these white masses; that Crusty and I shouldered our canoe between us, after having placed our guns, etcetera, in it, and walked lightly down to the river bank under our burden. It is needless, I say, to describe all this minutely, as it would be unnecessary waste of pen, ink, and paper. It is sufficient to say that we were soon out in the middle of the stream, floating gently down the current towards the Point of Marsh, which was to be the scene of our exploits.

The day was indeed beautiful, and so very calm and still that the glassy water reflected every little cloud in the sky; and on the seaward horizon everything was quivering and magically turned upside down—islands, trees, icebergs, and all! A solitary gull, which stood not far off upon a stone, looked so preposterously huge from the same atmospherical cause, that I would have laughed immoderately, had I had energy to do so; but I was too much wrapped in placid enjoyment of the scene to give way to boisterous mirth. The air was so calm that the plaintive cries of thousands of wildfowl which covered the Point of Marsh struck faintly on our ears. "Ah!" thought I—

But I need not say what I thought. I grasped my powder-flask and shook it; it was full—crammed full! I felt my shot-belt; it was fat, very fat, bursting with shot! Our two guns lay side by side, vying in brightness; their flints quite new and sharp, and standing up in a lively wide-awake sort of way, as much as to say, "If you do not let me go, I'll go bang off by myself!" Happiness is sometimes too strong to be enjoyed quietly; and Crusty and I, feeling that we could keep it down no longer, burst simultaneously into a yell that rent the air, and, seizing the paddles, made our light canoe spring over the water, while we vented our feelings in a lively song, which reaching the astonished ears of the afore-mentioned preposterously large gull, caused its precipitate departure.

In half an hour we reached the point; dragged the canoe above high-water mark; shouldered our guns, and, with long strides, proceeded over the swamp in search of game.

We had little doubt of having good sport, for the whole point away to the horizon was teeming with ducks and plo-ver. We had scarcely gone a hundred yards ere a large widgeon rose from behind a bush, and Crusty, who was in advance, brought it down. As we plodded on, the faint cry of a wild-goose caused us to squat down suddenly behind a neighbour-ing bush, from which retreat we gazed round to see where our friends were. Another cry from behind attracted our atten-tion; and far away on the horizon we saw a large flock of geese flying in a mathematically correct triangle. Now, although far out of shot, and almost out of sight, we did not despair of get-ting one of these birds; for, by imitating their cry, there was a possibility of attracting them towards us. Geese often answer to a call in this way, if well imitated; particularly in spring, as they imagine that their friends have found a good feeding-place, and wish them to alight. Knowing this, Crusty and I continued in our squatting position—utterly unmindful, in the excitement of the moment, of the fact that the water of the swamp lay in the same proximity to our persons as a chair does when we sit down on it—and commenced to yell and scream vociferously in imitation of geese; for which, doubtless, many people unacquainted with our purpose would have taken us. At first our call seemed to make no impression on them; but gradually they bent into a curve, and, sweeping round in a long circle, came nearer to us, while we continued to shout at the top of our voices. How they ever mistook our bad imitation of the cry for the voices of real geese, I cannot tell—probably they thought we had colds or sore throats; at any rate they came nearer and nearer, screaming to us in return, till at last they ceased to flap their wings, and sailed slowly over the bush behind which we were ensconced, with their long necks stretched straight out, and their heads a little to one side, looking down for their friends. Upon discovering their mistake, and beholding two human beings instead of geese within a few yards of them, the sensation created among them was tremendous, and the racket they kicked up in trying to fly from us was terrific; but it was too late. The moment we saw that they had discovered us, our guns poured forth their contents, and two out of the flock fell with a lumbering smash upon the ground, while a third went off wounded, and, after wavering in its flight for a little, sank slowly to the ground.

Having bagged our game, we proceeded, and ere long filled our bags with ducks, geese, and plover. Towards the afternoon we arrived at a tent belonging to an old Indian called Morris. With this dingy gentleman we agreed to dine, and accordingly bent our steps towards his habitation. Here we found the old Indian and his wife squatting down on the floor and wreathed in smoke, partly from the wood-fire which burned in the middle of the tent, and partly from the tobacco-pipes stuck in their respective mouths. Old Morris was engaged in preparing a kettle of pea-soup, in which were boiled several plover and a large white owl; which latter, when lifted out of the pot, looked so very like a skinned baby that we could scarcely believe they were not guilty of cannibalism. His wife was engaged in ornamenting a pair of moccasins with dyed quills. On our entrance, the old man removed his pipe, and cast an inquiring glance into the soup-kettle; this apparently gave him immense satisfaction, as he turned to us with a smiling countenance, and remarked (for he could speak capital English, having spent the most of his life near York Factory) that "duck plenty, but he too hold to shoot much; obliged to heat howl." This we agreed was uncommonly hard, and after presenting him with several ducks and a goose, proposed an inspection of the contents of the kettle, which being agreed to, we demolished nearly half of the soup, and left him and his

AT THE POINT OF MARSH

wife to "heat" the "howl."

After resting an hour with this hospitable fellow, we departed, to prepare our encampment ere it became dark, as we intended passing the night in the swamps, under our canoe. Near the tent we passed a fox-trap set on the top of a pole, and, on inquiring, found that this was the machine in which old Morris caught his "*h*owls." The white owl is a very large and beautiful bird, sometimes nearly as large as a swan. I shot one which measured five feet three inches across the wings, when expanded. They are in the habit of alighting upon the tops of blighted trees, and poles of any kind, which happen to stand conspicuously apart from the forest trees—for the purpose, probably, of watching for mice and little birds, on which they prey. Taking advantage of this habit, the Indian plants his trap on the top of a bare tree, so that when the owl alights it is generally caught by the legs.

Our walk back to the place where we had left the canoe was very exhausting, as we had nearly tired ourselves out before thinking of returning. This is very often the case with eager sportsmen, as they follow the game till quite exhausted, and only then it strikes them that they have got as long a walk back as they had in going out. I recollect this happening once to myself. I had walked so far away into the forest after wild-fowl, that I forgot time and distance in the ardour of the pursuit, and only thought of returning when quite knocked up. The walk back was truly wretched. I was obliged to rest every ten minutes, as, besides being tired, I became faint from hunger. On the way I stumbled on the nest of a plover, with one egg in it. This was a great acquisition; so seating myself on a stone, I made my dinner of it raw. Being very small, it did not do me much good, but it inspired me with courage;

and, making a last effort, I reached the encampment in a very unenviable state of exhaustion.

After an hour's walk, Crusty and I arrived at the place where we left the canoe.

Our first care was to select a dry spot whereon to sleep, which was not an easy matter in such a swampy place. We found one at last, however, under the shelter of a small willow bush. Thither we dragged the canoe, and turned it bottom up, intending to creep in below it when we retired to rest. After a long search on the sea-shore, we found a sufficiency of drift-wood to make a fire, which we carried up to the encampment, and placed in a heap in front of the canoe. This was soon kindled by means of a flint and steel, and the forked flames began in a few minutes to rise and leap around the branches, throwing the swampy point into deeper shadow, making the sea look cold and black, and the ice upon its surface ghost-like. The interior of our inverted canoe looked really quite cheerful and snug, under the influence of the fire's rosy light. And when we had spread our blankets under it, plucked and cleaned two of the fattest ducks, and stuck them on sticks before the blaze to roast, we agreed that there were worse things in nature than an encampment in the swamps.

Ere long the night became pitchy dark; but although we could see nothing, yet ever and anon the whistling wings of ducks became audible, as they passed in flocks overhead. So often did they pass in this way, that at last I was tempted to try to get a shot at them, notwithstanding the apparent hopelessness of such an attempt. Seizing my gun, and leaving strict injunctions with Crusty to attend to the roasting of my widgeon, I sallied forth, and, after getting beyond the light of the fire, endeavoured to peer through the gloom. Nothing was to be seen, however. Flocks of ducks were passing quite near, for I heard their wings whizzing as they flew, but they were quite invisible; so at last, becoming tired of standing up to my knees in water, I pointed my gun at random at the next flock that passed, and fired. After the shot, I listened intently for a few seconds, and the next moment a splash in the water apprised me that the shot had taken effect. After a long search I found the bird, and returned to my friend Crusty, whom I threw into a state of consternation by pitching the dead duck into his lap as he sat winking and rubbing his hands before the warm blaze.

Supper in these out-of-the-way regions is never long in the eating, and on the present occasion we finished it very quickly, being both hungry and fatigued. That over, we heaped fresh logs upon the fire, wrapped our green blankets round us, and nestling close together, as much underneath our canoe as possible, courted the drowsy god. In this courtship I was unsuccessful for some time, and lay gazing on the flick-ering flames of the watch-fire, which illuminated the grass of the marsh a little distance round, and listening, in a sort of dreamy felicity, to the occasional cry of a wakeful plover, or starting suddenly at the flapping wings of a huge owl, which, attracted by the light of our fire, wheeled slowly round, gaz-ing on us in a kind of solemn astonishment, till, scared by the sounds that proceeded from Crusty's nasal organ, it flew with a scream into the dark night air; and again all was silent save the protracted, solemn, sweeping boom of the distant waves, as they rolled at long intervals upon the sea-shore. During the night we were awakened by a shower of rain falling upon our feet and as much of our legs as the canoe was incapable of pro-tecting. Pulling them up more under shelter, at the expense of exposing our knees and elbows—for the canoe could not completely cover us—we each gave a mournful grunt, and dropped off again.

Morning broke with unclouded splendour, and we rose from our grassy couch with alacrity to resume our sport; but I will not again drag my patient reader through the Point of Marsh.

In the afternoon, having spent our ammunition, we launched our light canoe, and after an hour's paddle up the river, arrived, laden with game and splashed with mud, at York Factory.

Note 1: Quicksilver easily freezes; and it has frequently been run into a bullet mould, exposed to the cold air till frozen, and in this state rammed down a gun barrel, and fired through a thick plank.

Note 2: The thousands of frogs that fill the swamps of America whistle or chirp so exactly like little birds, that many people, upon hearing them for the first time, have mistaken them for the feathered songsters of the groves. Their only fault is that they scarcely ever cease singing.

Note 3: The traveller sits, or rather lies in it, wrapped in buffalo robes; while the dogs are urged forward by a man who walks behind, and prevents the machine from upsetting, which it is very liable to do, from the inequalities of the ground over which it sometimes passes.

9

VOYAGE FROM YORK FACTORY TO NORWAY HOUSE IN A SMALL INDIAN CANOE

—Departure—Life in the Woods—Difficulties of Canoe Navigation—Outwit the Mosquitoes—"Lève! lève! lève!" —Music in the Pot and on the Organ

ON THE AFTERNOON of the 20th of June 1845, I sat in my room at York Fort, musing on the probability of my being dispatched to some other part of the Company's wide dominions.

The season approached when changes from one part of the country to another might be expected, and boats began to arrive from the interior. Two years of fun and frolic had I spent on the coast, and I was beginning to wish to be sent once more upon my travels, particularly as the busy season was about to commence, and the hot weather to set in.

As I sat cogitating, my brother scribblers called me to join

185

them in a short promenade upon the wharf, preparatory to resuming our pens. Just as we reached it, a small Indian canoe from the interior swept round the point above the factory, and came rapidly forward, the sparkling water foaming past her sharp bow as she made towards the landing.

At almost any time an arrival causes a great deal of interest in this out-of-the-way place; but an arrival of this sort— for the canoe was evidently an *express*—threw us into a fever of excitement, which was greatly increased when we found that it contained dispatches from headquarters; and many speculative remarks passed among us as we hurried up to our hall, there to wait in anxious expectation for a letter or an order to appear *instanter* before Mr Grave. Our patience was severely tried, however, and we began to think there was no news at all, when Gibeault, the butler, turned the corner, and came towards our door. We immediately rushed towards it in breathless expectation, and a row of eager faces appeared as he walked slowly up and said, "Mr Grave wishes to see Mr Ballantyne immediately." On hearing this I assumed an appearance of calm indifference I was far from feeling, put on my cap, and obeyed the order.

Upon entering Mr Grave's presence, he received me with a benign, patronising air, and requested me to be seated. He then went on to inform me that letters had just arrived, requesting that I might be sent off immediately to Norway House, where I should be enlightened as to my ultimate destination. This piece of news I received with mingled surprise and delight, at the same time exclaiming "Indeed!" with peculiar emphasis; and then, becoming suddenly aware of the impropriety of the expression, I endeavoured to follow it up with a look of sorrow at the prospect of leaving my friends, combined with resignation to the will of the Honourable Hudson Bay Company, in which attempt I failed most signally. After receiving orders to prepare for an immediate start, I rushed out in a state of high excitement, to acquaint my comrades with my good fortune. On entering the hall, I found them as anxious to know where I was destined to vegetate next winter, as they before had been to learn who was going off. Having satisfied them on this point, or rather told them as much as I knew myself regarding it, I proceeded to pack up.

It happened just at this time that a brigade of inland boats was on the eve of starting for the distant regions of the interior; and as the little canoe, destined to carry myself, was much too small to take such an unwieldy article as my "cassette," I gladly availed myself of the opportunity to forward it by the boats, as they would have to pass Norway House *en route*. It would be endless to detail how I spent the next three days: how I never appeared in public without walking very fast, as if pressed with a superhuman amount of business; how I rummaged about here and there, seeing that everything was prepared; looking vastly important, and thinking I was immensely busy, when in reality I was doing next to nothing. I shall, therefore, without further preface, proceed to describe my travelling equipments.

The canoe in which I and two Indians were to travel from York Factory to Norway House, a distance of nearly three hundred miles, measured between five and six yards long, by two feet and a half broad in the middle, tapering from thence to *nothing* at each end. It was made of birch bark, and could with great ease be carried by one man. In this we were to embark, with ten days' provisions for three men, three blankets, three small bundles, and a little travelling-case belonging to myself; besides three paddles wherewith to propel us forward, a tin kettle for cooking, and an iron one for boiling water. Our craft being too small to permit my taking the usual allowance of what are called luxuries, I determined to take pot-luck with my men, so that our existence for the next eight or ten days was to depend upon the nutritive properties contained in a few pounds of pemmican, a little biscuit, one pound of butter, and a very small quantity of tea and sugar. With all this, in addition to ourselves, we calculated upon being pretty deeply laden.

My men were of the tribe called Swampy Crees—and truly, to judge merely from appearance, they would have been the very last I should have picked out to travel with; for one was old, apparently upwards of fifty, and the other, though young, was a cripple. Nevertheless, they were good, hard-working men, as I afterwards experienced. I did not take a tent with me, our craft requiring to be as light as possible, but I rolled up a mosquito-net in my blanket, that being a light affair of gauze, capable of compression into very small compass. Such were our equipments; and on the 23rd of June we started for the interior.

A melancholy feeling came over me as I turned and looked for the last time upon York Factory, where I had spent so many happy days with the young men who now stood waving their handkerchiefs from the wharf. Mr Grave, too, stood among them, and as I looked on his benevolent, manly countenance, I felt that I should ever remember with gratitude his kindness to me while we resided together on the shores of Hudson Bay. A few minutes more, and the fort was hid from my sight for ever.

My disposition is not a sorrowful one; I never did and

never could remain long in a melancholy mood, which will account for the state of feeling I enjoyed half an hour after losing sight of my late home. The day was fine, and I began to anticipate a pleasant journey, and to speculate as to what part of the country I might be sent to. The whole wide continent of North America was now open to the excursive flights of my imagination, as there was a possibility of my being sent to any one of the numerous stations in the extensive territories of the Hudson Bay Company. Sometimes I fancied myself ranging through the wild district of Mackenzie River, admiring the scenery described by Franklin and Back in their travels of discovery; and anon, as the tales of my companions occurred to me, I was bounding over the prairies of the Saskatchewan in chase of the buffalo, or descending the rapid waters of the Columbia to the Pacific Ocean. Again my fancy wandered, and I imagined myself hunting the grizzly bear in the woods of Athabasca—when a heavy lurch of the canoe awakened me to the fact that I was only ascending the sluggish waters of Hayes River.

The banks of the river were covered with huge blocks of ice, and scarcely a leaf had as yet made its appearance. Not a bird was to be seen, except a few crows and whisky-jacks, which chattered among the branches of the trees; and Nature appeared as if undecided whether or not she should take another nap, ere she bedecked herself in the garments of spring. My Indians paddled slowly against the stream, and I lay back, with a leg cocked over each gunwale, watching the sombre pines as they dropped slowly astern. On our way we passed two landslips which encroached a good deal on the river, each forming a small rapid round its base. The trees with which they had formerly been clothed were now scattered about in chaotic confusion, leafless, and covered with mud; some more than half buried, and others standing with their roots in the air. There is a tradition among the natives that a whole camp of Indians was overwhelmed in the falling of these slips.

A good deal of danger is incurred in passing up these rivers, owing to the number of small landslips which occur annually. The banks, being principally composed of sandy clay, are loosened, and rendered almost fluid in many places, upon the melting of the snow in spring; and the ice, during the general disruption, tears away large masses of the lower part of the banks, which renders the superincumbent clay liable to slip, upon the first heavy shower of rain, with considerable force into the stream.

About sixteen miles from York Factory we ran against a stone, and tore a small hole in the bottom of our canoe. This obliged us to put ashore immediately, when I had an opportunity of watching the swiftness and dexterity of the Indians in repairing the damage. A small hole, about three inches long and one inch wide, had been torn in the bottom of the canoe, through which the water squirted with considerable rapidity. Into this hole they fitted a piece of bark, sewed it with wattape (the fibrous roots of the pine-tree), made a small fire, melted gum, and plastered the place so as to be effectually water-tight, all in about the space of an hour.

During the day we passed a brigade of boats bound for the factory; but being too far off, and in a rapid part of the river we did not hail them. About nine o'clock we put ashore for the night, having travelled nearly twenty miles. The weather was pleasantly cool, so that we were free from mosquitoes. The spot we chose for our encampment was on the edge of a high bank, being the only place within three miles where

ASCENDING THE RIVER.

we could carry up our provisions; and even here the ascent
was bad enough. But after we were up, the top proved a good
spot, covered with soft moss, and well sheltered by trees and
bushes. A brook of fresh water rippled at the foot of the bank,
and a few decayed trees afforded us excellent firewood. Here,
then, in the bosom of the wilderness, with the silvery light of
the moon for our lamp, and serenaded by a solitary owl, we
made our first bivouac. Supper was neatly laid out on an oilcloth, spread before a blazing fire. A huge junk of pemmican
graced the centre of our rustic table, flanked by a small pile

191

of ship's biscuit on one side, and a lump of salt butter on the other; while a large iron kettle filled with hot water, slightly flavoured with tea-leaves, brought up the rear. Two tin pots and a tumbler performed outpost duty, and were soon smoking full of warm tea. We made an excellent supper, after which the Indians proceeded to solace themselves with a whiff, while I lay on my blanket enjoying the warmth of the fire, and admiring the apparently extreme felicity of the men, as they sat, with half-closed eyes, watching the smoke curling in snowy wreaths from their pipes, and varying their employment now and then with a pull at the tin pots, which seemed to afford them extreme satisfaction. In this manner we lay till the moon waned; and the owl having finished his overture, we rolled ourselves in our blankets, and watched the twinkling star, till sleep closed our eyelids.

Next morning, between two and three o'clock, we began to stretch our limbs, and after a few ill-humoured grunts prepared for a start. The morning was foggy when we embarked and once more began to ascend the stream. Everything was obscure and indistinct till about six o'clock, when the powerful rays of the rising sun dispelled the mist, and Nature was herself again. A good deal of ice still lined the shores; but what astonished me most was the advanced state of vegetation apparent as we proceeded inland. When we left York Factory, not a leaf had been visible; but here, though only thirty miles inland, the trees, and more particularly the bushes, were well covered with beautiful light green foliage, which appeared to me quite delightful after the patches of snow and leafless willows on the shores of Hudson Bay.

At eight o'clock we put ashore for breakfast—which was just a repetition of the supper of the preceding night, with this

ENCAMPMENT ON HAYES RIVER.

exception, that we discussed it a little more hurriedly—and then proceeded on our way.

Shortly afterwards we met a small canoe, about the size of our own, which contained a postmaster and two Indians, on their way to York Factory with a few packs of otters. After five minutes' conversation we parted, and were soon out of sight of each other. The day, which had hitherto been agreeable, now became oppressively sultry: not a breath of wind ruffled the water; and as the sun shone down with intense heat from a perfectly cloudless sky, it became almost insufferable. I tried all methods to cool myself, by lying in every position I could think of, sometimes even hanging both legs and arms over the sides of the canoe and trailing them through the water. I had a racking headache, and, to add to my misery, as the sun sank the mosquitoes rose and bit ferociously. The Indians, however, did not appear to suffer much, being accustomed, no doubt, to these little annoyances, much in the same way as eels are to being skinned.

In the afternoon we arrived at the forks of Hayes and Steel Rivers, and ascended the latter, till the increasing darkness and our quickening appetites reminded us that it was time to put ashore. We made a hearty supper, having eaten nothing since breakfast; dinner, while travelling in a light canoe, being considered quite superfluous.

Our persevering foes, the mosquitoes, now thought it high time to make their supper also, and attacked us in myriads whenever we dared to venture near the woods; so we were fain to sleep as best we could on the open beach, without any fire—being much too warm for that. But even there they found us out, and most effectually prevented us from sleeping.

On the morning of the 25th, we arose very little refreshed by our short nap, and continued our journey. The weather was still warm, but a little more bearable, owing to a light, grateful breeze that came down the river. After breakfast—which we took at the usual hour, and in the usual way—while proceeding slowly up the current, we descried, on rounding a point, a brigade of boats close to the bank, on the opposite side of the river; so we embarked our man, who was tracking us up with a line (the current being too rapid for the continued use of the paddle), and crossed over to see who they were. On landing, we found it was the Norway House brigade, in charge of George Kippling, a Red River settler. He shook hands with us, and then commenced an animated discourse with my two men in the Indian language, which being perfectly unintelligible to me, I amused myself by watching the operations of the men, who were in the act of cooking breakfast.

Nothing can be more picturesque than a band of *voyageurs* breakfasting on the banks of a pretty river. The spot they had chosen was a little above the Burntwood Creek, on a projecting grassy point, pretty clear of underwood. Each boat's crew—of which there were three—had a fire to itself, and over these fires were placed gipsy-like tripods, from which huge tin kettles depended; and above them hovered three volunteer cooks, who were employed stirring their contents with persevering industry. The curling wreaths of smoke formed a black cloud among the numerous fleecy ones in the blue sky, while all around, in every imaginable attitude, sat, stood, and reclined the sunburnt, savage-looking half-breeds, chatting, laughing, and smoking in perfect happiness. They were all dressed alike, in light cloth capotes with hoods, corduroy trousers, striped shirts open in front, with cotton kerchiefs tied sailor-fashion loosely round their swarthy necks. A scarlet worsted belt strapped each man's coat tightly to his body, and Indian moccasins defended their feet. Their head-dresses were as various as fanciful—some wore caps of coarse cloth; others coloured handkerchiefs, twisted turban-fashion round their heads; and one or two, who might be looked upon as voyageur-fops, sported tall black hats, covered so plenteously with bullion tassels and feathers as to be scarcely recognisable.

The breakfast consisted solely of pemmican and flour, boiled into the sort of thick soup dignified by the name of *robbiboo*. As might be expected, it is not a very delicate dish, but is, nevertheless, exceedingly nutritious; and those who have lived long in the country, particularly the Canadians, are very fond of it. I think, however, that another of their dishes, composed of the same materials, but fried instead of boiled, is much superior to it. They call it *richeau*; it is uncommonly rich, and very little will suffice for an ordinary man.

After staying about a quarter of an hour, chatting with Kippling about the good folk of Red River and Norway House, we took our departure, just as they commenced the first vigorous attack upon the capacious kettles of robbiboo.

Shortly after, we arrived at the mouth of Hill River, which we began to ascend. The face of the country was now greatly changed, and it was evident that here spring had long ago dethroned winter. The banks of the river were covered from top to bottom with the most luxuriant foliage, while dark clumps of spruce-fir varied and improved the landscape. In many places the banks, which appeared to be upwards of a hundred feet high, ran almost perpendicularly down to the water's edge, perfectly devoid of vegetation, except at the top, where large trees overhung the precipice, some clinging by their roots and ready to fall. In other places the bank sloped from nearly the same height, gradually, and with slight undulations, down to the stream, thickly covered with vegetation, and teeming with little birds, whose merry voices, warbling a cheerful welcome to the opening buds, greatly enhanced the pleasures of the scene.

We soon began to experience great difficulty in tracking the canoe against the rapid stream that now opposed us. From the steepness of the banks in some places, and their being clothed with thick willows in others, it became a slow and fatiguing process for the men to drag us against the strong current; and sometimes the poor Indians had to cling like flies against nearly perpendicular cliffs of slippery clay, whilst at others they tore their way through almost impervious bushes. They relieved each other by turns every hour at this work, the one steering the canoe while the other tracked; and they took no rest during the whole day, except when at breakfast. Indeed, any proposal to do so would have been received by them with great contempt, as a very improper and useless waste of time.

When the track happened to be at all passable, I used to get out and walk, to relieve them a little, as well as to stretch my cramped limbs, it being almost impossible, when there is any luggage in a small Indian canoe, to attain a comfortable position.

At sunset we put ashore for the night, on a point covered with a great number of *lopsticks*. These are tall pine-trees, denuded of their lower branches, a small tuft being left at the top. They are generally made to serve as landmarks; and sometimes the *voyageurs* make them in honour of gentlemen who happen to be travelling for the first time along the route—and those trees are chosen which, from their being on elevated ground, are conspicuous objects. The traveller for whom they are made is always expected to acknowledge his sense of the honour conferred upon him by presenting the boat's crew with a pint of grog, either on the spot or at the first establishment they meet with. He is then considered as having paid for his footing, and may ever afterwards pass scot-free.

We soon had our encampment prepared, and the fire

blazing: but hundreds of mosquitoes were, as usual, awaiting our arrival, and we found it utterly impossible to sup, so
fiercely did they attack us. We at last went to leeward of the
fire, and devoured it hastily in the smoke—preferring to risk
being suffocated or smoke-dried to being eaten up alive! It was
certainly amusing to see us rushing into the thick smoke, bolt
a few mouthfuls of pemmican, and then rush out again for
fresh air; our hands swinging like the sails of a windmill round
our heads, while every now and then, as a mosquito fastened
on a tender part, we gave ourselves a resounding slap on the

RUNNING THE RAPID.

side of the head, which, had it come from the hand of another, would certainly have raised in us a most pugnacious spirit of resentment. In this manner we continued rushing out of and into the smoke till supper was finished, and then prepared for sleep. This time, however, I was determined not to be tormented; so I cut four stakes, drove them into the ground, and threw over them my gauze mosquito-net, previously making a small fire, with wet grass on it, to raise a smoke and prevent intruders from entering while I was in the act of putting it on; then, cautiously raising one end, I bolted in after the most approved harlequinian style, leaving my discomfited tormentors wondering at the audacity of a man who could snore in a state of unconcerned felicity in the very midst of the enemy's camp.

On the following morning we started at an early hour. The day was delightfully cool, and mosquitoes were scarce, so that we felt considerably comfortable as we glided quietly up the current. In this way we proceeded till after breakfast, when we came in sight of the first portage, on which we landed. In a surprisingly short time our luggage, etcetera, was pitched ashore, and the canoe carried over by the Indians, while I followed with some of the baggage; and in half an hour we were ready to start from the upper end of the portage. While carrying across the last few articles, one of the Indians killed two fish called suckers, which they boiled on the spot and devoured immediately.

Towards sunset we paddled quietly up to the "White Mud Portage," where there is a fall, of about seven or eight feet, of extreme rapidity, shooting over the edge in an arch of solid water, which falls hissing and curling into the stream below. Here we intended to encamp. As we approached the cataract, a boat suddenly appeared on the top of it, and shot with the speed of lightning into the boiling water beneath, its reckless crew shouting, pulling, laughing, and hallooing, as it swept round a small point at the foot of the fall and ran aground in a bay or hollow, where the eddying water, still covered with patches of foam after its mighty leap, floated quietly round the shore. They had scarcely landed when another boat appeared on the brink, and, hovering for an instant, as if to prepare itself for the leap, flashed through the water, and the next moment was aground beside the first. In this manner seven boats successively ran the fall, and grounded in the bay.

Upon our arriving, we found them to be a part of the Saskatchewan brigade, on its way to the common point of rendezvous, York Factory. It was in charge of two friends of mine; so I accosted them, without introducing myself, and chatted for some time about the occurrences of the voyage. They appeared a little disconcerted, however, and looked very earnestly at me two or three times. At last they confessed they had forgotten me altogether! And, indeed, it was no wonder, for the sun had burned me nearly as black as my Indian friends, while my dress consisted of a blue capote, sadly singed by the fire; a straw hat, whose shape, from exposure and bad usage, was utterly indescribable; a pair of corduroys, and Indian moccasins; which so metamorphosed me, that my friends, who perfectly recollected me the moment I mentioned my name, might have remained in ignorance to this day had I not enlightened them on the subject.

After supper one of these gentlemen offered me a share of his tent, and we turned in together, but not to sleep; for we continued gossiping till long after the noisy voices of the men had ceased to disturb the tranquillity of night.

At the first peep of day our ears were saluted with the

usual unpleasant sound of "*Lève! lève! lève!*" issuing from the leathern throat of the guide. Now this same "*Lève!*" is in my ears a peculiarly harsh and disagreeable word, being associated with frosty mornings, uncomfortable beds, and getting up in the dark before half enough of sleep has been obtained. The way in which it is uttered, too, is particularly exasperating; and often, when partially awakened by a stump boring a hole in my side, have I listened with dread to hear the detested sound, and then, fancying it must surely be too early to rise, have fallen gently over on the other side, when a low muffled sound, as if some one were throwing off his blanket, would strike upon my ear, then a cough or grunt, and finally, as if from the bowels of the earth, a low and scarcely audible "*Lève! lève!*" would break the universal stillness—growing rapidly louder, "*Lève! lève! lève!*" and louder, "*Lève! lève!*" till at last a final stentorian "*Lève! lève! lève!*" brought the hateful sound to a close, and was succeeded by a confused collection of grunts, groans, coughs, grumbles, and sneezes from the unfortunate sleepers thus rudely roused from their slumbers. The disinclination to rise, however, was soon overcome; and up we got, merry as larks, the men loading their boats, while I and my Indians carried our luggage, etcetera, over the portage.

Our troubles now commenced: the longest and most difficult part of the route lay before us, and we prepared for a day of toil. Far as the eye could reach, the river was white with boiling rapids and foaming cascades, which, though small, were much too large to ascend, and consequently we were obliged to make portages at almost every two or three hundred yards. Rapid after rapid was surmounted; yet still, as we rounded every point and curve, rapids and falls rose, in apparently endless succession, before our wearied eyes. My Indians, however, knew exactly the number they had to ascend, so they set themselves manfully to the task. I could not help admiring the dexterous way in which they guided the canoe among the rapids. Upon arriving at one, the old Indian, who always sat in the bow (this being the principal seat in canoe travelling), rose up on his knees and stretched out his neck to take a look before commencing the attempt; and then, sinking down again, seized his paddle, and pointing significantly to the chaos of boiling waters that rushed swiftly past us (thus indicating the route he intended to pursue to his partner in the stern), dashed into the stream. At first we were borne down with the speed of lightning, while the water hissed and boiled to within an inch of the gunwale, and a person unaccustomed to such navigation would have thought it folly our attempting to ascend; but a second glance would prove that our Indians had not acted rashly. In the centre of the impetuous current a large rock rose above the surface, and from its lower end a long eddy ran like the tail of a comet for about twenty yards down the river. It was just opposite this rock that we entered the rapid, and paddled for it with all our might. The current, however, as I said before, swept us down; and when we got to the middle of the stream, we just reached the extreme point of the eddy, and after a few vigorous strokes of the paddles were floating quietly in the lee of the rock. We did not stay long, however—just long enough to look for another stone; and the old Indian soon pitched upon one a few yards higher up, but a good deal to one side; so, dipping our paddles once more, we pushed out into the stream again, and soon reached the second rock. In this way, yard by yard, did we ascend for miles, sometimes scarcely gaining a foot in a minute, and at others, as a favouring bay or curve presented a long piece of smooth water, advancing more rapidly. In fact, our progress could not be likened to anything more aptly than to the ascent of a salmon as he darts rapidly from eddy to eddy, taking advantage of every stone and hollow that he finds: and the simile may be still further carried out; for, as the salmon is sometimes driven back *tail* foremost in attempting to leap a fall, so were we, in a similar attempt, driven back by the overpowering force of the water.

It happened thus: We had surmounted a good many rapids, and made a few portages, when we arrived at a perpendicular fall of about two feet in height, but from the rapidity of the current it formed only a very steep shoot. Here the Indians paused to breathe, and seemed to doubt the possibility of ascent; however, after a little conversation on the subject, they determined to try it, and got out their poles for the purpose (poles being always used when the current is too strong for the paddles). We now made a dash, and turning the bow to the current, the Indians fixed their poles firmly in the ground, while the water rushed like a mill-race past us. They then pushed forward, one keeping his pole fixed, while the other refixed his a little more ahead. In this way we advanced inch by inch, and had almost got up—the water rushing past us in a thick, black body, hissing sharply in passing the side of our canoe, which trembled like a reed before the powerful current—when suddenly the pole of the Indian in the stern slipped; and almost before I knew what had happened, we were floating down the stream about a hundred yards below the fall. Fortunately the canoe went stern foremost, so that we got down in safety. Had it turned round even a little in its descent, it would have been rolled over and over like a cask. Our second attempt proved more successful; and after a good deal of straining and puffing we arrived at the top, where the sight of a longer stretch than usual of calm and placid water rewarded us for our exertions during the day.

In passing over a portage we met the English River brigade; and after a little conversation, we parted. The evening was deliciously cool and serene as we glided quietly up the now tranquil river. Numbers of little islets, covered to the very edge of the rippling water with luxuriant vegetation, rose like emeralds from the bosom of the broad river, shining brightly in the rays of the setting sun; sometimes so closely scattered as to veil the real size of the river, which, upon our again emerging from among them, burst upon our delighted vision a broad sheet of clear pellucid water, with beautiful fresh banks covered with foliage of every shade, from the dark and sombre pine to the light drooping willow; while near the shore a matronly-looking duck swam solemnly along, casting now and then a look of warning to a numerous family of little yellow ducklings that frisked and gambolled in very wantonness, as if they too enjoyed and appreciated the beauties of the scene. Through this terrestrial paradise we wended our way, till rapids again began to disturb the water, and a portage at last brought us to a stand. Here we found McNab, who had left York Factory three days before us with his brigade, just going to encamp; so we also brought up for the night. When supper was ready, I sent an invitation to McNab to come and sup with me, which he accepted, at the same time bringing his brother with him. The elder was a bluff, good-natured Red River settler, with whom I had become acquainted while in the colony; and we chatted of bygone times and mutual acquaintances over a cup of excellent tea, till long after the sun had gone down, leaving the blazing camp-fires to illuminate the scene.

Next morning we started at the same time with the boats; but our little canoe soon passed them in the rapids, and we saw no more of them. Our way was not now so much impeded by rapids as it had hitherto been; and by breakfast-time we had surmounted them all and arrived at the Dram-stone, where we put ashore for our morning meal. In the morning I shot a duck, being the first that had come within range since I left York Factory. Ducks were very scarce, and the few that we did see were generally accompanied by a numerous offspring not much bigger than the eggs which originally contained them. While taking breakfast we were surprised by hearing a quick rushing sound a little above us, and the next moment a light canoe came sweeping round a point and made towards us. It was one of those called "north canoes," which are calculated to carry eight men as a crew, besides three passengers. The one now before us was built much the same as an Indian canoe, but somewhat neater, and ornamented with sundry ingenious devices painted in gaudy colours on the bows and stern. It was manned by eight men and apparently one passenger, to whom I hallooed once or twice; but they took me, no doubt, for an Indian, and so passed on without taking any notice of us. As the noble bark bounded quickly forward and was hid by intervening trees, I bent a look savouring slightly of contempt upon our little Indian canoe, and proceeded to finish breakfast.

A solitary north canoe, however, passing thus in silence, can give but a faint idea of the sensation felt on seeing a brigade of them arriving at a post after a long journey. It is then that they appear in wild perfection. The *voyageurs* upon such occasions are dressed in their best clothes; and gaudy feathers, ribbons, and tassels stream in abundance from their caps and garters. Painted gaily, and ranged side by side, like contending chargers, the light canoes skim swiftly over the water, bounding under the vigorous and rapid strokes of the small but numerous paddles, while the powerful *voyageurs* strain every muscle to urge them quickly on. And while yet in the distance, the beautifully simple and lively yet plaintive paddling song, so well suited to the surrounding scenery, and so different from any other air, breaks sweetly on the ear; and one reflects, with a kind of subdued and pleasing melancholy, how far the singers are from their native land, and how many long and weary days of danger and of toil will pass before they can rest once more in their Canadian homes. How strangely, too, upon their nearer approach, is this feeling changed for one of exultation, as the deep and manly voices swell in chorus over the placid waters, while a competition arises among them who shall first arrive; and the canoes dash over the water with arrow-speed to the very edge of the wharf, where they come suddenly, and as by magic, to a pause. This is effected by each man backing water with his utmost force; after which they roll their paddles on the gunwale simultaneously, enveloping themselves in a shower of spray as they shake the dripping water from the bright vermilion blades. Truly it is an animating, inspiriting scene, the arrival of a brigade of light canoes.

Our route now lay through a number of small lakes and rivers, with scarcely any current in them; so we proceeded happily on our way with the cheering prospect of uninterrupted travelling. We had crossed Swampy Lake, and, after making one or two insignificant portages, entered Knee Lake. This body of water obtained its name from turning at a sharp angle near its centre, and stretching out in an opposite direction from its preceding course; thus forming something like a knee. Late in the evening we encamped on one of the small islands with which it is here and there dotted. Nothing could exceed the beauty of the view we had of the lake from our encampment. Not a breath of wind stirred its glassy surface, which shone in the ruddy rays of the sun setting on its bosom in the distant horizon; and I sat long upon the rocks admiring the lovely scene, while one of my Indians filled the tea-kettle, and the other was busily engaged in skinning a minx for supper. Our evening meal was further enriched by the addition of a great many small gulls' eggs, which we had found on an island during the day—which, saving one or two that showed evident symptoms of being far advanced towards birdhood, were excellent.

On the following morning the scene was entirely changed. Dark and lowering clouds flew across the sky, and the wind blew furiously, with a melancholy moaning sound, through the trees. The lake, which the night before had been so calm and tranquil, was now of a dark leaden hue, and covered with foaming waves. However, we determined to proceed, and launched our canoe accordingly; but soon finding the wind too strong for us, we put ashore on a small island and break-fasted. As the weather moderated after breakfast, we made another attempt to advance. Numerous islets studded the lake, and on one of them we landed to collect gulls' eggs. Of these we found enough; but among them were a number of little yellow gulls, chattering vociferously, and in terrible consternation at our approach, while the old ones kept uttering the most plaintive cries overhead. The eggs were very small, being those of a small species of gull which frequents those inland lakes in great numbers. The wind again began to rise; and after a little consultation on the subject we landed, intending to spend the remainder of the day on shore.

We now, for the first time since leaving York Factory, prepared dinner, which we expected would be quite a sumptuous one, having collected a good many eggs in the morning; so we set about it with alacrity. A fire was quickly made, the tea-kettle on, and a huge pot containing upwards of a hundred eggs placed upon the fire. These we intended to boil hard and carry with us. Being very hungry, I watched the progress of dinner with much interest, while the Indians smoked in silence. While sitting thus, my attention was attracted by a loud whistling sound that greatly perplexed me, as I could not discover whence it proceeded—I got up once or twice to see what it could be, but found nothing, although it sounded as if close beside me. At last one of the Indians rose, and, standing close to the fire, bent in a very attentive attitude over the kettle; and, after listening a little while, took up one of the eggs and broke it, when out came a young gull with a monstrous head and no feathers, squeaking and chirping in a most indefatigable manner! "So much for our dinner!" thought I, as he threw the bird into the lake, and took out a handful of eggs, which all proved to be much in the same condition. The warmth of the water put life into the little birds, which, however, was speedily destroyed when it began to boil. We did not despair, nevertheless, of finding a few good ones amongst them; so, after they were well cooked, we all sat round the kettle and commenced operations. Some were good and others slightly spoiled, while many were intersected with red veins, but the greater part contained boiled birds. The Indians were not nice, however, and we managed to make a good dinner off them after all.

In the afternoon the weather cleared up and the wind

ENCAMPED ON AN ISLAND IN KNEE LAKE.

moderated, but we had scarcely got under weigh again when a thunderstorm arose and obliged us to put ashore; and there we remained for four hours sitting under a tree, while the rain poured in torrents. In the evening Nature tired of teasing us; and the sun shone brightly out as we once more resumed our paddles. To make up for lost time, we travelled until about two o'clock next morning, when we put ashore to rest a little; and, as the night was fine, we just threw our blankets over our shoulders and tumbled down on the first convenient spot we could find, without making a fire or taking any supper. We had not lain long, however, when I felt a curious chilly sensation all along my side, which effectually awakened me; and then I saw, or rather heard, that a perfect deluge of rain was descending upon our luckless heads, and that I had been reposing in the centre of a large puddle. This state of things was desperate; and as the poor Indians seemed to be as thoroughly uncomfortable as they possibly could be, I proposed to start again—which we did, and before daylight were many a mile from our wretched encampment. As the sun rose the weather cleared up, and soon after we came to the end of Knee Lake and commenced the ascent of Trout River. Here I made a sketch of the Trout Falls while the men made a portage to avoid them. With a few Indians encamped on this portage we exchanged a little pemmican for some excellent white-fish, a great treat to us after living so long on pemmican and tea. Our biscuit had run short a few days before, and the pound of butter which we brought from York Factory had melted into oil from the excessive heat, and vanished through the bottom of the canvas bag containing it. Trout River, though short, has a pretty fair share of falls and rapids, which we continued ascending all day. The scenery was pleasing and romantic; but there was nothing of grandeur in it, the country being low, flat, and, excepting on the banks of the river, uninteresting. In the afternoon we came to the end of this short river, and arrived at Oxford House. We landed in silence, and I walked slowly up the hill, but not a soul appeared. At last, as I neared the house, I caught a glimpse of a little boy's face at the window, who no sooner saw me than his eyes opened to their widest extent, while his mouth followed their example, and he disappeared with a precipitancy that convinced me he was off to tell his mother the astounding news that somebody had arrived. The next moment I was shaking hands with my old friend Mrs Gordon and her two daughters, whom I found engaged in the interesting occupation of preparing tea. From them I learned that they were entirely alone, with only one man to take care of the post—Mr Gordon, whom they expected back every day, having gone to Norway House.

I spent a delightful evening with this kind and hospitable family, talking of our mutual friends, and discussing the affairs of the country, till a tall box in a corner of the room attracted my attention. This I discovered to my delight was no less than a barrel-organ, on which one of the young ladies at my request played a few tunes. Now, barrel-organs, be it known, were things that I had detested from my infancy upwards; but this dislike arose principally from my having been brought up in the dear town o' Auld Reekie, where barrel-organ music is, as it were, crammed down one's throat without permission being asked or received, and even, indeed, where it is decidedly objected to. Everybody said, too, that barrel-organs were a nuisance, and of course I believed them; so that I left my home with a decided dislike to barrel-organs in general. Four years' residence, however, in the bush had rendered me much less fastidious in music, as well as in many other things; and during the two last years spent at York Factory, not a solitary note of melody had soothed my longing ear, so that it was with a species of rapture that I now ground away at the handle of this organ, which happened to be a very good one, and played in perfect tune. "God Save the Queen," "Rule Britannia," "Lord McDonald's Reel," and the "Blue Bells of Scotland" were played over and over again; and, old and threadbare though they be, to me they were replete with endearing associations, and sounded like the well-known voices of long, long absent friends. I spent indeed a delightful evening; and its pleasures were the more enhanced from the circumstance of its being the first, after a banishment of two years, which I had spent in the society of the fair sex.

Next morning was fine, though the wind blew pretty fresh, and we started before breakfast, having taken leave of the family the night before. This was the 1st of July. We had been eight days on the route, which is rather a long time for a canoe to take to reach Oxford House; but as most of the portages were now over, we calculated upon arriving at Norway House in two or three days.

In the afternoon the wind blew again, and obliged us to encamp on a small island, where we remained all day. While there, a couple of Indians visited us, and gave us an immense trout in exchange for some pemmican. This trout I neglected to measure, but I am convinced it was more than three feet long and half a foot broad: it was very good, and we made a capital dinner off it. During the day, as it was very warm, I had a delightful swim in the lake, on the lee of the island.

The wind moderated a little in the evening, and we again embarked, making up for lost time by travelling till midnight, when we put ashore and went to sleep without making a fire or taking any supper. About four o'clock we started again, and in a couple of hours came to the end of Oxford Lake, after which we travelled through a number of small swamps or reedy lakes, and stagnant rivers, among which I got so bewildered that I gave up the attempt to chronicle their names as hopeless; and indeed it was scarcely worth while, as they were so small and overgrown with bulrushes that they were no more worthy of a name in such a place as America than a *dub* would be in Scotland. The weather was delightfully cool, and mosquitoes not troublesome, so that we proceeded with pleasure and rapidity.

While thus threading our way through narrow channels and passages, upon turning a point we met three light canoes just on the point of putting ashore for breakfast, so I told my Indians to run ashore near them. As we approached, I saw that there were five gentlemen assembled, with whom I was acquainted, so that I was rather anxious to get ashore; but, alas! fortune had determined to play me a scurvy trick, for no sooner had my foot touched the slippery stone on which I intended to land, than down I came squash on my breast in a most humiliating manner, while my legs kept playfully waving about in the cooling element. This unfortunate accident, I saw, occasioned a strange elongation in the lateral dimensions of the mouths of the party on shore, who stood in silence admiring the scene. I knew, however, that to appear annoyed would only make matters worse; so, with a desperate effort to appear at ease, I rose, and while shaking hands with them, expressed my belief that there was nothing so conducive to health as a cold bath in the morning. After a laugh at my expense, we sat down to breakfast. One of the gentlemen gave me a letter from the Governor, and I now learned, for the first time, that I was to take a passage in one of the light canoes for Montreal. Here, then, was a termination to my imaginary rambles on the Rocky Mountains, or on the undulating prairies of the Saskatchewan; and instead of massacring buffalo and deer in the bush, I was in a short time to endeavour to render myself a respectable member of civilized society. I was delighted with the idea of the change, however, and it was with a firmer step and lighter heart that I took my leave and once more stepped into the canoe.

After passing through a succession of swamps and narrow channels, we arrived at Robinson's Portage, where we found *voyageurs* running about in all directions, some with goods on their backs, and others returning light to the other end of the portage. We found that they belonged to the Oxford House boats, which had just arrived at the other end of the portage, where they intended to encamp, as it was now late. Robinson's Portage is the longest on the route, being nearly a mile in length; and as all the brigades going to York Factory must pass over it twice—in going and returning—the track is beaten into a good broad road, and pretty firm, although it is rather uneven, and during heavy rains somewhat muddy. Over this all the boats are dragged, and launched at the upper or lower end of the portage, as the brigades may happen to be ascending or descending the stream. Then all the cargoes are in like manner carried over. Packs of furs and bales of goods are generally from 80 to 100 pounds weight each; and every man who does not wish to be considered a lazy fellow, or to be ridiculed by his companions, carries two of these *pieces*, as they are called, across all portages. The boats are capable of containing from seventy to ninety of these pieces, so that it will be easily conceived that a *voyageur's* life is anything but an easy one; indeed, it is one of constant and harassing toil, even were the trouble of ascending rapid rivers, where he is often obliged to jump into the water at a moment's notice, to lighten the boat in shallows, left entirely out of the question. This portage is made to avoid what are called the White Falls—a succession of cataracts up which nothing but a fish could possibly ascend. After carrying over our canoe and luggage, we encamped at the upper end. The river we commenced ascending next morning was pretty broad, and after a short paddle in it we entered the Echimamis. This is a sluggish serpentine stream, about five or six yards broad, though in some places so narrow that boats scrape the banks on either side. What little current there is runs in a contrary direction to the rivers we had been ascending. Mosquitoes again attacked us as we glided down its gloomy current, and nothing but swamps, filled with immense bulrushes, were visible around. Here, in days of yore, the beaver had a flourishing colony, and numbers of their dams and cuttings were yet visible; but they have long since deserted this much-frequented waste, and one of their principal dams now serves to heighten the water, which is not deep, for the passage of brigades in dry seasons. At night, when we encamped on its low, damp banks, we were attacked by myriads of mosquitoes, so that we could only sleep by making several fires round us, the smoke from which partially protected us. About three o'clock in the morning, which was very warm, we re-embarked, and at noon arrived at the Sea Portage (why so called I know not, as it is hundreds of miles inland), which is the last on the route. This portage is very short, and is made to surmount a pretty large waterfall. Almost immediately afterwards we entered Playgreen Lake, and put ashore on a small island, to alter our attire before arriving at Norway House.

Here, with the woods for our closet, and the clear lake for our basin as well as looking-glass, we proceeded to scrub our sunburnt faces; and in half an hour, having made ourselves as respectable as circumstances would permit, we paddled swiftly over the lake. It is pretty long, and it was not until evening that I caught the first glimpse of the bright spire of the Wesleyan Church at Rossville.

WESLEYAN INDIAN VILLAGE OF ROSSVILLE.

We now approached the termination of our journey, for the time at least; and it was with pleasing recollections that I recognised the well-known rocks where I had so often wandered three years before. When we came in sight of the fort, it was in a state of bustle and excitement as usual, and I could perceive from the vigorous shaking of hands going forward, from the number of *voyageurs* collected on the landing-place, and of boats assembled at the wharf, that there had just been an arrival. Our poor little canoe was not taken any notice of as it neared the wharf, until some of the people on shore observed that there was some one in the middle of it sitting in a very lazy, indolent position, which is quite uncommon among Indians. In another minute we gained the bank, and I grasped the hand of my kind friend and former chief, Mr Russ.

We had now been travelling twelve days, and had passed over upwards of thirty portages during the voyage.

We ought to have performed this voyage in a much shorter time, as canoes proceed faster than boats, which seldom take longer to complete this voyage than we did; but this arose from our detention during high winds in several of the lakes.

10

VOYAGE TO CANADA BY THE GREAT LAKES OF THE INTERIOR

*—A Black Bear—Harassing Detentions—Another Bear
—Meet Dr Rae, the Arctic Discoverer
—The Guide's Story—Meet Indians
—Running the Rapid—Lake Superior
—A Squall—The Ottawa—Civilized Life Again
—Sleighing in Canada*

AT NORWAY HOUSE I remained for nearly a month with my old friend Mr Russ, who in a former part of this veracious book is described as being a very ardent and scientific fisher, extremely partial to strong rods and lines, and entertaining a powerful antipathy to slender rods and flies!

Little change had taken place in the appearance of the fort. The clerks' house was still as full, and as noisy, as when Polly told frightful stories to the greenhorns on the point of setting out for the wild countries of Mackenzie River and New

219

Caledonia. The Indians of the village at Rossville plodded on in their usual peaceful way, under the guidance of their former pastor; and the ladies of the establishment were as blooming as ever.

One fine morning, just as Mr Russ and I were sauntering down to the river with our rods, a north canoe, full of men, swept round the point above the fort, and grounded near the wharf. Our rods were soon cast aside, and we were speedily congratulating Mr and Mrs Bain on their safe arrival. These were to be my companions on the impending voyage to Canada, and the canoe in which they had arrived was to be our conveyance.

Mr Bain was a good-natured, light-hearted Highlander, and his lady a pretty lass of twenty-three.

On the following morning all was ready; and soon after breakfast we were escorted down to the wharf by all the people in the fort, who crowded to the rocks to witness our departure.

Our men, eight in number, stood leaning on their paddles near the wharf; and, truly, a fine athletic set of fellows they were. The beautifully-shaped canoe floated lightly on the river, notwithstanding her heavy cargo, and the water rippled gently against her sides as it swept slowly past. This frail bark, on which our safety and progression depended, was made of birch bark sewed together, lined in the inside with thin laths of wood, and pitched on the seams with gum. It was about thirty-six feet long, and five broad in the middle, from whence it tapered either way to a sharp edge. It was calculated to carry from twenty to twenty-five hundredweight, with eight or nine men, besides three passengers, and provisions for nearly a month. And yet, so light was it, that two men could carry it

OUR NIGHT ENCAMPMENT.

a quarter of a mile without resting. Such was the machine in which, on the 20th August 1845, we embarked; and, after bidding our friends at Norway House adieu, departed for Canada, a distance of nearly two thousand three hundred miles through the uninhabited forests of America.

Our first day was propitious, being warm and clear; and we travelled a good distance ere the rapidly thickening shades of evening obliged us to put ashore for the night. The place on which we encamped was a flat rock which lay close to the river's bank, and behind it the thick forest formed a screen from the north wind. It looked gloomy enough on landing; but, ere long, a huge fire was kindled on the rock, our two snow-white tents pitched, and supper in course of preparation, so that things soon began to wear a gayer aspect. Supper was spread in Mr Bain's tent by one of the men, whom we appointed to the office of cook and waiter. And when we were seated on our blankets and cloaks upon the ground, and Mr Bain had stared placidly at the fire for five minutes, and then at his wife (who presided at the *board)* for ten, we began to feel quite jolly, and gazed with infinite satisfaction at the men, who ate their supper out of the same kettle, in the warm light of the camp-fire. Our first bed was typical of the voyage, being hard and rough, but withal much more comfortable than many others we slept upon afterwards; and we were all soon as sound asleep upon the rock in the forest as if we had been in feather-beds at home.

The beds on which a traveller in this country sleeps are various and strange. Sometimes he reposes on a pile of branches of the pine-tree; sometimes on soft downy moss; occasionally on a pebbly beach or a flat rock; and not unfrequently on rough gravel and sand. Of these the moss bed is the most agreeable, and the sandy one the worst.

Early on the following morning, long before daylight, we were roused from our slumbers to re-embark; and now our journey may be said to have commenced in earnest. Slowly and silently we stepped into the canoe, and sat down in our allotted places, while the men advanced in silence, and paddled up the quiet river in a very melancholy sort of mood. The rising sun, however, dissipated these gloomy feelings; and after breakfast, which we took on a small island near the head of Jack River, we revived at once, and started with a cheering song, in which all joined. Soon after, we rounded a point of the river, and Lake Winnipeg, calm and clear as crystal, glittering in the beams of the morning sun, lay stretched out before us to the distant and scarcely perceptible horizon. Every

pleasure has its alloy, and the glorious calm, on which we felicitated ourselves not a little, was soon ruffled by a breeze,
which speedily increased so much as to oblige us to encamp
near Montreal Point, being too strong for us to venture across
the traverse of five or six miles now before us. Here, then, we
remained the rest of the day and night, rather disappointed
that delay should have occurred so soon.

Next day we left our encampment early, and travelled
prosperously till about noon, when the wind again increased
to such a degree that we were forced to put ashore on a point,
where we remained for the next two days in grumbling inac-
tivity.

There is nothing more distressing and annoying than being wind-bound in these wild and uninhabited regions. One
has no amusement except reading, or promenading about the
shore of the lake. Now, although this may be very delightful
to a person of a romantic disposition, it was anything but
agreeable to us, as the season was pretty far advanced, and
the voyage long; besides, I had no gun, having parted with
mine before leaving Norway House, and no books had been
brought, as we did not calculate upon being wind-bound. I
was particularly disappointed at not having brought my gun,
for while we lay upon the rocks one fine day, gazing gloomily
on the foaming lake, a black bear was perceived walking slowly
round the bottom of the bay formed by the point on which we
were encamped. It was hopeless to attempt killing him, as Mr
Bruin was not fool enough to permit us to attack him with
axes. After this a regular course of high winds commenced,
which retarded us very much, and gave us much uneasiness as
well as annoyance. A good idea of the harassing nature of our
voyage across Lake Winnipeg may be obtained from the fol-

lowing page or two of my journal, as I wrote it on the spot:—

Monday, 25th August.—The wind having moderated this morning, we left the encampment at an early hour, and travelled uninterruptedly till nearly eight o'clock, when it began to blow so furiously that we were obliged to run ashore and encamp. All day the gale continued, but in the evening it moderated, and we were enabled to proceed a good way ere night closed in.

Tuesday, 26th.—Rain fell in torrents during the night. The wind, too, was high, and we did not leave our encampment till after breakfast. We made a good day's journey, however, travelling about forty miles; and at night pitched our tents on a point of rock, the only camping-place, as our guide told us, within ten miles. No dry ground was to be found in the vicinity, so we were fain to sleep upon the flattest rock we could find, with only one blanket under us. This bed, however, was not so disagreeable as might be imagined; its principal disadvantage being that, should it happen to rain, the water, instead of sinking into the ground, forms a little pond below you, deep or shallow, according to the hollowness or flatness of the rock on which you repose.

Wednesday, 27th.—Set out early this morning, and travelled till noon, when the wind *again* drove us ashore, where we remained, in no very happy humour, all day. Mr Bain and I played the flute for pastime.

Thursday, 28th.—The persevering wind blew so hard that we remained in the encampment all day. This was indeed a dismal day; for, independently of being delayed, which is bad enough, the rain fell so heavily that it began to penetrate through our tents; and, as if not content with this, a gust of wind more violent than usual tore the fastenings of my tent

A SUDDEN SQUALL.

out of the ground, and dashed it over my head, leaving me exposed to the pitiless pelting of the storm. Mr Bain's tent, being in a more sheltered spot, fortunately escaped.

Friday, 29th.—The weather was much improved to-day, but it still continued to blow sufficiently to prevent our starting. As the wind moderated, however, in the evening, the men carried the baggage down to the beach, to have it in readiness for an early start on the morrow.

Saturday, 30th.—In the morning we found that the wind had *again* risen, so as to prevent our leaving the encampment. This detention is really very tiresome. We have no amusement except reading a few uninteresting books, eating without appetite, and sleeping inordinately. Oh that I were possessed of the Arabian Nights' *mat*, which transported its owner whithersoever he listed! There is nothing for it, however, but patience; and assuredly I have a good example in poor Mrs Bain, who, though little accustomed to such work, has not given utterance to a word of complaint since we left Norway House. It is now four days since we pitched our tents on this vile point. How long we may still remain is yet to be seen.

Thursday, September 4th.—The wind was still very strong this morning; but so impatient had we become at our repeated detentions, that, with one accord, we consented to do or die! So, after launching and loading the canoe with great difficulty, owing to the immense waves that thundered against the shore, we all embarked and pushed off. After severe exertion, and much shipping of water, we at length came to the mouth of the Winnipeg River, up which we proceeded a short distance, and arrived at Fort Alexander.

Thus had we taken fifteen days to coast along Lake Winnipeg, a journey that is usually performed in a third of that time.

Fort Alexander belongs to the Lac la Pluie district; but being a small post, neither famous for trade nor for appearance, I will not take the trouble of describing it. We only remained a couple of hours to take in provisions in the shape of a ham, a little pork, and some flour, and then re-embarking, commenced the ascent of Winnipeg River.

The travelling now before us was widely different from that of the last fifteen days. Our men could no longer rest upon their paddles when tired, as they used to do on the level waters of the lake. The river was a rapid one; and towards evening we had an earnest of the rough work in store for us, by meeting in rapid succession with three waterfalls, to surmount which we were obliged to carry the canoe and cargo over the rocks, and launch them above the falls. While the men were engaged in this laborious duty, Mr Bain and I discovered a great many plum-trees laden with excellent fruit, of which we ate as many as we conveniently could, and then filling our caps and handkerchiefs, embarked with our prize. They were a great treat to us, after our long abstinence from everything but salt food; and I believe we demolished enough to have killed a whole parish school-boys, master, usher, and all! But in voyages like these one may take great liberties with one's interior with perfect impunity.

About sunset we encamped in a picturesque spot near the top of a huge waterfall, whose thundering roar, as it mingled with the sighing of the night wind through the bushes and among the precipitous rocks around us, formed an appropriate and somewhat romantic lullaby.

On the following morning we were aroused from our slumbers at daybreak; and in ten minutes our tents were down and ourselves in the canoe, bounding merrily up the river, while the echoing woods and dells responded to the lively air of "Rose Blanche," sung by the men as we swept round point after point and curve after curve of the noble river, which displayed to our admiring gaze every variety of wild and woodland scenery—now opening up a long vista of sloping groves of graceful trees, beautifully variegated with the tints of autumnal foliage, and sprinkled with a profusion of wildflowers; and anon surrounding us with immense cliffs and precipitous banks of the grandest and most majestic aspect, at the foot of which the black waters rushed impetuously past, and gurgling into white foam as they sped through a broken and more interrupted channel, finally sprang over a mist-shrouded clift and, after boiling madly onwards for a short space, resumed their silent, quiet course through peaceful scenery. As if to enhance the romantic wildness of the scene, upon rounding a point we came suddenly upon a large black bear, which was walking leisurely along the bank of the river. He gazed at us in surprise for a moment; and then, as if it had suddenly occurred to him that guns *might* be in the canoe, away he went helter-skelter up the bank, tearing up the ground in his precipitate retreat, and vanished among the bushes. Fortunately for him, there was not a gun in the canoe, else his chance of escape would have been very small indeed, as he was only fifty yards or so from us when we first discovered him.

We made ten portages of various lengths during the course of the day: none of them exceeded a quarter of a mile, while the most were merely a few yards. They were very harassing, however, being close to each other; and often we loaded, unloaded, and carried the canoe and cargo overland several times in the distance of half a mile.

On the 7th we left the encampment at an early hour, and made one short portage a few minutes after starting. After breakfast, as we paddled quietly along, we descried three canoes coming towards us, filled with Indians of the Seauteaux tribe. They gave us a few fresh ducks in exchange for some pork and tobacco, with which they were much delighted. After a short conversation between them and one of our men, who understood the language, we parted, and proceeded on our way. A little rain fell during the day, but in the afternoon the sun shone out and lighted up the scenery. The forests about this part of the river wore a much more cheerful aspect than those of the lower countries, being composed chiefly of poplar, birch, oak, and willows, whose beautiful light-green foliage had a very pleasing effect upon eyes long accustomed to the dark pines along the shores of Hudson Bay.

In the afternoon we met another canoe, in which we saw a gentleman sitting. This strange sight set us all speculating as to who it could be, for we knew that all the canoes accustomed annually to go through these wilds had long since passed. We were soon enlightened, however, on the subject. Both canoes made towards a flat rock that offered a convenient spot for landing on; and the stranger introduced himself as Dr Rae. He was on his way to York Factory, for the purpose of fitting out at that post an expedition for the survey of the small part of the North American coast left unexplored by Messrs Dease and Simpson, which will then prove beyond a doubt whether or not there is a communication by water between the Atlantic and Pacific Oceans round the north of America. Dr Rae appeared to be just the man for such an expedition. He was very muscular and active, full of animal spirits, and had a fine intellectual countenance. He was considered, by those who knew him well, to be one of the best snow-shoe walkers in the service, was also an excellent rifle-shot, and could stand an immense amount of fatigue. Poor fellow! greatly will he require to exert all his abilities and powers of endurance. He does not proceed as other expeditions have done—namely, with large supplies of provisions and men—but merely takes a very small supply of provisions, and ten or twelve men. These, however, are all to be of his own choosing, and will doubtless be men of great experience in travelling among the wild regions of North America. The whole expedition is fitted out at the expense of the Hudson Bay Company. The party are to depend almost entirely on their guns for provisions; and after proceeding in two open boats round the north-western shores of Hudson Bay as far as they may find it expedient or practicable, are to land, place their boats in security for the winter, and then penetrate into these unexplored regions on foot. After having done as much as possible towards the forwarding of the object of his journey, Dr Rae and his party are to spend the long dreary winter with the Esquimaux, and commence operations again early in the spring. He is of such a pushing, energetic character, however, that there is every probability he will endeavour to prosecute his discoveries during winter, if at all practicable. How long he will remain exploring among these wild regions is uncertain; but he may be two, perhaps three years. There is every reason to believe that this expedition will be successful, as it is fitted out by a Company intimately acquainted with the difficulties and dangers of the country through which it will have to pass, and the best methods of overcoming and avoiding them. Besides, the doctor himself is well accustomed to the life he will have to lead; and enters upon it, not with the vague and uncertain notions of Back and Franklin, but with a pretty correct apprehension of the probable routine of procedure, and the experience of a great many years spent in the service of the Hudson Bay Company (see note 1). After a few minutes' conversation we parted, and pursued our respective journeys.

SUPPER IN OUR TENT.

Towards sunset we encamped on the margin of a small lake, or expanse of the river; and soon the silence of the forest was broken by the merry voices of our men, and by the crashing of the stately trees, as they fell under the axes of the *voyageurs*. The sun's last rays streamed across the water in a broad red glare, as if jealous of the huge campfire, which now rose crackling among the trees, casting a ruddy glow upon our huts, and lighting up the swarthy faces of our men as they as-

231

sembled round it to rest their weary limbs, and to watch the operations of the cook while he prepared their evening meal.

In less than an hour after we landed, the floor of our tent was covered with a smoking dish of fried pork, a huge ham, a monstrous teapot, and various massive slices of bread, with butter to match. To partake of these delicacies, we seated ourselves in Oriental fashion, and sipped our tea in contemplative silence, as we listened to the gentle murmur of a neighbouring brook, and gazed through the opening of our tent at the *voyageurs*, while they ate their supper round the fire, or, reclining at length upon the grass, smoked their pipes in silence.

Supper was soon over, and I went out to warm myself, preparatory to turning in for the night. The men had supped, and their huge forms were now stretched around the fire, enveloped in clouds of tobacco smoke, which curled in volumes from their unshaven lips. They were chatting and laughing over tales of bygone days; and just as I came up they were begging Pierre the guide to relate a tale of some sort or other. "Come, Pierre," said a tall, dark-looking fellow, whose pipe, eyes, and hair were of the same jetty hue, "tell us how that Ingin was killed on the Labrador coast by a black bear. Baptiste, here, never heard how it happened, and you know he's fond of wild stories."

"Well," returned the guide, "since you must have it, I'll do what I can; but don't be disappointed if it isn't so interesting as you would wish. It's a simple tale, and not over-long." So saying, the guide disposed himself in a more comfortable attitude, refilled his pipe, and after blowing two or three thick clouds to make sure of its keeping alight, gave, in nearly the following words, an account of:—

The Death of Wapwian:

"It is now twenty years since I saw Wapwian, and during that time I have travelled far and wide in the plains and forests of America. I have hunted the buffalo with the Seauteaux, in the prairies of the Saskatchewan; I have crossed the Rocky Mountains with the Blackfeet, and killed the black bear with the Abinikies, on the coasts of Labrador; but never, among all the tribes that I have visited, have I met an Indian like Wapwian. It was not his form or his strength that I admired, though the first was graceful, and the latter immense; but his disposition was so kind, and affectionate, and noble, that all who came in contact with him loved and respected him. Yet, strange to say, he was never converted by the Roman Catholic missionaries who from time to time visited his village. He listened to them with respectful attention, but always answered that he could worship the Great Manitou better as a hunter in the forest than as a farmer in the settlements of the white men.

"Well do I remember the first time I stumbled upon the Indian village in which he lived. I had set out from Montreal with two trappers to pay a visit to the Labrador coast; we had travelled most of the way in a small Indian canoe, coasting along the northern shore of the Gulf of St. Lawrence, and reconnoitring in the woods for portages to avoid rounding long capes and points of land, and sometimes in search of game; for we depended almost entirely upon our guns for food.

"It was upon one of the latter occasions that I went off, accompanied by one of the trappers, while the other remained to watch the canoe and prepare our encampment for the night. We were unsuccessful, and after a long walk thought of returning to our camp empty-handed, when a loud whirring sound in the bushes attracted our attention, and two partridges perched upon a tree quite near us. We shot them, and fixing them in our belts, retraced our way towards the coast with lighter hearts. Just as we emerged from the dense forest, however, on one side of an open space, a tall muscular Indian strode from among the bushes and stood before us. He was dressed in the blanket capote, cloth leggins, and scarlet cap usually worn by the Abinikies, and other tribes of the Labrador coast. A red deer-skin shot-pouch and a powder-horn hung round his neck, and at his side were a beautifully ornamented fire-bag and scalping-knife. A common gun lay in the hollow of his left arm, and a pair of ornamented moccasins covered his feet. He was, indeed, a handsome-looking fellow, as he stood scanning us rapidly with his jet-black eyes while we approached him. We accosted him, and informed him (for he understood a little French) whence we came, and our object in visiting his part of the country. He received our advances kindly, accepted a piece of tobacco that we offered him, and told us that his name was Wapwian, and that we were welcome to remain at his village—to which he offered to conduct us—as long as we pleased. After a little hesitation we accepted his invitation to remain a few days; the more so, as by so doing we would have an opportunity of getting some provisions to enable us to continue our journey. In half an hour we reached the brow of a small eminence, whence the curling smoke of the wigwams was visible. The tents were pitched on the shores of a small bay or inlet, guarded from the east wind by a high precipice of rugged rocks, around which hundreds of sea-fowl sailed in graceful flights. Beyond this headland stretched the majestic Gulf of St. Lawrence; while to the left the village was shaded by the spruce-fir, of which most of this part of the forest is composed. There were, in all, about a dozen tents, made of dressed deerskin; at the openings of which might be seen groups of little children playing about on the grass, or running after their mothers as they went to the neighbouring rivulet for water, or launched their canoes to examine the nets in the bay.

"Wapwian paused to gaze an instant on the scene, and then, descending the hill with rapid strides, entered the village, and dispatched a little boy for our companion in the encampment.

"We were ushered into a tent somewhat elevated above the others, and soon were reclining on a soft pile of pine branches, smoking in company with our friend Wapwian, while his pretty little squaw prepared a kettle of fish for supper.

"We spent two happy days in the village, hunting deer with our Indian friend, and assisting the squaws in their fishing operations. On the third morning we remained in the camp to dry the venison, and prepare for our departure; while Wapwian shouldered his gun, and calling to his nephew, a slim, active youth of eighteen, bade him follow with his gun, as he intended to bring back a few ducks for his white brothers.

"The two Indians proceeded for a time along the shore, and then striking off into the forest, threaded their way among the thick bushes in the direction of a chain of small lakes where wild-fowl were numerous.

"For some time they moved rapidly along under the sombre shade of the trees, casting from time to time sharp glances into the surrounding underwood. Suddenly the elder Indian paused and threw forward his gun, as a slight rustling in the bushes struck his ear. The boughs bent and crackled a few yards in advance, and a large black bear crossed the path and entered the underwood on the other side. Wapwian fired at him instantly, and a savage growl told that the shot had taken effect. The gun, however, had been loaded with small shot; and although, when he fired, the bear was only a few yards off, yet the improbability of its having wounded him badly, and the distance they had to go ere they reached the lakes, inclined him to give up the chase. While Wapwian was loading his gun, Miniquan (his nephew) had been examining the bear's track, and returned, saying that he was sure the animal must be badly wounded, for there was much blood on the track. At first the elder Indian refused to follow it; but seeing that his nephew wished very much to kill the brute, he at last consented. As the trail of the bear was much covered with blood, they found no difficulty in tracking it; and after a short walk they found him extended on his side at the foot of a large tree, apparently lifeless. Wapwian, however, was too experienced a hunter to trust himself incautiously within its reach, so he examined the priming of his gun, and then, advancing slowly to the animal, pushed it with the muzzle. In an instant the bear sprang upon him, regardless of the shot lodged in its breast, and in another moment Wapwian lay stunned and bleeding at the monster's feet. Miniquan was at first so thunderstruck, as he gazed in horror at the savage animal tearing with bloody jaws the senseless form of his uncle, that he stood rooted to the ground. It was only for a moment—the next, his gun was at his shoulder, and after firing at, but unfortunately, in the excitement of the moment, missing the bear, he attacked it with the butt of his gun, which he soon shivered to pieces on its skull. This drew the animal for a few moments from Wapwian; and Miniquan, in hopes of leading it from the place, ran off in the direction of the village. The bear, however, soon gave up the chase, and returned again to its victim. Miniquan now saw that the only chance of saving his relative was to alarm the village; so, tightening his belt, he set off with the speed of the hunted deer in the direction of the camp. In an incredibly short time he arrived, and soon returned with the trappers and myself. Alas! alas!" said the guide with a deep sigh, "it was too late. Upon arriving at the spot, we found the bear quite dead, and the noble, generous Wapwian extended by its side, torn and lacerated in such a manner that we could scarcely recognise him. He still breathed a little, however, and appeared to know me, as I bent over him and tried to close his gaping wounds. We constructed a rude couch of branches, and conveyed him slowly to the village. No word of complaint or cry of sorrow escaped from his wife as we laid his bleeding form in her tent. She seemed to have lost the power of speech, as she sat, hour after hour, gazing in unutterable despair on the mangled form of her husband. Poor Wapwian lingered for a week in a state of unconsciousness. His skull had been fractured, and he lay almost in a state of insensibility, and never spoke, save when, in a fit of delirium, his fancy wandered back to bygone days, when he ranged the forest with a tiny bow in chase of little birds and squirrels, strode in the vigour of early manhood over frozen plains of snow, or dashed down foaming currents and mighty rivers in his light canoe. Then a shade would cross his brow as he thought, perhaps, of his recent struggle with the bear, and he would again relapse into silence.

"He recovered slightly before his death; and once he smiled, as if he recognised his wife, but he never spoke to any one. We scarcely know when his spirit fled, so calm and peaceful was his end.

"His body now reposes beneath the spreading branches of

a lordly pine, near the scenes of his childhood, where he had spent his youth, and where he met his untimely end."

The guide paused, and looked round upon his auditors. Alas! for the sympathy of man—the half of them had gone to sleep; and Baptiste, for whose benefit the story had been related, lay, or rather sprawled, upon the turf behind the fire, his shaggy head resting on the decayed stump of an old tree, and his empty pipe hanging gracefully from his half-open mouth. A slight "humph" escaped the worthy guide as he shook the ashes from his pipe, and rolling his blanket round him, laid his head upon the ground.

Early the following morning we raised the camp and continued our journey. The scenery had now become more wild and picturesque. Large pines became numerous; and the rocky fissures, through which the river rushed in a black unbroken mass, cast a gloomy shadow upon us as we struggled to ascend. Sometimes we managed to get up these rapids with the paddles; and when the current was too powerful, with long poles, which the men fixed in the ground, and thus pushed slowly up; but when both of these failed, we resorted to the tracking line, upon which occasions four of the men went on shore and dragged us up, leaving four in the canoe to paddle and steer it. When the current was too strong for this, they used to carry parts of the cargo to the smooth water further up, and drag the canoe up light, or, taking it on their shoulders, carry it overland. We made nine or ten of these portages in two days. In the afternoon we came in view of a Roman Catholic mission station, snugly situated at the bottom of a small bay or creek; but as it was a little out of our way, and from its quiet appearance seemed deserted, we did not stop.

In the afternoon of the following day, the 9th of September, we arrived at the Company's post, called Rat Portage House, where we were hospitably entertained for a few hours by Mr McKenzie, the gentleman in charge. On the portage, over which we had to carry our canoe and baggage, a large party of Indians of both sexes and all ages were collected to witness our departure; and Mr McKenzie advised us to keep a sharp lookout, as they were much addicted to appropriating the property of others to their own private use, provided they could find an opportunity of doing so unobserved; so, while our men were running backwards and forwards, carrying the things over the rocks, Mr Bain and his lady remained at one end to guard them, and I at the other. Everything, however, was got safely across; the Indians merely stood looking on, apparently much amused with our proceedings, and nothing seemed further from their thoughts than stealing. Just as we paddled from the bank, one of our men threw them a handful of tobacco, for which there was a great scramble, and their noisy voices died away in the distance as we rounded an abrupt point of rocks, and floated out upon the glorious expanse of Lac du Bois, or, as it is more frequently called, the Lake of the Woods.

There is nothing, I think, better calculated to awaken the more solemn feelings of our nature (unless, indeed, it be the thrilling tones of sacred music) than these noble lakes, studded with innumerable islets, suddenly bursting on the traveller's view as he emerges from the sombre forest-rivers of the American wilderness. The clear unruffled water, stretching out to the horizon—here, embracing the heavy and luxuriant foliage of a hundred wooded isles, or reflecting the wood-clad mountains on its margin, clothed in all the variegated hues of autumn; and there, glittering with dazzling brilliancy in the bright rays of the evening sun, or rippling among the reeds and rushes of some shallow bay, where hundreds of wild-fowl chatter, as they feed, with varied cry, rendering more apparent, rather than disturbing, the solemn stillness of the scene: all tends to "raise the soul from nature up to nature's God," and reminds one of the beautiful passage of Scripture, "O Lord, how manifold are thy works! in wisdom hast thou made them all: the earth is full of thy riches." At the same time, when one considers how very few of the human race cast even a passing glance on the beauties of nature around, one cannot but be impressed with the truth of the lines—

> Full many a flower is born to blush unseen,
> And waste its sweetness on the desert air.

At night we encamped at the furthest extremity of the lake, on a very exposed spot, whence we looked out upon the starlit scene, while our supper was spread before us in the warm light of the fire, which blazed and crackled as the men heaped log after log upon it, sending up clouds of bright sparks into the sky.

Next morning we commenced the ascent of Lac la Pluie River. This is decidedly the most beautiful river we had yet traversed—not only on account of the luxuriant foliage of every hue with which its noble banks are covered, but chiefly from the resemblance it bears in many places to the scenery of England, recalling to mind the grassy lawns and verdant banks of Britain's streams, and transporting the beholder from the wild scenes of the western world to his native home. The trees along its banks were larger and more varied than any we had hitherto seen—ash, poplar, cedar, red and white pines, oak, and birch being abundant, whilst flowers of gaudy hues enhanced the beauty of the scene. Towards noon our guide kept a sharp lookout for a convenient spot whereon to dine; and ere long a flat shelving rock, partly shaded by trees and partly exposed to the blaze of the sun, presented itself to view. The canoe was soon alongside of it, and kept floating about half a foot from the edge by means of two branches, the two ends of which were fastened to the bow and stern of the canoe, and the other two to the ground by means of huge stones. It is necessary to be thus careful with canoes, as the gum or pitch with which the seams are plastered breaks off in lumps, particularly in cold weather, and makes the craft leaky. A snow-white napkin was spread on the flattest part of the rock, and so arranged that, as we reclined around it, on cloaks and blankets, our bodies down to the knees were shaded by the luxuriant foliage behind us, while our feet were basking in the solar rays! Upon the napkin were presently placed, by our active waiter Gibault, three pewter plates, a decanter of port wine, and a large ham, together with a turret of salt butter, and a loaf of bread, to the demolition of which viands we devoted ourselves with great earnestness. At a short distance the men circled round a huge lump of boiled pork, each with a large slice of bread in one hand and a knife in the other, with which he *porked* his bread in the same way that civilized people *butter* theirs! Half an hour concluded our mid-day meal; and then, casting off the branches from the canoe, we were out of sight of our temporary dining-room in five minutes.

On the evening of the following day we arrived at the Company's post, Fort Frances. The fort is rather an old building, situated at the bottom of a small bay or curve in the river, near the foot of a waterfall, whose thundering roar forms a ceaseless music to the inhabitants. We found the post in charge of a chief trader, who had no other society than that of three or four labouring men; so, as may be supposed, he was delighted to see us. Our men carried the canoe, etcetera, over the portage to avoid the waterfall, and as it was then too late to proceed further that night, we accepted his pressing invitation to pass the night at the fort. There was only one spare bed in the house, but this was a matter of little moment to us after the variety of beds we had had since starting; so, spreading a buffalo robe on the floor for a mattress, I rolled myself in my blanket and tried to sleep. At first I could not manage it, owing to the unearthly stillness of a room, after being so long accustomed to the open air and the noise of rivers and cataracts, but at last succeeded, and slept soundly till morning.

Dame Fortune does not always persecute her friends; and although she had retarded us hitherto a good deal with contrary winds and rains, she kindly assisted us when we commenced crossing Lac la Pluie next morning, by raising a stiff, fair breeze. Now, be it known that a canoe, from having no keel, and a round bottom, cannot venture to hoist a sail unless the wind is directly astern—the least bit to one side would be sure to capsize it; so that our getting the wind precisely in the proper direction at the commencement was a great piece of good fortune, inasmuch as it enabled us to cross the lake in six hours, instead of (as is generally the case) taking one, two, or three days.

In the evening we arrived, in high spirits, at a portage, on which we encamped.

Our progress now became a little more interrupted by portages and small lakes, or rather ponds, through which we sometimes passed with difficulty, owing to the shallowness of the water in many places. Soon after this we came to the

Mecan River, which we prepared to ascend. In making a portage, we suddenly discovered a little Indian boy, dressed in the extreme of the Indian summer fashion—in other words, he was in a state of perfect nakedness, with the exception of a breech-cloth; and upon casting our eyes across the river we beheld his worthy father, in a similar costume, busily employed in catching fish with a hand-net. He was really a wild, picturesque-looking fellow, notwithstanding the scantiness of his dress; and I was much interested in his proceedings. When I first saw him, he was standing upon a rock close to the edge of a foaming rapid, into the eddies of which he gazed intently, with the net raised in the air, and his muscular frame motionless, as if petrified while in the act of striking. Suddenly the net swung through the air, and his body quivered as he strained every sinew to force it quickly through the water: in a moment it came out with a beautiful white-fish, upwards of a foot long, glittering like silver as it struggled in the meshes. In the space of half an hour he had caught half a dozen in this manner, and we bought three or four of the finest for a few plugs of tobacco. His wigwam and family were close at hand; so, while our men crossed the portage, I ran up to see them.

The tent, which was made of sheets of birch bark sewed together, was pitched beneath the branches of a gigantic pine, upon the lower limbs of which hung a pair of worn-out snowshoes, a very dirty blanket, and a short bow, with a quiver of arrows near it. At the foot of it, upon the ground, were scattered a few tin pots, several pairs of old moccasins, and a gun; while against it leaned an Indian cradle, in which a small, very brown baby, with jet-black eyes and hair, stood bolt upright, basking in the sun's rays, and bearing a comical resemblance to an Egyptian mummy. At the door of the tent a child of riper years amused itself by rolling about among the chips of wood, useless bits of deer-skin, and filth always strewn around a wigwam. On the right hand lay a pile of firewood, with an axe beside it, near which crouched a half-starved, wretched-looking nondescript dog, who commenced barking vociferously the moment he cast eyes upon me. Such was the outside. The interior, filled with smoke from the fire and Indians' pipes, was, if possible, even dirtier. Amid a large pile of rabbit-skins reclined an old woman, busily plucking the feathers from a fine duck, which she carefully preserved (the feathers, not the duck) in a bag, for the purpose of trading them with the Company at a future period. Her dress was a coat of rabbit-skins, so strangely shaped that no one could possibly tell how she ever got it off or on. This, however, was doubtless a matter of little consequence to her, as Indians seldom take the trouble of changing their clothes, or even of undressing at all. The coat was fearfully dirty, and hung upon her in a way that led me to suppose she had worn it for six months, and that it would fall off her in a few days. A pair of faded blue cloth leggins completed her costume—her dirty shoulders, arms, and feet being quite destitute of covering; while her long black hair fell in tangled masses upon her neck, and it was evidently a long time since a comb had passed through it. On the other side sat a younger woman similarly attired, employed in mending a hand-net; and on a very much worn buffalo robe sat a young man (probably the brother of the one we had seen fishing), wrapped in a blanket, smoking his pipe in silence. A few dirty little half-naked boys lay sprawling among several packages of furs tied up in birch bark, and disputed with two or three ill-looking dogs the most commodious place whereon to lie. The fire in the middle of the tent sent up a cloud of smoke, which escaped through an aperture at the top; and from a cross-bar depended a few slices of deer-meat, undergoing the process of smoking.

I had merely time to note all this, and say, "What cheer!" to the Indians, who returned the compliment with a grunt, when the loud voice of our guide ringing through the glades of the forest informed me that the canoe was ready to proceed.

The country through which we now passed was very interesting, on account of the variety of the scenes and places through which we wound our way. At times we were paddling with difficulty against the strong current of a narrow river, which, on our turning a point of land, suddenly became a large lake; and then, after crossing this, we arrived at a portage. After passing over it, there came a series of small ponds and little creeks, through which we pushed our way with difficulty; and then arrived at another lake, and more little rivers, with numerous portages. Sometimes ludicrous accidents happened to us—bad enough at the time, but subjects of mirth afterwards.

One cold, frosty morning (for the weather had now become cold, from the elevation of the country through which we were passing), while the canoe was going quietly over a small reedy lake or ford, I was awakened out of a nap, and told that the canoe was aground, and I must get out and walk a little way to lighten her. Hastily pulling up my trousers for I always travelled barefoot—I sprang over the side into the water, and the canoe left me. Now, all this happened so quickly that I was scarcely awake; but the bitterly cold water, which nearly reached my knees, cleared up my faculties most effectually, and I then found that I was fifty yards from the shore, with an unknown depth of water around me, the canoe out of sight ahead of me, and Mr Bain—who had been turned out while half asleep also—standing with a rueful expression of countenance beside me. After feeling our way cautiously—for the bottom was soft and muddy—we reached the shore; and then, thinking that all was right, proceeded to walk round to join the canoe. Alas! we found the bushes so thick that they were very nearly impenetrable; and, worse than all, that they, as well as the ground, were covered with thorns, which scratched and lacerated our feet most fearfully at every step. There was nothing for it, however, but to persevere; and after a painful walk of a quarter of a mile we overtook the canoe, vowing never to leap before we looked upon any other occasion whatsoever.

In this way we proceeded—literally over hill and dale—in our canoe; and in the course of a few days ascended Mecan River, and traversed Cross Lake, Malign River, Sturgeon Lake, Lac du Mort, Mille Lac, besides a great number of smaller sheets of water without names, and many portages of various lengths and descriptions, till the evening of the 19th, when we ascended the beautiful little river called the Savan, and arrived at the Savan Portage.

Many years ago, in the time of the North-West Company, the echoes among these wild solitudes were far oftener and more loudly awakened than they are now. The reason of it was this. The North-West Company, having their head quarters at Montreal, and being composed chiefly of Canadian adventurers, imported their whole supplies into the country and exported all their furs out of it in north canoes, by the same route over which we now travelled. As they carried on business on a large scale, it may be supposed that the traffic was correspondingly great. No less than ten brigades, each numbering twenty canoes, used to pass through these scenes during the summer months. No one who has not experienced it can form an adequate idea of the thrilling effect the passing of these brigades must have had upon a stranger. I have seen four canoes sweep round a promontory suddenly, and burst upon my view, while at the same moment the wild romantic song of the *voyageurs*, as they plied their brisk paddles, struck upon my ear; and I have felt thrilling enthusiasm on witnessing such a scene. What, then, must have been the feelings of those who had spent a long, dreary winter in the wild North-West, far removed from the bustle and excitement of the civilized world, when thirty or forty of these picturesque canoes burst unexpectedly upon them, half shrouded in the spray that flew from the bright vermilion paddles; while the men, who had overcome difficulties and dangers innumerable during a long voyage through the wilderness, urged their light craft over the troubled water with the speed of the reindeer, and, with hearts joyful at the happy termination of their trials and privations, sang, with all the force of three hundred manly voices, one of their lively airs, which, rising and falling faintly in the distance as it was borne, first lightly on the breeze, and then more steadily as they approached, swelled out in the rich tones of many a mellow voice, and burst at last into a long enthusiastic shout of joy!

Alas! the forests no longer echo to such sounds. The passage of three or four canoes once or twice a year is all that breaks the stillness of the scene; and nought, save narrow pathways over the portages, and rough wooden crosses over the graves of the travellers who perished by the way, remains to mark that such things were. Of these marks, the Savan Portage, at which we had arrived, was one of the most striking. A long succession of boiling rapids and waterfalls having in days of yore obstructed the passage of the fur-traders, they had landed at the top of them, and cut a pathway through the woods, which happened at this place to be exceedingly swampy: hence the name Savan (or *swampy*) Portage. To render the road more passable, they had cut down trees, which they placed side by side along its whole extent—which was about three miles—and over this wooden platform carried their canoes and cargoes with perfect ease. After the coalition of the two companies, and the consequent carriage of the furs to England by Hudson Bay—instead of to Canada, by the lakes and rivers of the interior—these roads were neglected, and got out of repair; and consequently we found the logs over the portage decayed and trees fallen across them, so that our men, instead of running quickly over them, were constantly breaking through the rotten wood, sinking up to the knees in mud, and scrambling over trees and branches. We got over at last, however—in about two hours; and after proceeding a little further, arrived at and encamped upon the Prairie Portage, by the side of a *voyageur's* grave, which was marked as usual with a wooden cross, on which some friendly hand had cut a rude inscription. Time had now rendered it quite illegible. This is the height of land dividing the waters which flow northward into Hudson Bay from those which flow in a southerly direction, through the great lakes, into the Atlantic Ocean.

A few pages from my journal here may serve to give a better idea of the characteristics of our voyage than could be conveyed in narrative:—

Saturday, 20th September.—We crossed the Prairie Portage this morning—a distance of between three and four miles—and breakfasted at the upper end of it. Amused myself by sketching the view from a neighbouring hill. After crossing two more portages and a variety of small lakes, we launched our canoe on the bosom of the river Du Chien, and began, for the first time since the commencement of our journey, to *descend*, having passed over the height of land. We saw several grey grouse here, and in the evening one of our men caught one in a curious manner. They were extremely tame, and allowed us to approach them very closely, so Baptiste determined to catch one for supper. Cutting a long branch from a neighbouring tree, he tied a running noose on one end of it, and going quietly up to the bird, put the noose gently over its head, and pulled it off the tree. This is a common practice among the Indians, particularly when they have run short of gunpowder.

Sunday, 21st.—Crossed Lac du Chien, and made the portage of the same name, from the top of which we had a most beautiful view of the whole country for miles round. Having crossed this portage, we proceeded down the Kamenistaquoia River, on the banks of which, after making another portage, we pitched our tents.

Monday, 22nd.—Rain obliged us to put ashore this morning. Nothing can be more wretched than travelling in rainy weather. The men, poor fellows, do not make the least attempt to keep themselves dry; but the passengers endeavour, by means of oiled cloths, to keep out the wet; and under this they broil and suffocate, till at last they are obliged to throw off the covering. Even were this not the case, we should still be wretched, as the rain always finds its way in somewhere or other; and I have been often awakened from a nap by the cold trickling of moisture down my back, and have discovered upon moving that I was lying in a pool of water. Ashore we are generally a little more comfortable, but not much. After din-

VIEW FROM PORTAGE DU CHIEN.

ner we again started, and advanced on our journey till sunset.

Tuesday, 23rd.—To-day we advanced very slowly, owing to the shallowness of the water, and crossed a number of portages. During the day we ran several rapids. This is very exciting work. Upon nearing the head of a large rapid, the men strain every muscle to urge the canoe forward more quickly than the water, so that it may steer better. The bowsman and steersman stand erect, guiding the frail bark through the more unbroken places in the fierce current, which hisses and foams around, as if eager to swallow us up. Now we rush with lightning force towards a rock, against which the water dashes in fury; and to an uninitiated traveller we appear to be on the point of destruction. But one vigorous stroke from the bowsman and steersman (for they always act in concert) sends the light craft at a sharp angle from the impending danger; and away we plunge again over the surging waters—sometimes floating for an instant in a small eddy, and hovering, as it were, to choose our path; and then plunging swiftly forward again through the windings of the stream, till, having passed the whole in safety, we float in the smooth water below.

Accidents, as may be supposed, often happen; and to-day we found that there is danger as well as pleasure in running the rapids. We had got over a great part of the day in safety, and were in the act of running the first part of the Rose Rapid, when our canoe struck upon a rock, and wheeling round with its broadside to the stream, began to fill quickly. I could hear the timbers cracking beneath me under the immense pressure. Another minute, and we should have been gone; but our men, who were active fellows, and well accustomed to such dangers, sprang simultaneously over the side of the canoe, which, being thus lightened, passed over the rock, and rushed down the remainder of the rapid stern foremost ere the men could scramble in and resume their paddles. When rapids were very dangerous, most of the cargo was generally disembarked; and while one half of the crew carried it round to the still water below, the other half ran down light.

Crossed two small portages and the Mountain Portage in the afternoon; on the latter of which I went to see a waterfall, which I was told was in its vicinity. I had great difficulty in finding it at first, but its thundering roar soon guided me to a spot from which it was visible. Truly, a grander waterfall I never saw. The whole river, which was pretty broad, plunged in one broad white sheet over a precipice, higher by a few feet than the famous Falls of Niagara; and the spray from the foot sprang high into the air, bedewing the wild, precipitous crags with which the fall is encompassed, and the gloomy pines that hang about the clefts and fissures of the rocks. Fur-traders have given it the name of the Mountain Fall, from a peculiar mountain in its vicinity; but the natives call it the *Kackabecka* Falls. After making a sketch of it, and getting myself thoroughly wet in so doing, I returned to the canoe.

In the evening we encamped within nine miles of Fort William, having lost one of our men, who went ashore to lighten the canoe while we ran a rapid. After a good deal of trouble we found him again, but too late to admit of our proceeding to the fort that night.

Wednesday, 24th.—Early this morning we left the encampment, and after two hours' paddling Fort William burst upon our gaze, mirrored in the limpid waters of Lake Superior—that immense fresh-water sea, whose rocky shores and rolling billows vie with the ocean itself in grandeur and magnificence.

Fort William was once one of the chief posts in the Indian country, and, when it belonged to the North-West Company, contained a great number of men. Now, however, much of its glory has departed. Many of the buildings have been pulled down, and those that remain are very rickety-looking affairs. It is still, however, a very important fishing station, and many hundreds of beautiful white-fish, with which Lake Superior

KACKABECKA FALLS.

swarms, are salted there annually for the Canada markets. These white-fish are indeed excellent; and it is difficult to say whether they or the immense trout, which are also caught in abundance, have the most delicate flavour. These trout, as well as white-fish, are caught in nets; and the former sometimes measure three feet long, and are proportionately broad. The one we had to breakfast on the morning of our arrival must have been very nearly this size.

The fur-trade of the post is not very good, but the furs traded are similar to those obtained in other parts of the country.

A number of *canôtes de maître*, or very large canoes, are always kept in store here, for the use of the Company's travellers. These canoes are of the largest size, exceeding the north canoe in length by several feet, besides being much broader and deeper. They are used solely for the purpose of travelling on Lake Superior, being much too large and cumbersome for travelling with through the interior. They are carried by four men instead of two, like the north canoe; and, besides being capable of carrying twice as much cargo, are paddled by fourteen or sixteen men. Travellers from Canada to the interior generally change their *canôtes de maître* for north canoes at Fort William, before entering upon the intricate navigation through which we had already passed; while those going from the interior to Canada change the small for the large canoe. As we had few men, however, and the weather appeared settled, we determined to risk coasting round the northern shore of the lake in our north canoe.

The scenery around the fort is very pretty. In its immediate vicinity the land is flat, covered with small trees and willows, which are agreeably suggestive of partridges and other game; but in the distance rise goodly-sized mountains; and on the left hand the noble expanse of the Lake Superior, with rocky islands on its mighty bosom and abrupt hills on its shores, stretches out to the horizon. The fort is built at the mouth of the Kamenistaquoia River, and from its palisades a beautiful view of the surrounding country can be obtained.

As the men wanted rest and our canoe a little repair, we determined to remain all day at Fort William; so some of the men employed themselves re-gumming the canoe, while others spread out our blankets and tents to dry. This last was very necessary as on the journey we have little time to spare from eating and sleeping while on shore; and many a time have I, in consequence, slept in a wet blanket.

The fair lady of the gentleman in charge of the fort was the *only lady* at the place, and indeed the only one within a circuit of six hundred miles—which space, being the primeval forest, was inhabited only by wild beasts and a few Indians. She was, consequently, very much delighted to meet with Mrs Bain, who, having for so many days seen no one but rough *voyageurs*, was equally delighted to meet her. While they went off to make the most of each other, Mr Bain and I sauntered about in the vicinity of the fort, admiring the beauty of the scenery, and paid numerous visits to a superb dairy in the fort, which overflowed with milk and cream. I rather think that we admired the dairy more than the scenery. There were a number of cows at the post, a few of which we encountered in our walk, and also a good many pigs and sheep. In the evening we returned, and at tea were introduced to a postmaster, who had been absent when we arrived. This postmaster turned out to be a first-rate player of Scotch reels on the violin. He was self-taught, and truly the sweetness and precision with which he played every note and trill of the rapid reel and strathspey might have made Neil Gow himself envious. So beautiful and inspiriting were they, that Mr Bain and our host, who were both genuine Highlanders, jumped simultaneously from their seats, in an ecstasy of enthusiasm, and danced to the lively music till the very walls shook; much to the amusement of the two ladies, who, having been both born in Canada, could not so well appreciate the music. Indeed, the musician himself looked a little astonished, being quite ignorant of the endearing recollections and associations recalled to the memory of the two Highlanders by the rapid notes of his violin. They were not, however, to be contented with one reel; so, after fruitlessly attempting to make the ladies join us, we sent over to the men's houses for the old Canadian wife of Pierre Lattinville and her two blooming daughters. They soon came, and after much coyness, blushing, and hesitation, at last stood up, and under the inspiring influence of the violin we:—

Danced, till we were like to fa',
The reel o' Tullochgorum!

And did not cease till the lateness of the hour and the exhaustion of our musician compelled us to give in.

On the following morning we bade adieu to the good people at Fort William, and began our journey along the northern shore of Lake Superior, which is upwards of three hundred miles in diameter. Fortune, however, is proverbially fickle, and she did not belie her character on this particular day. The weather, when we started, was calm and clear, which pleased us much, as we had to make what is called a traverse— that is, to cross from one point of land to another, instead of coasting round a very deep bay. The traverse which we set out to make on leaving Fort William was fourteen miles broad, which made it of some consequence our having a calm day to cross it in our little egg-shell of a canoe. Away we went, then, over the clear lake, singing "Rose Blanche" vociferously. We had already gone a few miles of the distance, when a dark cloud rose on the seaward horizon. Presently the water darkened under the influence of a stiff breeze, and in less than

half an hour the waves were rolling and boiling around us like those of the Atlantic. Ahead of us lay a small island, about a mile distant; and towards this the canoe was steered, while the men urged it forward as quickly as the roughness of the sea would allow. Still the wind increased, and the island was not yet gained. Some of the waves had broken over the edge of the canoe, and she was getting filled with water; but a kind Providence permitted us to reach the island in safety, though not in comfort, as most of the men were much wet, and many of them a good deal frightened.

On landing, we pitched our tents, made a fire, and proceeded to dry ourselves, and in less than an hour were as comfortable as possible. The island on which we had encamped was a small rocky one, covered with short heathery-looking shrubs, among which we found thousands of blaeberries. On walking round to the other side of it, I discovered an Indian encamped with his family. He supplied us with a fine whitefish, for which our men gave him a little tobacco and a bit of the fresh mutton which we had brought with us from Fort William.

Three days did we remain on this island, while the wind and waves continued unceasingly to howl and lash around it, as if they wished, in their disappointment, to beat it down and swallow us up, island and all; but towards the close of the third day the gale moderated, and we ventured again to attempt the traverse. This time we succeeded, and in two hours passed Thunder Point, on the other side of which we encamped.

The next day we could only travel till breakfast-time, as the wind again increased so much as to oblige us to put ashore. We comforted ourselves, however, with the prospect of a good mutton-chop.

The fire was soon made, the kettle on, and everything in preparation, when the dreadful discovery was made that the whole of the fresh mutton had been forgotten! Words cannot paint our consternation at this discovery. Poor Mrs Bain sat in mute despair, thinking of the misery of being reduced again to salt pork; while her husband, who had hitherto stood aghast, jumped suddenly forward, and seizing a bag of fine potatoes that had been given to the men, threw it, in a transport of rage, into the lake, vowing that as we were, by their negligence, to be deprived of our mutton, they certainly should also be sufferers with us.

It was very laughable to behold the rueful countenances of the men as their beautiful, large white potatoes sank to the bottom of the clear lake, and shone brightly there, as if to tantalise them, while the rippling water caused them to quiver so much that the lake seemed to rest on a pavement of huge potatoes! None dared, however, attempt to recover one; but after a while, when Mr Bain's back was turned, a man crept cautiously down to the water's edge, and gathered as many as were within reach—always, however, keeping an eye on his master, and stooping in an attitude that would permit of his bolting up on the slightest indication of a wrathful movement.

It would be tedious, as well as unnecessary, to recount here all the minutiae of our voyage across Lake Superior; I shall merely touch on a few of the more particular incidents.

On the 1st of October we arrived at the Pic House (see note 2), where we spent the night; and, after a rough voyage, reached Michipicoton on the 4th. Our voyage along Lake Superior was very stormy and harassing, reminding us often of Lake Winnipeg. Sometimes we were paddling along over the smooth water, and at other times *lying-by*, while the lake was lashed into a mass of foam and billows by a strong gale. So much detention, and the lateness of the season, rendered it necessary to take advantage of every lull and calm hour that occurred, so that we travelled a good deal during the night. This sort of travelling was very romantic.

On one occasion, after having been ashore two days, the wind moderated in the afternoon, and we determined to proceed, if possible. The sun set gloriously, giving promise of fine weather. The sky was clear and cloudless, and the lake calm. For an hour or so the men sang as they paddled, but as the shades of evening fell they ceased; and as it was getting rather chilly, I wrapped myself in my green blanket (which served me for a boat-cloak as well as a bed), and soon fell fast asleep.

How long I slept I know not; but when I awoke, the regular, rapid hiss of the paddles struck upon my ear, and upon throwing off the blanket the first thing that met my eye was the dark sky, spangled with the most gorgeous and brilliant stars I ever beheld. The whole scene, indeed, was one of the most magnificent and awful that can be imagined. On our left hand rose tremendous precipices and cliffs, around the bottom and among the caverns of which the black waters of the lake curled quietly (for a most death-like, unearthly calm prevailed), sending forth a faint hollow murmur, which ended, at long intervals, in a low melancholy cadence. Before and behind us abrupt craggy islands rose from the water, assuming every imaginable and unimaginable shape in the uncertain light; while on the right the eye ranged over the inky lake till it was lost in thick darkness. A thin, transparent night-fog added to the mystical appearance of the scene, upon which I looked with mingled feelings of wonder and awe. The only distinct sound that could be heard was the measured sound of the paddles, which the men plied in silence, as if unwilling to break the stillness of the night. Suddenly the guide uttered in a hoarse whisper, "*A terre!*" startling the sleepy men, and rendering the succeeding silence still more impressive.

The canoe glided noiselessly through a maze of narrow passages among the tall cliffs, and grounded on a stony beach. Everything was then carried up, and the tents pitched in the dark, as no wood could be conveniently found for the purpose of making a fire; and without taking any supper, or even breaking the solemn silence of the night, we spread our beds as we best could upon the round stones (some of which were larger than a man's fist), and sank into repose. About a couple of hours afterwards we were roused by the anxious guide, and told to embark again. In this way we travelled at night or by day, as the weather permitted—and even, upon one or two occasions, both night and day—till the 12th of October, when we arrived at the *Sault de Ste. Marie*, which is situated at the termination of Lake Superior, just as our provisions were exhausted.

We had thus taken eighteen days to coast the lake. This

was very slow going indeed, the usual time for coasting the lake in a north canoe being from eight to ten days.

The Sault de Ste. Marie is a large rapid, which carries the waters of Lake Superior into Lake Huron. It separates the British from the American possessions, and is fortified on the American side by a large wooden fort, in which a body of soldiers are constantly resident. There is also a pretty large village of Americans, which is rapidly increasing. The British side is not fortified; and, indeed, there are no houses of any kind except the few belonging to the Hudson Bay Company. This may be considered the extreme outskirts of civilisation, being the first place where I had seen any number of people collected together who were unconnected with the Hudson Bay Company.

I was not destined, however, to enjoy the sight of new faces long, for next morning we started to coast round the northern and uninhabited shores of Lake Huron, and so down the Ottawa to Montreal. Mr and Mrs Bain left me here, and proceeded by the route of the Lakes.

During the next few days we travelled through a number of rivers and lakes of various sizes; among the latter were Lakes Huron and Nipisingue. In crossing the latter, I observed a point on which were erected fourteen rough wooden crosses. Such an unusual sight excited my curiosity, and upon inquiring I found that they were planted there to mark the place where a canoe, containing fourteen men, had been upset in a gale, and every soul lost. The lake was clear and smooth when we passed the melancholy spot, and many a rolling year has defaced and cast down the crosses since the unfortunate men whose sad fate they commemorate perished in the storm.

While searching about the shore one night for wood to

make a fire, one of our men found a large basket, made of bark, and filled with fine bears'-grease, which had been hid by some Indians. This was considered a great windfall; and ere two days were passed the whole of it was eaten by the men, who buttered their flour cakes with it profusely.

Not long after this we passed a large waterfall, where a friend of mine was once very nearly lost. A projecting point obliges the traveller to run his canoe rather near the head of the fall, for the purpose of landing to make the portage. From long habit the guides had been accustomed to this, and always effected the doubling of the point in safety. Upon this occasion, however, either from carelessness or accident, the canoe got into the strong current, and almost in an instant was swept down towards the fall. To turn the head of the canoe up the stream, and paddle for their lives, was the work of a moment; but before they got it fairly round they were on the very brink of the cataract, which, had they gone over it, would have dashed them to a thousand atoms. They paddled with the strength of desperation, but so strong was the current that they remained almost stationary. At last they began slowly to ascend—an inch at a time—and finally reached the bank in safety.

On Sunday the 19th of October we commenced descending the magnificent river Ottawa, and began to feel that we were at last approaching the civilized nations of the earth. During the day we passed several small log-huts, or shanties, which are the temporary dwelling-places of men who penetrate thus far into the forest for the purpose of cutting timber. A canoe full of these adventurous pioneers also passed us; and in the evening we reached Fort Mattawan, one of the Company's stations. At night we encamped along with a party who

A NARROW ESCAPE.

were taking provisions to the wood-cutters.

The scenery on the Ottawa is beautiful, and as we descended the stream it was rendered more picturesque and interesting by the appearance, occasionally, of that, to us, unusual sight, a farmhouse. They were too few and far between, however, to permit of our taking advantage of the inhabitants' hospitality, and for the next four days we continued to make our encampments in the woods as heretofore. At one of these frontier farms our worthy guide discovered, to his unutterable astonishment and delight, an old friend and fellow-voyageur, to greet whom he put ashore. The meeting was strange: instead of shaking hands warmly, as I had expected, they stood for a moment gazing in astonishment, and then, with perfect solemnity, kissed each other—not gently on the cheek, but with a good hearty smack on their sunburnt lips. After conversing for a little, they parted with another kiss.

On the fourth day after this event we came in sight of the village of Aylmer, which lay calmly on the sloping banks of the river, its church spire glittering in the sun, and its white houses reflected in the stream.

It is difficult to express the feelings of delight with which I gazed upon this little village, after my long banishment from the civilized world. It was like recovering from a trance of four long dreamy years; and I wandered about the streets, gazing in joy and admiration upon everything and everybody, but especially upon the ladies, who appeared quite a strange race of beings to me—and all of them looked so beautiful in my eyes (long accustomed to Indian dames), that I fell in love with every one individually that passed me in the village. In this happy mood I sauntered about, utterly oblivious of the fact that my men had been left in a public-house, and would infallibly, if not prevented, get dead drunk. I was soon awakened to this startling probability by the guide, who walked up the road in a very solemn I'm-not-at-all-drunk sort of a manner, peering about on every side, evidently in search of me. Having found me, he burst into an expression of unbounded joy; and then, recollecting that this was inconsistent with his assumed character of sobriety, became awfully grave, and told me that we must start soon, as the men were all getting tipsy.

The following day we arrived at Bytown.

This town is picturesquely situated on the brow of a stupendous cliff, which descends precipitously into the Ottawa. Just above the town a handsome bridge stretches across the river, near which the Kettle Fall thunders over a high cliff. We only stayed a few minutes here, and then proceeded on our way.

During the day we passed the locks of the Rideau Canal, which rise, to the number of eight or ten, one over another like steps; and immediately below them appeared the Curtain Falls. These falls are not very picturesque, but their great height and curtain-like smoothness render them an interesting object. After this, villages and detached houses became numerous all the way down the river; and late in the evening of the 24th we arrived at a station belonging to the Hudson Bay Company, on the Lake of the Two Mountains, where we passed the remainder of the night.

Here, for the first time since leaving home, I was ushered into a civilized drawing-room; and when I found myself seated on a *cushioned* chair, with my moccasined feet pressing a soft carpet, and several real, *bonâ fide ladies* (the wife and daughters of my entertainer) sitting before me, and asking hundreds of questions about my long voyage, the strange species of unbelief in the possibility of again seeing the civilized world, which had beset me for the last three years, began slowly to give way, and at last entirely vanished when my host showed me into a handsomely furnished bedroom, and left me for the night.

The first thing that struck me on entering the bedroom was the appearance of one of our *voyageurs*, dressed in a soiled blue capote, dilapidated corduroy trousers, and moccasins; while his deeply sunburnt face, under a mass of long straggling hair, stared at me in astonishment! It will doubtless be supposed that I was much horrified at this apparition. I was, indeed, much surprised; but, seeing that it was my own image reflected in a full-length looking-glass, I cannot say that I felt extremely horrified. This was the first time that I had seen myself—if I may so speak—since leaving Norway House; and, truly, I had no reason to feel proud of my appearance.

The following morning, at four o'clock, we left the Lake of the Two Mountains; and in the afternoon of the 25th October, 1845, arrived at Lachine, where, for the time, my travels came to a close—having been journeying in the wilderness for sixty-six days.

Soon after my arrival winter set in, and I became acquainted with a few of the inhabitants of Lachine. The moment the snow fell, wheeled carriages were superseded by carioles and sleighs of all descriptions. These beautiful vehicles are mounted on runners, or large skates, and slide very smoothly and easily over the snow, except when the road is bad; and then, owing to the want of springs, sleighs become very rough carriages indeed. They are usually drawn by one horse, the harness and trappings of which are profusely covered with small round bells. These bells are very necessary appendages, as little noise is made by the approach of a sleigh over the soft snow, and they serve to warn travellers in the dark. The cheerful tinkling music thus occasioned on the Canadian roads is very pleasing. Sleighs vary a good deal in structure and costliness of decoration; and one often meets a rough, cheerful Canadian *ha-*

CANADIAN SLEIGH.

bitant sitting in his small box of a sledge (painted sometimes red and sometimes green), lashing away at his shaggy pony in a fruitless attempt to keep up with the large graceful sleigh of a wealthy inhabitant of Montreal, who, wrapped up in furs, drives tandem, with two strong horses, and loudly tinkling bells.

Reader, I had very nearly come to the resolution of giving you a long account of Canada and the Canadians, but I dare not venture on it. I feel that it would be encroaching upon the ground of civilized authors; and as I do not belong to this class, but profess to write of savage life, and nothing but savage life, I hope you will extend to me your kind forgiveness if I conclude this chapter rather abruptly.

It is a true saying that the cup of happiness is often dashed from the lips that are about to taste it. I have sometimes proved this to be the case. The cup of happiness, on the present occasion, was the enjoyment of civilized and social life; and the dashing of it away was my being sent, with very short warning, to an out-of-the-way station, whose name, to me, was strange—distance uncertain, but long—appearance unknown, and geographical position a most profound mystery.

Note 1: Since the above was written, many years have passed, and Dr Rae's name has become famous, not only on account of successful discovery, but also in connection with the expeditions sent out in search of Sir John Franklin.

Note 2: It must be borne in mind that all the establishments we passed on the way belonged to the Hudson Bay Company.

11

WINTER-TRAVELLING
IN CANADA

*—Departure from Lachine—Scenery Along the Road
—"Incidents" by the Way—Arrival at Tadousac
—Mr Stone's Adventure with Indians—Clubbing Seals*

IT WAS ON A BRIGHT winter's day in the month of January 1846 that I was sent for by the Governor, and told to hold myself in readiness to start early the following morning with Mr Stone for Tadousac—adding, that probably I should spend the approaching summer at Seven Islands.

Tadousac, be it known, is a station about three hundred miles below Montreal, at the mouth of the river Saguenay, and Seven Islands is two hundred miles below Tadousac; so that the journey is not a short one. The greater part of the road runs through an uninhabited country, and the travelling is bad.

In preparation for this journey, then, I employed myself during the remainder of the day; and before night all was ready.

Next morning I found that our journey was postponed to the following day, so I went into Montreal to make a few purchases, and passed the rest of the day in a state of intense thought, endeavouring to find out if anything had been forgotten. Nothing, however, recurred to my memory; and going to bed only half undressed, in order to be ready at a moment's notice, I soon fell into a short disturbed slumber, from which the servant awakened me long before daylight, by announcing that the sleigh was at the door. In ten minutes I was downstairs, where Mr Stone shortly afterwards joined me; and after seeing our traps safely deposited in the bottom of the sleigh, we jumped in, and slid noiselessly over the quiet street of Lachine.

The stars shone brightly as we glided over the crunching snow, and the sleigh-bells tinkled merrily as our horse sped over the deserted road. Groups of white cottages and solitary gigantic trees flew past us, looking, in the uncertain light, like large snow-drifts; save where the twinkling of a candle, or the first blue flames of the morning fire, indicated that the industrious *habitant* had risen to his daily toil. In silence we glided on our way, till the distant lights of Montreal awakened us from our reveries, and we met at intervals a solitary pedestrian, or a sleigh-load of laughing, fur-encompassed faces returning from an evening party.

About seven o'clock we arrived at the hotel from which the stage was to start for Quebec—but when did stage-coach, or sleigh either, keep to its time? No sign of it was to be seen, and it required no small application of our knuckles and toes at the door to make the lazy waiter turn out to let us in. No misery, save being too late, can equal that of being too soon; at least, so I thought while walking up and down the coffee-room of the hotel, upon the table of which were scattered the remains of last night's supper, amid a confusion of newspapers and fag-ends of cigars; while the sleepy waiter made unavailing efforts to coax a small spark of fire to contribute some warmth to one or two damp billets of wood.

About an hour after its appointed time, the sleigh drove up to the door, and we hastened to take our places. The stage, however, was full, but the driver informed us that an "extra" (or separate sleigh of smaller dimensions than the stage) had been provided for us; so that we enjoyed the enviable advantage of having it all to ourselves. Crack went the whip, and off went the leader with a bound, the wheeler following at a pace between a trot and a gallop, and our "extra" keeping close in the rear. The lamps were still burning as we left the city, although the first streaks of dawn illumined the eastern sky. In fifteen minutes more we had left Montreal far behind.

There is something very agreeable in the motion of a sleigh along a good road. The soft muffled sound of the runners gliding over the snow harmonises well with the tinkling bells; and the rapid motion through the frosty air, together with the occasional jolt of going into a hollow or over a hillock, is very exhilarating, and we enjoyed our drive very much for the first hour or so. But, alas! human happiness is seldom of long duration, as we soon discovered; for, just as I was falling into a comfortable doze, bang! went the sleigh into a deep "cahoe," which most effectually wakened me. Now these same "cahoes" are among the disadvantages attending sleigh-travelling in Canada. They are nothing more or less than deep hollows or undulations in the road, into which the sleighs unexpectedly plunge, thereby pitching the traveller roughly forward; and upon the horses jerking the vehicles out of them, throwing him backward in a way that is pretty sure to bring his head into closer acquaintance with the back of the sleigh than is quite agreeable, particularly if he be a novice in sleigh-travelling. Those which we now encountered were certainly the worst I ever travelled over, rising in succession like the waves of the sea, and making our conveyance plunge sometimes so roughly that I expected it to go to pieces. Indeed, I cannot understand how wood and iron could stand the crashes to which we were exposed. In this way we jolted along, sometimes over good, sometimes over bad roads, till about nine o'clock, when we stopped at a neat, comfortable-looking inn, where the driver changed his horses, and the passengers sat down to a hurried breakfast.

The morning turned out beautifully clear and warm, at least in comparison with what it had been; and upon re-entering the sleigh we all looked extremely happy, and disposed to be pleased with everything and everybody. The country through which we now passed was picturesque and varied. Hills and valleys, covered with glittering snow and dark pines, followed each other in endless succession; while in every valley, and from every mountain-top, we saw hundreds of hamlets and villages, whose little streets and thoroughfares were crowded with busy *habitants*, engaged in their various occupations and winter traffic.

The laughing voices of merry little children romping along the roads accorded harmoniously with the lively tinkling of their parents' sleigh-bells as they set out for the market with the produce of their farms, or, dressed in their whitest blanket capotes and smartest *bonnets rouges*, accompanied their wives and daughters to a marriage or a festival. The scene was rendered still more pleasing by the extreme clearness of the frosty air and the deep blue of the sky; while the weather was just cold enough to make the rapid motion of our sleighs agreeable and necessary.

In some places the roads were extremely precipitous; and when we arrived at the foot of a large hill we used generally to get out and walk, preferring this to being dragged slowly up by the jaded horses.

During the day our sleighs were upset several times; but Mr Stone and I, in the "extra," suffered more in this way than those of the regular stage, as it was much narrower, and, consequently, more liable to tip over. Upon upsetting, it unaccountably happened that poor Mr Stone was always undermost. But he submitted to his fate most stoically; though from the nature of things my elbow invariably thrust him deep into the snow, on which, after being extricated, a splendid profile impression was left, to serve as a warning to other travellers, and to show them that a gentleman had been *cast* there.

As very little danger, however, attended these accidents, they only afforded subject for mirth at the time, and conversation at the end of the stage—except once, when the sleigh turned over so rapidly, that I was thrown with considerable force against the roof, which, being of a kind of slight framework, covered with painted canvas, offered but small opposition to my flight; my head, consequently, went quite through it, and my unfortunate nose was divested to rather an alarming extent of its cutaneous covering. With this exception, we proceeded safely and merrily along, and about seven o'clock in the evening arrived at the small town of Three Rivers.

Early next morning we resumed our journey, and about four in the afternoon arrived at the famous city of Quebec, without having encountered any very interesting adventures by the way.

The first sight we had of Quebec was certainly anything but prepossessing. A recent fire in the lower town had completely destroyed a large portion of it; and the first street I passed through was nothing but a gaunt row of blackened chimneys and skeleton houses, which had a very melancholy, ghostlike appearance when contrasted with the white snow. As we advanced, however, to where the fire had been checked, the streets assumed a more agreeable aspect—shops were open here and there, and workmen busily employed in repairing damaged houses and pulling down dangerous ones. Upon arriving at the steep street which leads from the lower town to within the walls, the immense strength of the ramparts and fortifications struck me forcibly. The road up which we passed to the gate was very narrow: on one side a steep hill descended to the lower town; and on the other towered the city walls, pierced all over with loopholes, and bristling with cannon. At the head of the road, in an angle of the wall, two silent but grim-looking guns pointed their muzzles directly down the road, so as to command it from one end to the other. All the other parts of the walls that I happened to see were even more strongly fortified than this.

The streets of Quebec are very steep, much more so than those of Edinburgh; and it requires no small exertion to mount one or two without stopping to breathe at the top. Upon the whole, it is anything but a pretty town (at least in winter), the houses being high, and the streets very narrow. The buildings, too, are commonplace; and the monument to Wolfe and Montcalm is a very insignificant affair. In fact, Quebec can boast of little else than the magnificent views it commands from the ramparts, and the impregnable strength of its fortifications. Some of the suburban villas, however, are very beautiful; and although I saw them in winter, yet I could form some idea of the enchanting places they must be in summer.

After spending three pleasant days here, we got into our sleigh again, and resumed our journey.

No stages ran below Quebec, so that we now travelled in the sleigh of a farmer, who happened to be going down part of the way.

Soon after leaving the city, we passed quite close to the famous Falls of Montmorenci. They are as high, if not higher, than those of Niagara, but I thought them rather tame, being nothing but a broad curtain of water falling over an even cliff, and quite devoid of picturesque scenery. A curious cone of ice, formed by the spray, rose nearly half-way up the falls.

The scenery below Quebec is much more rugged and mountainous than that above; and as we advanced the marks of civilisation began gradually to disappear—villages became scarcer, and roads worse, till at last we came to the shanties of the wood-cutters, with here and there a solitary farmhouse. Still, however, we occasionally met a few sleighs, with the conductors of which our driver seemed to be intimately acquainted. These little interruptions broke, in a great degree, the monotony of the journey; and we always felt happier for an hour after having passed and exchanged with a Canadian a cheerful *bonjour*.

Our driver happened to be a very agreeable man, and more intelligent than most Canadians of his class; moreover, he had a good voice, and when we came to a level part of the road I requested him to sing me a song—which he did at once, singing with a clear, strong, manly voice the most beautiful French air I ever heard; both the name and air, however, I have now forgotten. He then asked me to sing—which I did without further ceremony, treating him to one of the ancient melodies of Scotland; and thus, with solos and duets, we beguiled the tedium of the road, and filled the woods with melody! much to the annoyance of the unmusical American feathered tribes, and to the edification of our horse, who pricked up his ears, and often glanced backwards, apparently in extreme surprise.

Towards evening the driver told us that we should soon arrive at Baie de St. Paul; and in half an hour more our weary horse dragged us slowly to the top of a hill, whence we had a splendid view of the village. In all the miles of country I had passed over, I had seen nothing to equal the exquisite beauty of the Vale of Baie de St. Paul. From the hill on which we stood the whole valley, of many miles in extent, was visible. It was perfectly level, and covered from end to end with thousands of little hamlets, and several churches, with here and there a few small patches of forest. The course of a little rivulet, which meanders through it in summer, was apparent, even though covered with snow. At the mouth of this several schooners and small vessels lay embedded in ice; beyond which rolled the dark, ice-laden waves of the Gulf of St. Lawrence. The whole valley teemed with human life. Hundreds of Canadians, in their graceful sleighs and carioles, flew over the numerous roads intersecting the country; and the faint sound of tinkling bells floated gently up the mountain-side, till it reached the elevated position on which we stood. The whole scene was exquisitely calm and peaceful, forming a strange and striking contrast to the country round it. Like the Happy Valley of Rasselas, it was surrounded by the most

FALLS OF MONTMORENCI

LUMBERERS.

wild and rugged mountains, which rose in endless succession, one behind another, stretching away in the distance till they resembled a faint blue wave on the horizon. In this beautiful place we spent the night, and the following at Mal Baie. This village was also pretty, but after Baie de St. Paul I could but little admire it.

Next night we slept in a shanty belonging to the timber-cutters on the coast of the gulf, which was truly the most wretched abode, except an Indian tent, I ever had the chance (or mischance) to sleep in. It was a small log-hut, with only one room; a low door—to enter which we had to stoop—and a solitary square window, filled with parchment in lieu of glass. The furniture was of the coarsest description, and certainly not too abundant. Everything was extremely dirty, and the close air was further adulterated with thick clouds of tobacco smoke, which curled from the pipes of half a dozen wood-choppers. Such was the place in which we passed the night; and glad was I when the first blush of day summoned us to resume our travels. We now entered our sleigh for the last time, and after a short drive arrived at the termination of the horse road. Here we got out, and rested a short time in a shanty, preparatory to taking to our snow-shoes.

The road now lay through the primeval forest, and fortunately it proved to be pretty well beaten, so we walked lightly along, with our snow-shoes under our arms. In the afternoon we arrived at another shanty, having walked about eighteen miles. Here we found a gentleman who superintended the operations of the lumberers, or wood-cutters. He kindly offered to drive us to Canard River, a place not far distant from the termination of our journey. I need scarcely say we gladly accepted his offer, and in a short time arrived at the river Saguenay.

This river, owing to its immense depth, never freezes over at its mouth; so we crossed it in a boat, and on the evening of the 7th of February we arrived at the post of Tadousac.

This establishment belongs to the Hudson Bay Company, and is situated at the bottom of a large and deep bay adjoining the mouth of the river Saguenay. Unlike the posts of the north, it is merely a group of houses, scattered about in a hollow of the mountains, without any attempt at arrangement, and without a stockade. The post, when viewed from one of the hills in the neighbourhood, is rather picturesque; it is seen embedded in the mountains, and its white-topped houses contrast prettily with the few pines around it. A little to the right rolls the deep, unfathomable Saguenay, at the base of precipitous rocks and abrupt mountains, covered in some places with stunted pines, but for the most part bald-fronted. Up the riv-

VIEW OF TADOUSAC.

er, the view is interrupted by a large rock, nearly round, which juts out into the stream, and is named the "Bull." To the right lies the Bay of St. Catherine, with a new settlement at its head; and above this flows the majestic St. Lawrence, compared to which the broad Saguenay is but a thread.

Tadousac Bay is one of the finest natural harbours in the St. Lawrence. Being very deep quite close to the shore, it is much frequented by vessels and craft of every description and dimension. Ships, schooners, barks, brigs, and bateaux lie calmly at anchor within a stone's-throw of the bushes on shore; others are seen beating about at the mouth of the harbour, attempting to enter; while numerous pilot boats sail up and down, almost under the windows of the house; and in the offing are hundreds of vessels, whose white sails glimmer on the horizon like the wings of sea-gulls, as they beat up for anchorage, or proceed on their course for England or Quebec. The magnificent panorama is closed by the distant hills of the opposite shore, blending with the azure sky. This, however, is the only view, the land being a monotonous repetition of bare granite hills and stunted pines (see note 1).

Here, then, for a time, my travels came to a close, and I set about making myself as comfortable in my new quarters as circumstances would permit.

Tadousac I found to be similar, in many respects, to the forts in the north. The country around was wild, mountainous, and inhabited only by a few Indians and wild animals. There was no society, excepting that of Mr Stone's family; the only other civilized being, above the rank of a labourer, being a gentleman who superintended a timber-cutting and log-sawing establishment, a quarter of a mile from the Company's post.

My *bourgeois*, Mr Stone, was a very kind man and an entertaining companion. He had left Scotland, his native land, when very young, and had ever since been travelling about and dwelling in the wild woods of America. A deep scar on the bridge of his nose showed that he had not passed through these savage countries scathless. The way in which he came by this scar was curious, so I may relate it here.

At one of the solitary forts in the wild regions on the west side of the Rocky Mountains, where my friend Mr Stone dwelt, the Indians were in the habit of selling horses, of which they had a great many, to the servants of the Hudson Bay Company. They had, however, an uncommonly disagreeable propensity to steal these horses again the moment a convenient opportunity presented itself; and to guard against the

gratification of this propensity was one of the many difficulties that the fur-traders had to encounter. Upon one occasion a fine horse was sold by an Indian to Mr Stone, the price
(probably several yards of cloth and a few pounds of tobacco)
paid, and the Indian went away. Not long after the horse was
stolen; but as this was an event that often happened, it was
soon forgotten. Winter passed away, spring thawed the lakes
and rivers, and soon a party of Indians arrived with furs and
horses to trade. They were of the Blackfoot tribe, and a wilder
set of fellows one would hardly wish to see. Being much in
the habit of fighting with the neighbouring tribes, they were
quite prepared for battle, and decorated with many of the tro-
phies of war. Scalp-locks hung from the skirts of their leather
shirts and leggins, eagles' feathers and beads ornamented their
heads, and their faces were painted with stripes of black and
red paint.

After conversing with them a short time, they were admitted through the wicket one by one, and their arms taken
from them and locked up. This precaution was rendered necessary at these posts, as the Indians used to buy spirits, and
often quarrelled with each other; but, having no arms, of
course they could do themselves little damage. When about
a dozen of them had entered, the gate was shut, and Mr Stone
proceeded to trade their furs and examine their horses, when
he beheld, to his surprise, the horse that had been stolen
from him the summer before; and upon asking to whom it
belonged, the same Indian who had formerly sold it to him
stood forward and said it was his. Mr Stone (an exceedingly
quiet, good-natured man, but, like many men of this stamp,
very passionate when roused) no sooner witnessed the fellow's
audacity than he seized a gun from one of his men and shot

the horse. The Indian instantly sprang upon him, but being a less powerful man than Mr Stone, and, withal, unaccustomed to use his fists, he was soon overcome, and pommelled out of the fort. Not content with this, Mr Stone followed him down to the Indian camp, pommelling him all the way. The instant, however, that the Indian found himself surrounded by his own friends, he faced about, and with a dozen warriors attacked Mr Stone and threw him on the ground, where they kicked and bruised him severely; whilst several boys of the tribe hovered around him with bows and arrows, waiting a favourable opportunity to shoot him. Suddenly a savage came forward with a large stone in his hand, and, standing over his fallen enemy, raised it high in the air and dashed it down upon his face. My friend, when telling me the story, said that he had just time, upon seeing the stone in the act of falling, to commend his spirit to God ere he was rendered insensible. The merciful God, to whom he thus looked for help at the eleventh hour, did not desert him. Several men belonging to the fort, seeing the turn things took, hastily armed themselves, and hurrying out to the rescue, arrived just at the critical moment when the stone was dashed in his face. Though too late to prevent this, they were in time to prevent a repetition of the blow; and after a short scuffle with the Indians, without any blood shed, they succeeded in carrying their master up to the fort, where he soon recovered. The deep cut made by the stone on the bridge of his nose left an indelible scar.

Besides Mr Stone, I had another companion—namely, Mr Jordan, a clerk, who inhabited the same office with me, and slept in the same bedroom, during the whole winter. He was a fine-looking athletic half-breed, who had been partially educated, but had spent much more of his life among

Indians than among civilized men. He used to be sent about the country to trade with the natives, and consequently led a much more active life than I did. One part of his business, during the early months of spring, was hunting seals. This was an amusing, though, withal, rather a murderous kind of sport. The manner of it was this:—

My friend Jordan chose a fine day for his excursion, and, embarking in a boat with six or seven men, sailed a few miles down the St. Lawrence, till he came to a low flat point. In a small bay near this he drew up the boat, and then went into the woods with his party, where each man cut a large pole or club. Arming themselves with these, they waited until the tide receded and left the point dry. In a short time one or two seals crawled out of the sea to bask upon the shore; soon several more appeared, and ere long a band of more than a hundred lay sunning themselves upon the beach. The ambuscade now prepared to attack the enemy. Creeping stealthily down as near as possible without being discovered, they simultaneously rushed upon the astonished animals; and the tragic scene of slaughter, mingled with melodramatic and comic incidents, that ensued, baffles all description. In one place might be seen my friend Jordan swinging a huge club round with his powerful arms, and dealing death and destruction at every blow; while in another place a poor weazened-looking Scotchman (who had formerly been a tailor! and to whom the work was new) advanced, with cautious trepidation, towards a huge seal, which spluttered and splashed fearfully in its endeavours to reach the sea, and dealt it a blow on the back. He might as well have hit a rock. The slight rap had only the effect of making the animal show its teeth; at which sight the tailor retreated precipitately, and, striking his heel against a rock, fell backwards into a pool of water, where he rolled over and over—impressed, apparently, with the idea that he was attacked by all the seals in the sea. His next essay, however, was more successful, and in a few minutes he killed several, having learned to hit on the head instead of on the back. In less than a quarter of an hour they killed between twenty and thirty seals, which were stowed in the boat and conveyed to the post.

Nothing worth mentioning took place at Tadousac during my residence there. The winter became severe and stormy, confining us much to the house, and obliging us to lead very humdrum sort of lives. Indeed, the only thing that I can recollect as being at all interesting or amusing—except, of coarse, the society of my scientific and agreeable friend, Mr Stone, and his amiable family—was a huge barrel-organ, which, like the one that I had found at Oxford House, played a rich variety of psalm tunes, and a choice selection of Scotch reels—the grinding out of which formed the chief solace of my life, until the arrival of an auspicious day when I received sudden orders to prepare for another journey.

Note 1: It may be well to say that the above description applied to the country only in the summer and autumn months. It is now, we believe, an important summer resort, and a comparatively populous place.

12

A JOURNEY ON SNOW-SHOES

*—Evils of Snow-Shoe Travelling in Spring
—Value of Tea to a Tired Man—Encamp in the Snow
—Isle Jérémie—Canoeing and Boating on
the Gulf of St. Lawrence—Amateur Navigating
—Seven Islands—A Narrow Escape—Conclusion*

IT WAS ON A COLD, bleak morning, about the beginning of March 1846, that I awoke from a comfortable snooze in my bedroom at Tadousac, and recollected that in a few hours I must take leave of my present quarters, and travel, on snow-shoes, sixty miles down the Gulf of St. Lawrence to the post of Isle Jérémie.

The wind howled mournfully through the leafless trees, and a few flakes of snow fell upon the window as I looked out upon the cheerless prospect. Winter—cold, biting, frosty winter—still reigned around. The shores of Tadousac Bay were still covered with the same coat of ice that had bound them up four months before; and the broad St. Lawrence still flowed on, black as ink, and laden with immense fields and hummocks of dirty ice, brought down from the banks of the river above. The land presented one uniform chilling prospect of bare trees and deep snow, over which I was soon to traverse many a weary mile.

There is nothing, however, like taking things philosophically; so, after venting my spite at the weather in one or two short grumbles, I sat down in a passable state of equanimity to breakfast. During the meal I discussed with Mr Stone the prospects of the impending journey, and indulged in a few excursive remarks upon snow-shoe travelling, whilst he related a few incidents of his own eventful career in the country.

On one occasion he was sent off upon a long journey over the snow, where the country was so mountainous that snowshoe walking was rendered exceedingly painful, by the feet slipping forward against the front bar of the shoe when descending the hills. After he had accomplished a good part of his journey, two large blisters rose under the nails of his great toes; and soon the nails themselves came off. Still he must go on, or die in the woods; so he was obliged to *tie* the nails on his toes each morning before starting, for the purpose of protecting the tender parts beneath; and every evening he wrapped them up carefully in a piece of rag, and put them into his waistcoat pocket—*being afraid of losing them if he kept them on all night.*

After breakfast I took leave of my friends at Tadousac, and, with a pair of snow-shoes under my arm, followed my companion Jordan to the boat which was to convey me the first twenty miles of the journey, and then land me, with one man, who was to be my only companion. In the boat was seated a Roman Catholic priest, on his way to visit a party of Indians a short distance down the gulf. The shivering men shipped their oars in silence, and we glided through the black water, while the ice grated harshly against the boat's sides as we rounded Point Rouge. Another pull, and Tadousac was hidden from our view.

Few things can be more comfortless or depressing than a sail down the Gulf of St. Lawrence on a gloomy winter's day, with the thermometer at zero! The water looks so black and cold, and the sky so gray, that it makes one shudder, and turn to look upon the land. But there no cheering prospect meets the view. Rocks—cold, hard, misanthropic rocks—grin from beneath volumes of snow; and the few stunted black-looking pines that dot the banks here and there only tend to render the scene more desolate. No birds fly about to enliven the traveller; and the only sound that meets the ear, besides the low sighing of the cold, cold wind, is the crashing of immense fields of ice, as they meet and war in the eddies of opposing currents. Fortunately, however, there was no ice near the shore, and we met with little interruption on the way. The priest bore the cold like a stoic; and my friend Jordan, being made, meta-phorically speaking, of iron, treated it with the contemptuous indifference that might be expected from such metal.

In the evening we arrived at Esquimain River, where we took up our quarters in a small log-hut belonging to a poor seal-fisher, whose family, and a few men who attended a saw-mill a short distance off, were the only inhabitants of this little hamlet. Here we remained all night, and prepared our snow-shoes for the morrow, as the boat was there to leave us and return to Tadousac. The night was calm and frosty, and everything gave promise of fine weather for our journey. But who can tell what an hour will bring forth? Before morning the weather became milder, and soon it began to *thaw*. A fine warm day, with a bright sun, be it known, is one of the most dreadful calamities that can befall a snowshoe traveller, as the snow then becomes soft and sticky, thereby drenching the feet and snow-shoes, which become painfully heavy from the quantity of snow which sticks to and falls upon them. In cold frosty weather the snow is dry, crisp, and fine, so that it falls through the network of the snow-shoe without leaving a feather's weight behind, while the feet are dry and warm; but a thaw!—oh! it is useless attempting to recapitulate the miseries attending a thaw; my next day's experience will show what it is.

Early on the following morning I jumped from my bed on the floor of the hut, and proceeded to equip myself for the march. The apartment in which I had passed the night presented a curious appearance. It measured about sixteen feet by twelve, and the greater part of this space was occupied by two beds, on which lay, in every imaginable position, the different members of the half-breed family to whom the mansion belonged. In the centre of the room stood a coarsely-constructed deal table, on which lay in confusion the remains of the preceding night's supper. On the right of this, a large gaudily-painted Yankee clock graced the wall, and stared down upon the sleeping figures of the men. This, with a few rough wooden chairs and a small cupboard, comprised all the furniture of the house.

I soon singled out *my* man from among the sleeping figures on the floor, and bade him equip himself for the road— or rather for the march, for road we had none. In half an hour we were ready; and having fortified ourselves with a cup of weak tea and a slice of bread, left the house and commenced our journey.

My man Bezeau (a French Canadian) was dressed in a blue striped cotton shirt, of very coarse quality, and a pair of corduroys, strapped round his waist with a scarlet belt. Over these he wore a pair of blue cloth leggins, neatly bound with orange-coloured ribbon. A Glengarry bonnet covered his head; and two pairs of flannel socks, under a pair of raw seal-skin shoes, protected his feet from the cold. His burden consisted of my carpet-bag, two days' provisions, and a blue cloth capote—which latter he carried over his shoulder, the weather being warm. My dress consisted of a scarlet flannel shirt, and a pair of *étoffe du pays* trousers, which were fastened round my waist by a leathern belt, from which depended a small hunting-knife; a foraging cap and deer-skin moccasins completed my costume. My burden was a large green blanket, a greatcoat, and a tin tea-kettle. Our only arms of offence or defence were the little hunting-knife before mentioned, and a small axe for felling trees, should we wish to make a fire. We brought no guns, as there was little prospect of meeting any game on the road; and it behoves one, when travelling on foot, to carry as little as possible.

Thus we started from Esquimain River. The best joke, however, of all was, that neither I nor my man had ever travelled that way before! All we knew was, that we had to walk fifty miles through an uninhabited country, and that then we should, or at least ought to, reach Isle Jérémie. There were two solitary houses, however, that we had to pass on the way; the one an outpost of the Hudson Bay Company, the other a saw-mill belonging to one of the lumber companies (or timber-traders) in Quebec. In fact, the best idea of our situation may be had from the following lines, which may be supposed

to have been uttered by the establishment to which we were
bound:—

> Through the woods, through the woods, follow and find me,
> Search every hollow, and dingle, and dell;
> To the right, left, or front, you may pass, or behind me,
> Unless you are careful, and look for me well.

The first part of our road lay along the shores of the St.
Lawrence.

The sun shone brightly, and the drifting ice in the gulf
glittered in its rays as it flowed slowly out to sea; but ere long
the warm rays acted upon the snow, and rendered walking
toilsome and fatiguing. After about an hour's walk along the
shore, we arrived at the last hut we were likely to see that day.
It was inhabited by an Indian and his family. Here we rested a
few minutes, and I renewed my snow-shoe lines, the old ones
having broken by the way.

Shortly after this we passed the wreck of what had once
been a fine ship. She lay crushed and dismasted among the
rocks and lumps of ice which lined the desolate shore, her
decks and the stumps of her masts drifted over with snow.
Six short months before, she had bounded over the Atlantic wave in all the panoply of sail and rigging pertaining to
a large three-master, inclosing in her sturdy hull full many a
daring heart beating high with sanguine hopes, and dreaming
of fame and glory, or perchance of home. But now, how great
the change!—her sails and masts uprooted, and her helm—
the seaman's confidence and safeguard—gone; her bed upon
the rocks and pebbles of a dreary shore; and her shattered hull
hung round with icicles, and wrapped in the cold embraces of
the wintry ocean. Few things, I think, can have a more inex-

pressibly melancholy appearance than a wreck upon a rocky and deserted shore in winter.

The road now began to get extremely bad. The ice, over which we had to walk for miles, had been covered with about six inches of water and snow. A sharp frost during the night had covered this with a cake of ice sufficiently strong to bear us up until we got fairly upon it, and were preparing to take another step, when down it went—so that we had a sort of natural treadmill to exercise ourselves upon all day; while every time we sank, as a matter of course our snowshoes were covered with a mixture of water, snow, and broken ice, to extricate our feet from which almost pulled our legs out of the sockets.

In this way we plodded slowly and painfully along, till we came to a part of the shore where the ice had been entirely carried off, leaving the sandy beach uncovered for about two miles. We gladly took advantage of this, and, pulling off our snow-shoes, walked along among the shells and tangle of the sea-shore. At this agreeable part of our journey, while we walked lightly along, with our snow-shoes under our arms, I fell into a reverie upon the superior advantages of travelling in cold weather, and the delights of walking on sandy beaches in contrast with wet snow. These cogitations, however, were suddenly interrupted by our arrival at the place where the ice had parted from the general mass; so, with a deep sigh, we resumed our snow-shoes. My feet, from the friction of the lines, now began to feel very painful; so, having walked about ten miles, I proposed taking a rest. To this my man, who seemed rather tired, gladly acceded, and we proceeded to light a fire under the stem of a fallen tree which opportunely presented itself.

Here we sat down comfortably together; and while our

ENCAMPED IN THE SNOW.

wet shoes and socks dried before the blazing fire, and our chafed toes wriggled joyously at being relieved from the painful harness of the snow-shoes, we swallowed a cup of congou with a degree of luxurious enjoyment, appreciable only by those who have walked themselves into a state of great exhaustion after a hurried breakfast.

Greatly refreshed by the tea, we resumed our journey in better spirits, and even affected to believe we were taking an agreeable afternoon walk for the first mile or so. We soon, however, fell to zero again, as we gazed wistfully upon the long line of coast stretching away to the horizon. But there was no help for it; on we splashed, sometimes through ice, water, and snow, and sometimes across the shingly beach, till the day was far spent, when I became so exhausted that I could scarcely drag one foot after the other, and moved along almost mechanically. My man, too, strong as he was, exhibited symptoms of fatigue; though, to do him justice, he was at least seven times more heavily laden than I.

While we jogged slowly along in this unenviable condition, a lump of ice offered so tempting a seat that we simultaneously proposed to sit down. This was very foolish. Resting without a fire is bad at all times; and the exhausted condition we were then in made it far worse, as I soon found to my cost. Tired as I was before, I could have walked a good deal farther; but no sooner did I rise again to my feet than an inexpressible weakness overcame me, and I felt that I could go no farther. This my man soon perceived, and proposed making a fire and having a cup of tea; and then, if I felt better, we might proceed. This I agreed to; so, entering the woods, we dug a hole in the snow, and in half an hour had a fire blazing in it that would have roasted an ox! In a short time a panful of snow was converted into hot tea; and as I sat sipping this, and watching the white smoke as it wreathed upwards from the pipe of my good-natured guide, I never felt rest more delightful.

The tea refreshed us so much that we resumed our journey, intending, if possible, to reach Port Neuf during the night; and as we calculated that we had walked between fifteen and eighteen miles, we hoped to reach it in a few hours.

Away, then, we went, and plodded on till dark without reaching the post; nevertheless, being determined to travel as long as we could, we pushed on till near midnight, when, being quite *done up*, and seeing no sign of the establishment, we called a council of war, and sat down on a lump of ice to discuss our difficulties. I suggested that if we had not already passed the post, in all probability we should do so, if we continued to travel any farther in the dark. My companion admitted that he entertained precisely the same views on the subject; and, furthermore, that as we both seemed pretty tired, and there happened to be a nice little clump of willows, intermixed with pine trees, close at hand, his opinion was that nothing better could be done than encamping for the night. I agreed to this; and the resolution being carried unanimously, the council adjourned, and we proceeded to make our encampment.

First of all, the snow was dug away from the foot of a large pine with our snow-shoes, which we used as spades; and when a space of about ten feet long, by six broad, was cleared, we covered it with pine branches at one end, and made a roaring fire against the tree at the other. The snow rose all around to the height of about four feet, so that when our fire blazed cheerily, and our supper was spread out before it upon my green blanket, we looked very comfortable indeed—and what was of much more consequence, *felt* so. Supper consisted of a cup of tea, a loaf of bread, and a lump of salt butter. After having partaken largely of these delicacies, we threw a fresh log upon the fire, and rolling ourselves in our blankets, were soon buried in repose.

Next morning, on awaking, the first thing I became aware of was the fact that it was raining, and heavily too, in the shape of a Scotch mist. I could scarcely believe it, and rubbed my eyes to make sure; but there was no mistake about it at all. The sky was gray, cold, and dismal, and the blanket quite wet! "Well," thought I, as I fell back in a sort of mute despair, "this is certainly precious weather for snow-shoe travelling!" I nudged my sleeping companion, and the look of melancholy resignation which he put on, as he became gradually aware of the state of matters, convinced me that bad as yesterday had been, to-day would be far worse.

When I got upon my legs, I found that every joint in my body was stiffer than the rustiest hinge ever heard of in the annals of doors! and my feet as tender as a chicken's, with huge blisters all over them. Bezeau, however, though a little stiff, was otherwise quite well, being well inured to hardships of every description.

It is needless to recount the miseries of the five miles' walk that we had to make before arriving at Port Neuf, over ground that was literally next to impassable. About nine o'clock we reached the house, and remained there for the rest of the day. Here, for three days, we were hospitably entertained by the Canadian family inhabiting the place; during this time it rained and thawed so heavily that we could not venture to re-sume our journey.

On the 16th the weather became colder, and Bezeau announced his opinion that we might venture to proceed. Glad to be once more on the move—for fears of being arrest-ed altogether by the setting-in of spring had begun to beset me—I once more put on my snow-shoes; and, bidding adieu to the hospitable inmates of Port Neuf, we again wended our weary way along the coast. Alas! our misfortunes had not yet ceased. The snow was much softer than we anticipated, and the blisters on my feet, which had nearly healed during the time we stayed at Port Neuf, were now torn open afresh. After a painful and laborious walk of eight or nine miles, we arrived at a small house, where a few enterprising men lived who had penetrated thus far down the gulf to erect a saw-mill.

Here we found, to our infinite joy, a small flat-bottomed boat, capable of carrying two or three men; so, without delay, we launched it, and putting our snow-shoes and provisions into it, my man and I jumped in, and pulled away down the gulf, intending to finish the twenty miles that still remained of our journey by water. We were obliged to pull a long way out to sea, to avoid the ice which lined the shore, and our course lay a good deal among drifting masses.

Half an hour after we embarked a snow-storm came on, but still we pulled along, preferring anything to resuming the snow-shoes.

After a few hours' rowing, we rested on our oars, and re-freshed ourselves with a slice of bread and a glass of rum—which latter, having forgotten to bring water with us, we were obliged to drink pure. We certainly cut a strange figure, while thus lunching in our little boat—surrounded by ice, and look-ing hazy through the thickly falling snow, which prevented us from seeing very far ahead, and made the mountains on shore look quite spectral.

For about five miles we pulled along in a straight line, af-ter which the ice trended outwards, and finally brought us to a stand-still by running straight out to sea. This was an inter-ruption we were not at all prepared for, and we felt rather un-decided how to proceed. After a little confabulation, we deter-mined to pull out, and see if the ice did not again turn in the proper direction; but after pulling straight out for a quarter of a mile, we perceived, or imagined we perceived, to our horror, that the ice, instead of being stationary, as we supposed it to be, was floating slowly out to sea with the wind, and carrying us along with it. No time was to be lost; so, wheeling about, we rowed with all our strength for the shore, and after a pretty stiff pull gained the solid ice. Here we hauled the flat up out of the water with great difficulty, and once more put on our snow-shoes.

Our road still lay along shore, and, as the weather was getting colder, we proceeded along much more easily than heretofore. In an hour or two the snow ceased to fall, and showed us that the ice was *not* drifting, but that it ran so far out to sea that it would have proved a bar to our further progress by water at any rate.

The last ten miles of our journey now lay before us; and we sat down, before starting, to have another bite of bread and a pull at the rum bottle; after which, we trudged along in silence. The peculiar compression of my guide's lips, and the length of step that he now adopted, showed me that he had made up his mind to get through the last part of the journey without stopping; so, tightening my belt, and bending my head forward, I plodded on, solacing myself as we advanced by humming, "Follow, follow, over mountain,—follow, follow, over sea!" etcetera.

About four or five o'clock in the afternoon, upon rounding a point, we were a little excited by perceiving evident signs of the axe having been at work in the forest; and a little farther on discovered, to our inexpressible joy, a small piece of ground enclosed as a garden. This led us to suppose that the post could not be far off, so we pushed forward rapidly; and upon gaining the summit of a small eminence, beheld with delight the post of Isle Jérémie.

This establishment, like most of the others on the St. Lawrence, is merely a collection of scattered buildings, most of which are storehouses and stables. It stands in a hollow of the mountains, and close to a large bay, where sundry small boats and a sloop lay quietly at anchor. Upon a little hillock close to the principal house is a Roman Catholic chapel; and behind it stretches away the broad St. Lawrence, the south shore of which is indistinctly seen on the horizon. We had not much inclination, however, to admire the scenery just then; so, hastening down the hill, my man walked into the men's house, where in five minutes he was busily engaged eating bread and pork, and recounting his adventures to a circle of admiring friends; while I warmed myself beside a comfortable fire in the hall, and chatted with the gentleman in charge of the establishment.

At Isle Jérémie I remained about six weeks; or rather, I should say, belonged to the establishment for that time, as during a great part of it I was absent from the post. Mr Coral, soon after my arrival, went to visit the Company's posts lower down the St. Lawrence, leaving me in charge of Isle Jérémie; and as I had little or nothing to do in the way of business (our Indians not having arrived from the interior), most of my time was spent in reading and shooting.

It was here I took my first lessons in navigation—I mean in a practical way; as for the scientific part of the business, that was deferred to a more favourable opportunity—and, truly, the lessons were rather rough. The way of it was this:— Our flour at Isle Jérémie had run out. Indians were arriving every day calling loudly for flour, and more were expected; so Mr Coral told me, one fine morning, to get ready to go to Tadousac in the boat for a load of flour. This I prepared to do at once, and started after breakfast in a large boat, manned by two men. The wind was fair, and I fired a couple of shots with my fowling-piece, as we cleared the harbour, in answer to an equal number of salutes from two iron cannons that stood in front of the house. By-the-bye, one of these guns had a melancholy interest attached to it a few months after this. While firing a salute of fourteen rounds, in honour of the arrival of a Roman Catholic bishop, one of them exploded while the man who acted as gunner was employed in ramming home the cartridge, and blew him about twenty yards down the bank. The unfortunate man expired in a few hours. Poor fellow! he was a fine little Canadian, and had sailed with me, not many weeks before, in a voyage up the St. Lawrence. But to return. Our voyage, during the first few days, was prosperous enough, and I amused myself in shooting the gulls which were foolish enough to come within range of my gun, and in recognizing the various places along shore where I had rested and slept on the memorable occasion of my snow-shoe trip.

But when did the St. Lawrence prove friendly for an entire voyage? Certainly not when I had the pleasure of ploughing its rascally waters! The remainder of our voyage was a succession of squalls, calms, contrary winds, sticking on shoals for hours, and being detained on shore, with an accompaniment of pitching, tossing, oscillation and botheration, that baffles all description. However, time brings the greatest miseries to an end; and in the process of time we arrived at Tadousac—loaded our boat deeply with flour—shook hands with our friends—related our adventures—bade them adieu—and again found ourselves scudding down the St. Lawrence, with a snoring breeze on our quarter.

Now this was truly a most delectable state of things, when contrasted with our wretched trip up; so we wrapped our blankets round us (for it was very cold), and felicitated ourselves considerably on such good fortune. It was rather premature, however; as, not long after, we had a very narrow escape from being swamped. The wind, as I said before, was pretty strong, and it continued so the whole way; so that on the evening of the second day we came within sight of Isle Jérémie, while running before a stiff breeze, through the green waves which were covered with foam. Our boat had a "drooping nose," and was extremely partial to what the men termed "drinking;" in other words, it shipped a good deal of water over the bows. Now it happened that while we were straining our eyes ahead, to catch a sight of our haven, an insidious squall was creeping fast down behind us. The first intimation we had of its presence was a loud and ominous hiss, which made us turn our heads round rather smartly; but it was too late—for with a howl, that appeared to be quite vicious the wind burst upon our sails, and buried the boat in the water, which rushed in a cataract over the bows, and nearly filled us in a moment, although the steersman threw her into the wind immediately. The sheets were instantly let go, and one of the men, who happened to be a sailor, jumped up, and, seizing an axe, began to cut down the main-mast, at the same time exclaiming to the steersman, "You've done for us now, Cooper!" He was mistaken, however, for the sails were taken in just in time to save us; and, while the boat lay tumbling in the sea, we all began to bail, with anything we could lay hands on, as fast as we could. In a few minutes the boat was lightened enough to allow of our hoisting the fore-sail; and about half an hour afterwards we were safely anchored in the harbour.

This happened within about three or four hundred yards of the shore; yet the best swimmer in the world would have been drowned ere he reached it, as the water was so bitterly cold, that when I was bailing for my life, and, consequently, in pretty violent exercise, my hands became quite benumbed and almost powerless.

Shortly after this I was again sent up to Tadousac, in charge of a small bateau, of about ten or fifteen tons, with a number of shipwrecked seamen on board. These unfortunate men had been cast on shore about the commencement of winter, on an uninhabited part of the coast, and had remained without provisions or fire for a long time, till they were discovered by a gentleman of the Hudson Bay Company, and conveyed over the snow in sleighs to the nearest establishment, which happened to be Isle Jérémie. Here they remained all winter, in a most dreadfully mutilated condition, some of them having been desperately frozen. One of the poor fellows, a negro, had one of his feet frozen off at the ankle, and had lost all the toes and the heel of the other, the bone being laid bare for about an inch and a half. Mr Coral, the gentleman who had saved them, did all in his power to relieve their distress—amputating their frozen limbs, and dressing their wounds, while they were provided with food and warm clothing. I am sorry to say, however, that these men, who would have perished had it not been for Mr Coral's care of them, were the first, upon arriving at Quebec the following spring, to open their mouths in violent reproach and bitter invective against him; forgetting that, while their only charge against him was a little severity in refusing them a few trifling and unnecessary luxuries, he had saved them from a painful and lingering death.

In a couple of days we arrived at Tadousac the second

time, to the no small astonishment of my brother scribbler residing there. After reloading our craft, we directed our course once more down the gulf.

This time the wind was also favourable, but, unfortunately, a little too strong; so we were obliged, in the evening, to come to an anchor in Esquimain River. This river has good anchorage close to the bank, but is very deep in the lead, or current; this, however, we did not know at the time, and seeing a small schooner close to shore, we rounded to a few fathoms outside of her, and let go our anchor. Whirr! went the chain—ten! twelve! sixteen! till at last forty fathoms ran out, and only a little bit remained on board, and still we had no bottom. After attaching our spare cable to the other one, the anchor at last grounded. This, however, was a dangerous situation to remain in, as, if the wind blew strong, we would have to run out to sea, and so much cable would take a long time to get in; so I ordered my two men, in a very pompous, despotic way, to heave up the anchor again. But not a bit would it budge. We all heaved at the windlass; still the obstinate anchor held fast. Again we gave another heave, and smashed both the handspikes.

In this dilemma I begged assistance from the neighbouring schooner, and they kindly sent all their men on board with new handspikes; but our refractory anchor would *not* let go, and at last it was conjectured that it had got foul of a rock, and that it was not in the power of mortal man to move it. Under these pleasant circumstances we went to bed, in hopes that the falling tide might swing us clear before morning. This turned out just as we expected—or, rather, a little better—for next morning, when I went on deck, I found that we were drifting quietly down the gulf, stern foremost, all the sails snugly tied up, and the long cable dragging at the bows! Towards evening we arrived at Jérémie, and I gladly resigned command of the vessel to my first lieutenant.

One afternoon, near the middle of April, I sat sunning myself in the veranda before the door of the principal house at Isle Jérémie, and watched the fields of ice, as they floated down the Gulf of St. Lawrence, occasionally disappearing behind the body of a large pig, which stood upon a hillock close in front of me, and then reappearing again as the current swept them slowly past the intervening obstacle.

Mr Coral, with whom I had been leading a very quiet, harmless sort of life for a couple of weeks past, leant against a wooden post, gazing wistfully out to sea. Suddenly he turned towards me, and with great gravity told me that, as there was nothing particular for me to do at the establishment, he meant to send me down to Seven Islands, to relieve the gentleman at that post of his charge; adding, that as he wished me to set off the following morning at an early hour, I had better pack up a few things to-night.

Now, this order may not seem, at the first glance, a very dreadful one; but taking into consideration that Seven Islands is one hundred and twenty miles below the post at which I then resided, it did appear as if one would wish to think about it a little before starting. Not having time to think about it, however, I merely, in a sort of bantering desperation, signified my readiness to undertake a voyage to any part of the undis-covered world, at any moment he (Mr Coral) might think proper, and then vanished, to prepare myself for the voyage.

It was optional with me whether I should walk through one hundred and twenty miles of primeval and most impass-able forest, or paddle over an equal number of miles of water.

Preferring the latter, as being at once the less disagreeable and more expeditious method, I accordingly, on the following morning, embarked in a small Indian canoe, similar to the one in which I had formerly travelled with two Indians in the North-West. My companions were—a Canadian, who acted as steersman; a genuine Patlander, who ostensibly acted as bowsman, but in reality was more useful in the way of ballast; and a young Newfoundland dog, which I had got as a present from Mr Stone while at Tadousac.

When we were all in our allotted places, the canoe was quite full; and we started from Isle Jérémie in good spirits, with the broad, sun-like face of Mike Lynch looming over the bows of the canoe, and the black muzzle of Humbug (the dog) resting on its gunwale.

It is needless to describe the voyage minutely. We had the usual amount of bad and good weather, and ran the risk several times of upsetting; we had, also, several breakfasts, dinners, suppers, and beds in the forest; and on the afternoon of the third day we arrived at Goodbout, an establishment nearly half-way between the post I had left and the one to which I was bound. Here we stayed all night, proposing to start again on the morrow. But the weather was so stormy as to prevent us for a couple of days trusting ourselves out in a frail bark canoe.

Early on the third morning, however, I took my place as steersman in the stern of our craft (my former guide being obliged to leave me here), and my man Mike squeezed his unwieldy person into the bow. In the middle lay our provisions and baggage, over which the black muzzle of Humbug peered anxiously out upon the ocean. In this trim we paddled from the beach, amid a shower of advice to keep close to shore, in case the *big-fish*—alias, the whales—might take a fancy to upset us.

After a long paddle of five or six hours we arrived at Pointe des Monts, where rough weather obliged us to put ashore. Here I remained all night, and slept in the lighthouse—a cylindrical building of moderate height, which stands on a rock off Pointe des Monte, and serves to warn sailors off the numerous shoals with which this part of the gulf is filled. In the morning we fortunately found an Indian with his boat, who was just starting for Seven Islands; and after a little higgling, at which Mike proved himself quite an adept, he agreed to give us a lift for a few pounds of tobacco. Away, then, we went, with:—

> A wet sheet and a flowing sea,
> And a wind that followed fast,
> ploughing through the water in beautiful style.

The interior of our boat presented a truly ludicrous, and rather filthy scene. The Indian, who was a fine-looking man of about thirty, had brought his whole family—sons, daughters, brothers, sisters, wife, and mother—and a more heterogeneous mass of dirty, dark-skinned humanity I never before had the ill-luck to travel with. The mother of the flock was the most extraordinary being that I ever beheld. She must have been very near a hundred years old, as black and wrinkled as a singed hide, yet active and playful as a kitten. She was a very bad sailor, however, and dived down into the bottom of the boat the moment a puff of wind arose. Indians have a most extraordinary knack of diminishing their bulk, which is very convenient sometimes. Upon this occasion it was amusing to watch them settling gradually down, upon the slightest appearance of wind, until you might almost believe they had squeezed themselves quite through the bottom of the boat, and left only a few dirty blankets to tell the tale. Truly, one rarely meets with such a compact mass of human ballast. If, however, a slight lull occurred, or the sun peeped out from behind a cloud, there was immediately a perceptible increase in the bulk of the mass, and gradually a few heads appeared, then a leg, and soon a few arms; till at last the whole batch were up, laughing, talking, singing, eating, and chattering in a most uproarious state of confusion!

After the usual amount of storms, calms, and contrary winds, we arrived in safety at the post of Seven Islands, where I threw my worthy friend Mr Anderson into a state of considerable surprise and agitation by informing him that in the individual before him he beheld his august successor!

The establishment of Seven Islands is anything but an inviting place, although pretty enough on a fine day; and the general appearance of the surrounding scenery is lonely, wild, and desolate. The houses are built on a low sandy beach, at the bottom of the large bay of Seven Islands. The trees around are thinly scattered, and very small. In the background, rugged hills stretch as far as the eye can see; and in front, seven lofty islands, from which the bay and post derive their name, obstruct the view, affording only a partial glimpse of the open sea beyond. No human habitations exist within seventy miles of the place. Being out of the line of sailing, no vessels ever visit it, except when driven to the bay for shelter; and the bay is so large, that many vessels come in and go out again without having been observed. Altogether, I found it a lonely and desolate place, during a residence of nearly four months.

An extensive salmon-fishery is carried on at a large river called the Moisie, about eighteen miles below the post, where the Company sometimes catch and salt upwards of eighty and ninety tierces of fish.

During my sojourn there, I made one or two excursions to the fishery, a description of which may perhaps prove interesting to those versed in the more practical branches of ichthyology.

It was a lovely morning in June when Mr Anderson and I set out from Seven Islands on foot, with our coats (for the weather was warm) slung across our backs, and walked rapidly along the beach in the direction of the river Moisie. The weather was very calm, and the mosquitoes, consequently, rather annoying; but, as our progressive motion disconcerted their operations a little, we did not mind them much. The beach all the way was composed of fine hard sand, so that we found the walk very agreeable. A few loons dived about in the sea, and we passed two or three flocks of black ducks, known in some parts of the country by the name of "old wives;" but, having brought no gun with us, the old ladies were permitted to proceed on their way unmolested. The land all along presented the same uniform line of forest, with the yellow sand of the beach glittering at its edge; and as we cleared the islands, the boundless ocean opened upon our view.

In about four hours or so we arrived at the mouth of the Moisie, where the first fishery is established. Here we found that our men had caught and salted a good many salmon, some of which had just come from the nets, and lay on the grass, plump and glittering, in their pristine freshness. They looked very tempting, and we had one put in the kettle immediately; which, when we set to work at him soon afterwards, certainly did not belie his looks. The salmon had only commenced to ascend the river that day, and were being taken by fifties at a haul in the nets. The fishery was attended by three men, who kept seven or eight nets constantly in the water, which gave them enough of employment—two of them attending to the nets, while the third split, salted, and packed the fish in large vats. Here we spent the night, and slept in a small house about ten feet long by eight broad, built for the accommodation of the fishermen.

Next morning we embarked in a boat belonging to a trapper, and went up the river with a fair wind, to visit the fisheries higher up. On the way we passed a seal-net belonging to the owner of the boat, and at our request he visited it, and found seven or eight fine seals in it: they were all dead, and full of water. Seal-nets are made the same as salmon-nets, except that the mesh is larger, the seal having a pretty good-sized cranium of his own. After a good deal of unravelling and pulling, we got them all out of the net, and proceeded onward with our cargo.

The scenery on the river Moisie is pleasing: the banks are moderately high, and covered to the foot with the richest and most variegated verdure; while here and there, upon rounding some of the curvatures of the stream, long vistas of the river may be seen, embedded in luxuriant foliage. Thirteen or fourteen miles up the river is the Frog Creek fishery, at which we arrived late in the afternoon, and found that the man superintending it had taken a good many fish, and expected more. He visited his nets while we were there, but returned with only a few salmon. Some of them were badly cut up by the seals, which are the most formidable enemies of fishermen, as they eat and destroy many salmon, besides breaking the nets. We were detained here by rain all night, and slept in the small fishing-house.

Travelling makes people acquainted with strange beds as well as strange bed-fellows; but I question if many people can boast of having slept on a bed of *nets*. This we were obliged to do here, having brought no blankets with us, as we expected to have returned to the Point fishery in the evening. The bedstead was a long low platform, in one end of the little cabin, and was big enough to let four people sleep in it—two of us lying abreast at one end, and two more at the other end, feet to feet. A large salmon-net formed a pretty good mattress; another, spread out on top of us, served as a blanket; and a couple of trout-nets were excellent as pillows. From this *piscatorial* couch we arose early on the following morning, and breakfasted on a splendid fresh salmon; after which we resumed our journey. In a couple of hours we arrived at the Rapid fishery, where I found that my old friend Mike, the Irishman, had caught a great number of salmon. He was very bitter, however, in his remarks upon the seals, which it seems had made great havoc among his nets during the last two days. A black bear, too, was in the habit of visiting his station every morning, and, sitting on a rock not far off, watched his motions with great apparent interest while he took the fish out of the nets. Mike, poor man, regretted very much that he had no gun, as he might perhaps shoot "the baste." Bears are very destructive at times to the salted salmon, paying visits during the night to the vats, and carrying off and tearing to pieces far more than they are capable of devouring.

While inspecting the nets here, we witnessed an interesting seal-hunt. Two Indians, in separate canoes, were floating quietly in a small eddy, with their guns cocked, ready to fire at the first unfortunate seal that should show his head on the surface of the stream. They had not waited long when one popped up his head, and instantly got a shot, which evidently hurt him, as he splashed a little, and then dived. In a minute the Indian reloaded his gun, and paddled out into the stream, in order to have another shot the moment the seal rose for air: this he did in a short time, when another shot was fired, which turned him over apparently lifeless. The Indian then laid down his gun, and seizing his paddle, made towards the spot where the seal lay. He had scarcely approached a few yards, however, when it recovered a little, and dived—much to the Indian's chagrin, who had approached too near the head of a small rapid, and went down, stern foremost, just at the moment his friend the seal did the same. On arriving at the bottom, the animal, after one or two kicks, expired, and the Indian at last secured his prize. After this, we embarked again in our boat; and the wind *for once* determined to be accommodating, as it shifted in our favour, almost at the same time that we turned to retrace our way. In a few hours we arrived at the fishery near the mouth of the river, where we found supper just ready.

After supper, which we had about eight o'clock, the night looked so fine, and the mosquitoes in the little smoky house were so troublesome, that we determined to walk up to the post; so, ordering one of the men to follow us, away we went along the beach. The night was fine, though dark, and we trudged rapidly along. It was very tiresome work, however, as, the tide being full, we were obliged to walk upon the soft sand. Everything along the beach looked huge and mystical in the uncertain light; and this, accompanied with the solemn boom of the waves as they fell at long intervals upon the shore, made the scene quite romantic. After five hours' sharp walking, with pocket-handkerchiefs tied round our heads to guard us from the attacks of mosquitoes, we arrived at Seven Islands between one and two in the morning.

Not long after this, a boat arrived with orders for my companion, Mr Anderson, to pack up his worldly goods and start for Tadousac. The same day he bade me adieu and set sail. In a few minutes the boat turned a point of land, and I lost sight of one of the most kindly and agreeable men whom I have had the good fortune to meet in the Nor'-West.

The situation in which I found myself was a novel, and, to say truth, not a very agreeable one. A short way off stood a man watching contemplatively the point round which the boat had just disappeared; and this man was my only companion in the world!—my Friday, in fact. Not another human being lived within sixty miles of our solitary habitation, with the exception of the few men at the distant fishery. In front of us, the mighty Gulf of St. Lawrence stretched out to the horizon, its swelling bosom unbroken, save by the dipping of a sea-gull or the fin of a whale. Behind lay the dense forest, stretching back, without a break in its primeval wildness, across the whole continent of America to the Pacific Ocean; while above and below lay the rugged mountains that form the shores of the gulf. As I walked up to the house, and wandered like a ghost through its empty rooms, I felt inexpressibly melancholy, and began to have unpleasant anticipations of spending the winter at this lonely spot.

Just as this thought occurred to me, my dog Humbug bounded into the room, and, looking with a comical expression up in my face for a moment, went bounding off again. This incident induced me to take a more philosophical view of affairs. I began to gaze round upon my domain, and whisper to myself that I was "monarch of all I surveyed." All the mighty trees in the wood were mine—if I chose to cut them down; all the fish in the sea were mine—if I could only catch them; and the palace of Seven Islands was also mine. The regal feeling inspired by the consideration of these things induced me to call in a very kingly tone of voice for my man (he was a French Canadian), who politely answered, "Oui, monsieur."

"Dinner!" said I, falling back in my throne, and contemplating through the palace window our vast dominions!

On the following day a small party of Indians arrived, and the bustle of trading their furs, and asking questions about their expectations of a good winter hunt, tended to disperse those unpleasant feelings of loneliness that at first assailed me.

One of these poor Indians had died while travelling, and his relatives brought the body to be interred in our little burying-ground. The poor creatures came in a very melancholy mood to ask me for a few planks to make a coffin for him. They soon constructed a rough wooden box, in which the corpse was placed, and then buried. No ceremony attended the interment of this poor savage; no prayer was uttered over the grave; and the only mark that the survivors left upon the place was a small wooden cross, which those Indians who have been visited by Roman Catholic priests are in the habit of erecting over their departed relatives.

The almost total absence of religion of any kind among these unhappy natives is truly melancholy. The very name of our blessed Saviour is almost unknown by the hundreds of Indians who inhabit the vast forests of North America. It is strange that, while so many missionaries have been sent to the southern parts of the earth, so few should have been sent to the northward. There are not, I believe, more than a dozen or so of Protestant clergymen over the whole wide northern continent.

For at least a century these North American Indians have hunted for the white men, and poured annually into Britain a copious stream of wealth. Surely it is the duty of *Christian* Britain, in return, to send out faithful servants of God to preach the gospel of our Lord throughout their land.

The Indians, after spending a couple of days at the establishment—during which time they sold me a great many furs—set out again to return to their distant wigwams. It is strange to contemplate the precision and certainty with which these men travel towards any part of the vast wilderness, even where their route lies across numerous intricate and serpentine rivers. But the strangest thing of all is, the savage's certainty of finding his way in winter through the trackless forest, to a place where, perhaps, he never was before, and of which he has had only a slight description. They have no compasses, but the means by which they discover the cardinal points is curious. If an Indian happens to become confused with regard to this, he lays down his burden, and, taking his axe, cuts through the bark of a tree; from the thickness or thinness of which he can tell the north point at once, the bark being thicker on that side.

For a couple of weeks after this, I remained at the post with my solitary man, endeavouring by all the means in my power to dispel ennui; but it was a hard task. Sometimes I shouldered my gun and ranged about the forest in search of game, and occasionally took a swim in the sea. *I* was ignorant at the time, however, that there were sharks in the Gulf of St. Lawrence, else I should have been more cautious. The Indians afterwards told me that they were often seen, and several gentlemen who had lived long on the coast corroborated their testimony. Several times Indians have left the shores of the gulf in their canoes, to go hunting, and have never been heard of again, although the weather at the time was calm; so that it was generally believed that shark had upset the canoes and devoured the men. An occurrence that afterwards happened to an Indian renders this supposition highly probable. This man had been travelling along the shores of the gulf with his family—a wife and several children—in a small canoe. Towards evening, as he was crossing a large bay, a shark rose near his canoe, and, after reconnoitring a short time, swam towards it, and endeavoured to upset it. The size of the canoe, however, rendered this impossible; so the ferocious monster actually began to break it to pieces, by rushing forcibly against it. The Indian fired at the shark when he first saw it, but without effect; and, not having time to reload, he seized his paddle and made for the shore. The canoe, however, from the repeated attacks of the fish, soon became leaky, and it was evident that in a few minutes more the whole party would be at the mercy of the infuriated monster. In this extremity the Indian took up his youngest child, an infant of a few months old, and dropped it overboard; and while the shark was devouring it, the rest of the party gained the shore.

I sat one morning ruminating on the pleasures of solitude in the *palace* of Seven Islands, and gazed through the window at my solitary man, who was just leaving an old boat he had been repairing, for the purpose of preparing dinner. The wide ocean, which rolled its waves almost to the door of the house, was calm and unruffled, and the yellow beach shone again in the sun's rays, while Humbug lay stretched out at full length before the door. After contemplating this scene for some time, I rose, and was just turning away from the window, when I descried a *man*, accompanied by a *boy*, walking along the sea-shore towards the house. This unusual sight created in me almost as strong, though not so unpleasant, a sensation as was awakened in the bosom of Robinson Crusoe when he discovered the footprint in the sand. Hastily putting on my cap, I ran out to meet him, and found, to my joy, that he was a trapper of my acquaintance; and, what added immensely to the novelty of the thing, he was also a *white* man and a gentleman! He had entered one of the fur companies on the coast at an early age, and, a few years afterwards, fell in love with an Indian girl, whom he married; and, ultimately, he became a trapper. He was a fine, good-natured man, and had been well educated: and to hear philosophical discourse proceeding from the lips of one who was, in outward appearance, a regular Indian, was very strange indeed. He was dressed in the usual capote, leggins, and moccasins of a hunter.

"What have you got for dinner?" was his first question, after shaking hands with me.

"Pork and pancakes," said I.

"Oh!" said the trapper; "the first salt, and the latter made of flour and water?"

"Just so; and, with the exception of some bread, and a few ground pease in lieu of coffee, this has been my diet for three weeks back."

"You might have done better," said the trapper, pointing towards a blue line in the sea; "look, there are fish enough, if you only took the trouble to catch them."

As he said this, I advanced to the edge of the water; and there, to my astonishment, discovered that what I had taken for seaweed was a shoal of kippling, so dense that they seemed scarcely able to move.

Upon beholding this, I recollected having seen a couple of old hand-nets in some of the stores, which we immediately sent the trapper's son (a youth of twelve) to fetch. In a few minutes he returned with them; so, tucking up our trousers, we both went into the water and scooped the fish out by dozens. It required great quickness, however, as they shot into deep water like lightning, and sometimes made us run in so deep that we wet ourselves considerably. Indeed, the sport became so exciting at last, that we gave over attempting to keep our clothes dry; and in an hour we returned home, laden with kippling, and wet to the skin.

The fish, which measured from four to five inches long, were really excellent, and lent an additional relish to the pork, pancakes, and *pease coffee*!

I prevailed upon the trapper to remain with me during the following week; and a very pleasant time we had of it, paddling about in a canoe, or walking through the woods, while my companion told me numerous anecdotes, with which his memory was stored. Some of these were grave, and some comical; especially one, in which he described a bear-hunt that he and his son had on the coast of Labrador.

He had been out on a shooting expedition, and was returning home in his canoe, when, on turning a headland, he discovered a black bear walking leisurely along the beach. Now the place where he discovered him was a very wild, rugged spot. At the bottom of the bay rose a high precipice, so that Bruin could not escape that way: along the beach, in the direction in which he had been walking, a cape, which the rising tide now washed, prevented his retreating; so that the only chance for the brute to escape was by running past the trapper, within a few yards of him. In this dilemma, the bear bethought himself of trying the precipice; so, collecting himself, he made a bolt for it, and actually managed to scramble up thirty or forty feet, when bang went the boy's gun; but the shot missed, and it appeared as if the beast would actually get away, when the trapper took a deliberate aim and fired. The effect of the shot was so comical, that the two hunters could scarcely re-load their guns for laughing. Bruin, upon receiving the shot, covered his head with his fore-paws, and, curling himself up like a ball, came thundering down the precipice head over heels, raising clouds of dust, and hurling showers of stones down in his descent, till he actually rolled at the trapper's feet; and then, getting slowly up, he looked at him with such a bewildered expression, that the man could scarcely refrain from laughter, even while in the act of blowing the beast's brains out.

This man had also a narrow escape of having a *boxing* match with a moose-deer or elk. The moose had a strange method of fighting with its fore feet, getting up on its hind legs, and boxing, as it were, with great energy and deadly force. The trapper, upon the occasion referred to, was travelling with an Indian, who, having discovered the track of a moose in the snow, set off in chase of it, while the trapper pursued his way with the Indian's pack of furs and provisions on his shoulders. He had not gone far when he heard a shot, and the next moment a moose-deer, as large as a horse, sprang through the bushes and stood in front of him. The animal came so suddenly on the trapper that it could not turn; so, rising up with a savage look, it prepared to strike him, when another shot was fired from among the bushes by the Indian, and the moose, springing nearly its own height into the air, fell dead upon the snow.

In chasing the moose during winter in some parts of these countries, where the ground is broken and rugged, the hunters are not unfrequently exposed to the danger of falling over the precipices which the deceptive glare of the snow conceals from view, until, too late, he finds the treacherous snow giving way beneath his feet. On one occasion a young man in the service of the Company received intelligence from an Indian that he had seen fresh tracks of a moose, and being an eager sportsman, he sallied forth, accompanied by the Indian, in chase of it. A long fatiguing walk on the Chipewyan snow-shoes, which are six feet long, brought them within sight of the deer. The young man fired, wounded the animal, and then dashed forward in pursuit. For a long way the deer kept well ahead of them. At length they began to overtake it; but when they were about to fire again, it stumbled and disappeared, sending up a cloud of snow in its fall. Supposing that it had sunk exhausted into one of the many hollows which were formed by the undulations of the ground, the young man rushed headlong towards it, followed at a slower pace by the Indian. Suddenly he stopped and cast a wild glance around him as he observed that he stood on the very brink of a precipice, at the foot of which the mangled carcass of the deer lay. Thick masses of snow had drifted over its edge until a solid wreath was formed, projecting several feet beyond it. On this wreath the young man stood with the points of his long snow-shoes overhanging the yawning abyss; to turn round was impossible, as the exertion requisite to wield such huge snow-shoes would, in all probability, have broken off the mass. To step gently backwards was equally impossible, in consequence of the heels of the shoes being sunk into the snow. In this awful position he stood until the Indian came up, and taking off his long sash, threw the end

AN AWFUL POSITION.

of it towards him; catching hold of this, he collected all his en-
ergies, and giving a desperate bound threw himself backwards
at full length. The Indian pulled with all his force on the belt,
and succeeded in drawing him out of danger, just as the mass
on which he had stood a moment before gave way, and thundered down the cliff, where it was dashed into clouds against

the projecting crags long before it reached the foot.

About a week after his arrival the trapper departed, and left me again in solitude.

The last voyage.—There is something very sad and melancholy in these words—the last! The last look, the last word, the last smile, even the last shilling, have all a peculiarly melancholy import; but the last *voyage*, to one who has lived, as it were, on travelling—who has slept for weeks and months under the shadow of the forest trees, and dwelt among the wild romantic scenes of the wilderness—has a peculiar and thrilling interest. Each tree I passed on leaving shook its boughs mournfully, as if it felt hurt at being thus forsaken. The very rocks seemed to frown reproachfully, while I stood up and gazed wistfully after each well-known object for the last time. Even the wind seemed to sympathise with the rest; for, while it urged the boat swiftly away from my late home, like a faithful friend holding steadfastly on its favouring course, still it fell occasionally, and rose again in gusts and sighs, as if it wished to woo me back again to solitude. I started on this, the last voyage, shortly after the departure of my friend the trapper, leaving the palace in charge of an unfortunate gentleman who brought a wife and five children with him, which rendered Seven Islands a little less gloomy than heretofore. Five men accompanied me in an open boat; and on the morning of the 25th August we took our departure for Tadousac. And, truly, Nature appeared to be aware that it was my *last* voyage, for she gave us the most unkind and harassing treatment that I ever experienced at her hands.

The first few miles were accomplished pleasantly enough. We had a fair breeze, and not too much of it; but towards the afternoon it shifted, and blew directly against us, so that the men were obliged to take to the oars; and, as the boat was large, it required them all to pull, while I steered.

The men were all French Canadians: a merry, careless, but persevering set of fellows, just cut out for the work they had to do, and, moreover, accustomed to it. The boat was a clumsy affair, with two spritsails and a jigger or mizzen; but, notwithstanding, she looked well at a distance, and though incapable of progressing very fast through the water, she could stand a pretty heavy sea. We were badly off, how ever, with regard to camp gear, having neither tent nor oilcloth to protect us should it rain—indeed, all we had to guard us from the inclemency of the weather at night was one blanket each man; but as the weather had been fine and settled for some time back, we hoped to get along pretty well.

As for provisions, we had pork and flour, besides a small quantity of burnt-pease coffee, which I treasured up as a great delicacy.

Our first encampment was a good one. The night, though dark, was fine and calm, so that we slept very comfortably upon the beach, every man with his feet towards the fire, from which we all radiated like the spokes of a wheel. But our next bivouac was not so good. The day had been very boisterous and wet, so that we lay down to rest in damp clothes, with the pleasant reflection that we had scarcely advanced ten miles. The miseries of our fifth day, however, were so numerous and complicated that it at last became absurd! It was a drizzly damp morning to begin with; soon this gave way to a gale of contrary wind, so that we could scarcely proceed at the rate of half a mile an hour; and in the evening we were under the necessity either of running *back* five miles to reach a harbour, or of anchoring off an exposed lee-shore. Preferring the latter course, even at the risk of losing our boat altogether, we cast anchor, and leaving a man in the boat, waded ashore. Here things looked very wretched indeed. Everything was wet and clammy. Very little firewood was to be found; and when it was found, we had the greatest difficulty in getting it to light. At last, however, the fire blazed up; and though it still rained, we began to feel, *comparatively speaking*, comfortable.

Now, it must have been about midnight when I awoke, wheezing and sniffling with a bad cold, and feeling uncommonly wretched—the fire having gone out, and the drizzly rain having increased—and while I was endeavouring to cover myself a little better with a wet blanket, the man who had been left to watch the boat rushed in among us, and said that it had been driven ashore, and would infallibly go to pieces if not shoved out to sea immediately. Up we all got, and rushing down to the beach, were speedily groping about *in* the dark, up to our waists in water, while the roaring breakers heaved the boat violently against our breasts. After at least an hour of this work, we got it afloat again, and returned to our beds, where we lay shivering in wet clothes till morning.

We had several other nights nearly as bad as this one; and once or twice narrowly escaped being smashed to pieces among rocks and shoals, while travelling in foggy weather.

Even the last day of the voyage had something unpleasant in store for us. As we neared the mouth of the river Saguenay the tide began to recede, and ere long the current became so strong that we could not make headway against it; we had no alternative, therefore, but to try to run ashore, there to remain until the tide should rise again. Now it so happened that a sand-bank caught our keel just as we turned broadside to the current, and the water, rushing against the boat with the force of a mill-race, turned it up on one side, till it stood quivering, as if undecided whether or not to roll over on top of us. A simultaneous rush of the men to the elevated side decided the question, and caused it to fall squash down on its keel again, where it lay for the next four or five hours, being left quite dry by the tide. As this happened within a few miles of our journey's end, I left the men to take care of the boat, and walked along the beach to Tadousac.

Here I remained some time, and then travelled through the beautiful lakes of Canada and the United States to New York. But here I must pause. As I said before, I write not of civilized but of savage life; and having now o'ershot the boundary, it is time to close.

On the 25th of May 1847 I bade adieu to the Western hemisphere, and sailed for England in the good ship *New York*. The air was light and warm, and the sun unclouded, as we floated slowly out to sea, and ere long the vessel bathed her swelling bows in the broad Atlantic.

Gradually, as if loath to part, the wood-clad shores of America grew faint and dim; I turned my eyes, for the last time, upon the distant shore: the blue hills quivered for a moment on the horizon, as if to bid us all a long farewell, and then sank into the liquid bosom of the ocean.

The End

About the Cántaro Institute
Inheriting, Informing, Inspiring

The Cántaro Institute is a confessional evangelical Christian organization established in 2020 that seeks to recover the riches of historic Protestantism for the renewal and edification of the contemporary church and to advance the comprehensive Christian philosophy of life for the religious reformation of the Western and Ibero-American world.

We believe that as the Christian church returns to the fount of Scripture as her ultimate authority for all knowing and living, and wisely applies God's truth to every aspect of life, faithful in spirit to the reformers, her missiological activity will result in not only the renewal of the human person but also the reformation of culture, an inevitable result when the true scope and nature of the gospel is made known and applied.